THE FRONTIERS SAGA
PART 3: FRINGE WORLDS
EPISODE 2

NO RISK TOO GREAT
RYK BROWN

The Frontiers Saga Part 3: Fringe Worlds
Episode #2: No Risk Too Great
Copyright © 2022 by Ryk Brown All rights reserved.

No part of this book may be reproduced, scanned, or distributed in any printed or electronic form without permission. Please do not participate in or encourage piracy of copyrighted materials in violation of the author's rights. Thank you for respecting the hard work of this author.

This is a work of fiction. Names, characters, places, and incidents either are the product of the author's imagination or are used fictitiously, and any resemblance to locales, events, business establishments, or actual persons—living or dead—is entirely coincidental.

CHAPTER ONE

Nathan stood at the top of the hill, overlooking the crash site. From this vantage point, he could see the entire Aurora, as well as the scar she had carved into the surface during her belly landing. His ship, only a few days old, already looked like hell. Overall, she was surprisingly intact. Most of the exterior damage was superficial, with various hull plates and emitters having been torn away, mostly along the sides and undersides of the ship, and mostly on the forward section. Vladimir's efforts to ensure that the Expedition-class ships were over-built had paid off. He doubted that an XK, as tough as they were, would have survived such a landing.

Landing. The thought made him laugh. No one would call that a landing, let alone a *good* one.

"Any landing you can walk away from," Cameron stated as she came up the hill.

Nathan smiled. "I suppose so," he agreed. "Although I doubt they'll ever add *that* approach to the flight manual."

"Vlad has deemed the ship safe," she told him. "His people are starting their damage assessment now."

"Any word from the Dragons?" Nathan wondered.

"Not yet, but it should take them a few hours to search the entire planet."

"I'll feel better once we know whether or not we can expect any visitors," Nathan said.

"Still set on *not* contacting the Alliance?"

"We can't take the chance. Not until we at least know *where* and *when* we are. For all we know, the

Alliance might no longer exist. God knows who would respond to our distress call."

"We can use the Dragons to do some deep space recon," Cameron suggested.

"Not until we know where we stand here and now. First order of business is survival. Once we get things under control here, then we can peek out into the galaxy and see what's going on."

"Laza has been trying to calculate how far forward we may have traveled in time, but so far she doesn't have enough data to make a solid estimate."

"Does she have ballpark?"

"I asked," Cameron said. "I had to press. Jung don't like to guess. She said *maybe* two hundred years."

"Vlad guessed two fifty," Nathan sighed.

Cameron looked at him. "It wasn't your fault, Nathan. There's no way you could've known..."

"I should have seen it," Nathan insisted. "It was all too easy. They *let* us waltz in there. They were tracking us the entire time. They used Jessica to play me. They *knew* I would come for her."

"Yeah, Jessica is beating herself up over this just as much as you are."

"*I'm* responsible for this," he said, pointing to the crash site. "All of these people have lost *everything*... their lives, their families, their careers...because I fucked up."

"I would've done the same thing."

"No you wouldn't have," Nathan insisted. "You wouldn't have risked your ship and crew for *one* person, not even for a friend."

"Like I took the Aurora on an illegal mission to support your fight against the Dusahn?"

"That was different," Nathan argued.

"No it wasn't," Cameron countered. "I risked my ship *and* my crew, and without hesitation."

"You gave your crew a *choice*," Nathan explained.

"I didn't."

"You didn't have time, and you weren't acting outside of your authority as captain. I was, which is why I gave my crew a choice. Apples and oranges, Nathan."

Nathan chuckled.

"Besides, it's all in the past now."

"About two hundred *years* in the past," Nathan corrected.

"Neli has turned the Mirai's cargo bay into a makeshift galley. She's serving emergency rations and hot coffee."

"I think, at this point, I'd rather just take a nap. It's been a long day." Nathan turned to head back down the hill. "Let me know if the Dragons find anything."

"Comm-sets are still down," Cameron reminded him. "Where will I find you?"

"Where else?" Nathan replied. "In my ready room."

* * *

"*I am detecting low-level energy signals at bearing one four seven, eighty-seven kilometers*," Talisha's AI reported.

"What kind of energy?" Talisha wondered.

"*Thermal energy, most likely from fire, low-level radio waves, and electro-magnetic fields similar to those created by small, portable fusion generators.*"

"Sounds like people," Talisha concluded.

"*That would be my guess,*" her AI agreed.

Talisha looked to her right at her wingman. "Niko,

I've got a possible surface contact at one four seven, eighty-seven clicks."

"*I've got it,*" Nikolas confirmed.

"We'll overfly at angels twenty, but at sub-mach. That way, they shouldn't notice us."

"*Recon pattern?*" Nikolas assumed.

"A-firm. Ten-click spacing should do it."

"*You got it,*" Nikolas replied as his Dragon fighter rolled right, turning away from Talisha. "*Turning to one four seven. See ya on the other side.*"

* * *

"What news would you like first?" Cameron asked as she entered the captain's ready room. "Good or bad?"

"Let's end on a good note," Nathan replied, downing the last of his coffee.

"Well, this ship isn't flying again any time soon. Every grav-lift emitter needs to be replaced, as do half of our jump-field emitters."

"What about shields?"

"Most of them are fine," Cameron replied. "We lost a few in battle, but not so many that we can't fill in the gaps. Of course, the shields won't be back to full strength *until* the damaged emitters are replaced."

"Well, at least they should keep native intruders away."

"ZPEDs are still down, but since we're not flying, the backup fusion reactor should suffice."

"Did Vlad get it back online?"

"He's working on it now. He thinks he can have it up before nightfall."

"Good. We have no idea what the nights are like here. Any clue *where* we are yet?"

"None. For that, we'll need to get back into space."

"So far, things don't seem that bad," Nathan decided.

"Well, I'll refrain from reading the preliminary damage report. Better you peruse that at your leisure, since it's quite lengthy."

"I see."

"We're also looking at a raw materials problem."

"I thought we departed with full load?"

"A *full load* isn't enough to fix *this* much damage," Cameron explained. "We don't even have enough aramenium to fabricate half of the blown-out grav-lift emitters. If we're ever going to get this ship back into space, we'll need to find resources."

"Not until we know more about where and when we are, and what the current state of the galaxy is."

"You really are concerned about that, aren't you?"

"It's not that I'm *concerned*," Nathan explained. "I just don't want to make any assumptions. Not while we're this vulnerable."

"Agreed."

"Is it time for the good news yet?" Nathan wondered.

"Let's see..." Cameron scanned her data pad, forwarding through several pages.

"That long, huh?"

Cameron continued forward, eventually reaching the final page of her report. "Ah, Doctor Chen reports that Chief Calis is stable. However, he is still considered critical."

"How many people did we lose?"

"Eighteen total," Cameron replied solemnly. "Four from the Selles, and fourteen of our own."

That news hit Nathan hard. He had lost people under his command before, but it had been years ago. For him, this was the worst part of *being* in command.

"Doc has them in cold storage, in case it turns out we're able to get their bodies back to Earth."

"Is that it?" Nathan wondered. "Is that all the *good* news?"

"Well, the ship is structurally intact, so we have good shelter, and we have at least a month's worth of food and water, which we can stretch to two. Oh, and we still have seventy-six percent of our propellant, so we can use the Dragons and shuttles quite a lot before we'll start running low."

"We should plan on keeping twenty-five percent as a reserve for when we do get this ship flying again."

"That's still an *if* at this point."

"Optimism, Cam," Nathan urged. "Optimism."

"*XO, Base,*" Ensign Dass called over Cameron's comm-set.

"Go ahead," Cameron answered.

"Comm-sets are up?" Nathan wondered.

"*Dragon One reports a surface contact. They're over the target now at angels twenty. We're getting their sensor feed.*"

"Can you send it to my data pad?"

"*Yes, sir.*"

"How'd you get the comm-sets back up?" Nathan asked.

"Ensign Dass has set up a comm-station in the Mirai," Cameron explained as she studied her data pad. "All our comm-sets are currently tuned into her comm-net. She goes by Aurora Base." Cameron offered her data pad to Nathan. "It seems we're not alone on this world."

Nathan studied the data pad for a moment. "Looks

like a small settlement of some kind," he said as he handed the data pad back to her.

Cameron studied the data pad a bit more. "Looks like maybe a thousand people. There's a fusion reactor on site, so they have some technology. A lot of thermal signatures from fires, probably for cooking."

"So not *too* much technology then." Nathan rose from the couch. "I guess we should check them out."

"Maybe we should wait," Cameron suggested. "I mean, from the looks of this, they don't have anything that could help us, so why risk contact?"

"To get intel," Nathan said. "Where are we, *when* are we, and what's the state of the galaxy…"

"You can't just go in there and ask such questions," Cameron insisted. "They'll think you're nuts."

"I'll be subtle," Nathan promised.

"Don't tell them that we crashed. If they're stranded and desperate, they might attack us to steal what we have."

"I'll take the Seiiki, and we'll go as civilians," Nathan told her.

"And don't tell them who you are for God's sake…"

"Cam, relax. I know how to be covert. I'll go as Connor Tuplo."

"And take Jessica," Cameron added.

"Like I have a choice," Nathan chuckled as he headed out.

* * *

The Aurora had ended up relatively level, with a slight list to port, making moving around inside of her not too difficult. However, she was still a big ship, and she was bellied down, which made getting in and out of her a challenge.

Luckily, one of Vladimir's first accomplishments had been getting the port cargo hatch opened and a makeshift ramp set up. The ramp went from the hatch to the berm that the Aurora had plowed up during her crash landing. From there, it was a short hike down the uneven berm to open ground.

The Seiiki and the Mirai were positioned to the Aurora's port side. Most of the crew were inside the Aurora, conducting damage inspections.

Nathan came down the berm toward the Seiiki, immediately spotting Jessica, Kit, Marcus, and Neli, all gathered at the base of the shuttle's cargo ramp. "Aren't we a motley-looking bunch," he commented, noting their civilian attire. "Where'd you get the civies?"

"Well, half your crew are civilians, so it wasn't hard," Jessica explained. "We got some for you, too," she added, tossing him a shirt and jacket.

"Why are we here?" Neli asked.

"If I'm going to be Connor Tuplo, then I need Marcus and Neli on my crew," Nathan told her. "Besides, you two look the least military of all of us, and we want them to think we're just a small privateer."

"There are plenty of civilians aboard who could've come," Marcus pointed out.

"Are you complaining?" Nathan wondered.

"Me? Never. Just sayin'."

"Besides, everyone likes Neli," Nathan added, putting his arm around her. "She's our icebreaker."

Jessica handed Nathan a gun belt.

"Is this necessary?" Nathan wondered.

"Did you wear one when you *were* a privateer?" Jessica asked.

Nathan took the gun belt and headed up the ramp. "Let's get this show on the road."

* * *

Robert had not had any time to spend with their three passengers since escaping the Ilyan. He and his crew had spent most of their time helping Vladimir and his team assess the damage to the Aurora. While the air was breathable, they had no idea what the weather patterns held in store for them. The sooner they could all get back inside the Aurora, the better off they'd all be.

Now that the initial inspection was over, Robert had returned to his task of seeing after their three passengers.

Martina had been easy. The Aurora had sailed with minimal medical staffing. Martina's previous med-tech training was proving invaluable in the ship's medical department. Hanna had also required no effort on his part. She was more than happy to pass the time studying the last thousand years of Earth history.

Erica, on the other hand, had been a bit more of a challenge. In fact, he had spent the last hour trying to locate her, finally finding her sitting by herself on a small rise in the distance off the downed Aurora's port side.

"What are you doing way out here by your lonesome?" Robert asked as he approached.

"Just enjoying the view," she replied.

Robert could tell by her expression that there was more going on. "She's a mighty fine ship," Robert said as he sat on the hill next to her, facing the distant ship. "This was her first mission, you know."

Erica looked at him. "*Seriously?*"

"Yup. First of her class, in fact. She wasn't even scheduled to depart until two days from now."

"Hell of a first flight," she commented.

"It kind of goes with her name," Robert chuckled, "as well as her captain."

Erica looked at him, confused.

"The original Aurora was also pressed into service ahead of schedule and suffered a similar catastrophic event."

"Seriously?"

"Yup. That's how Captain Scott ended up in command. He was just a scrub lieutenant, fresh out of the academy at the time."

"I know how that feels," Erica said. "The Lokken was only my second *actual* flight."

"Really?"

"Yup. I only graduated flight school about a year... Wait, I guess that would be like, a thousand years ago?"

"We're guessing closer to twelve hundred at this point."

Erica sighed. "All I wanted was to get on the crew of an outbound colony mission. Now I wish I was back on McFallon."

"You're from McFallon?"

"I'm afraid so."

"Nice world. Why'd you want to leave?"

"You've been there?" she wondered.

"Several times."

"And you thought it was *nice?*"

"Well, I was there about a thousand years after you left, so I'm sure a lot had changed."

"It was just a fringe world in my day," Erica explained. "A few hundred thousand people at the most. Cargo ships only stopped by a few times a year at best."

"And they still had a flight academy?"

"Actually, it was just one instructor with a really nice simulator that he'd built himself. He was fully certified by the INA, though."

"I'm sure he taught you well."

"How many people lived on McFallon when *you* were there?"

"A few million, at least," Robert replied. "Fully industrialized and self-sufficient as best I could tell. She was a member of the Sol Alliance."

Erica rolled her eyes. "Then I was right by leaving."

"What do you mean?"

McFallon was becoming controlled by the Core Systems Alliance. That's why I left. I wanted to be someplace truly free."

"Well, in a roundabout way, you may have succeeded," Robert admitted.

"Maybe," Erica chuckled, her attention turning back to the Aurora. "You think she'll fly again?"

"If she holds true to her namesake, she will."

"I don't know; she looks pretty banged up.

"Well, her chief engineer was one of the original designers of this class, so if anyone can get her flying again, it's him."

"I'd love to get a look at her helm someday," Erica admitted.

"I'm sure that can be arranged," Robert told her.

"*Seriously?*"

"I think I can do one better, in fact. How'd you like to learn how to fly her?"

"I'd love to," she replied enthusiastically.

"Once Commander Kamenetskiy gets main power restored, we'll get you in the simulator."

"There's a *simulator* on board?"

"Full immersion," Robert assured her. "All five senses. It even hurts when you die."

"Maybe we can turn that setting off?"

"Most people do," Robert assured her. "You can learn to fly pretty much any ship in that thing. The Aurora, the Navarro-class shuttle, the Dragon fighter; you name it."

"I'd enjoy that." Erica looked back at the Aurora. "Not that those skills will ever be of much use."

"Says who?" Robert replied.

"What do you mean?"

"We're stranded God knows where and God knows when. We've got two good working shuttles and eleven Dragon fighters. We can use all the pilots we can get."

"*Seriously?*" Erica asked, genuinely afraid that he was joking.

"You really like that word, don't you?" Robert teased.

* * *

"I still think we should've set down a click or two outside of town," Jessica grumbled as they moved aft through the Seiiki toward her cargo bay.

"*Got a few people headed our way,*" Josh warned over comm-sets.

"From what direction?" Jessica asked.

"*All directions, and some of them are packin'.*"

"Told ya," Jessica said as they entered the cargo bay.

"What's the sit?" Kit asked as he checked his sidearm.

"We've drawn some interest," Jessica replied. "*Armed* interest."

"Tell me again why we had to set down in town?" Marcus complained.

"For the last time, if we had set down incognito and walked in, it would've looked suspicious," Nathan explained. "I mean, they have to know that they're the only ones on this rock. They'd damn well know that strangers had to come by ship."

"Yeah, but they wouldn't know *where* our ship was or what *kind* of ship we were flying," Jessica argued.

"We're here to get intel, Jess. People are more willing to talk to friends than enemies."

"And they're more willing to *kill* strangers."

Nathan rolled his eyes. "Open the hatch," he instructed Marcus.

"You sure?"

Nathan just glared at him.

"Just askin'," Marcus grumbled as he activated the hatch.

The aft cargo ramp that served as the hatch over the entire bay split across the top as it began to slowly swing away and head down.

Jessica reached down and fingered the safety and charge buttons on her sidearm, preparing for the worst.

"Don't *shoot* anyone," Nathan told her.

"I won't if they won't."

Nathan looked to Kit for support.

"Don't look at me," Kit told him. "I'm on her side."

Before the ramp deployed enough for them to be seen, Jessica reached over and mussed up Nathan's hair.

"What are you doing?" Nathan inquired, batting her hand away.

"Making you look less military," she explained. "You should've left it long."

The ramp continued its downward swing, revealing the heads of those gathered outside. Nathan offered a friendly wave as the ramp continued downward. But the moment the locals could see that Nathan and his crew were armed, their hands went to their sidearms.

Nathan put up both his hands as the ramp came to a stop. "We're not looking for trouble," he assured them as he headed slowly down the ramp.

"Then why are you strapped?" a man at the forefront of those gathered replied.

"Why are you?" Jessica snapped back, her hand also on her sidearm, just in case.

"Jess," Nathan said under his breath.

Jessica squinted as she scanned every man there and then lit on the one standing to the speaker's right. The man's hand was hovering just above his gun, twitching. "Kit," she said as she drew her weapon with lightning speed.

Kit did the same, so quickly in fact, that the man with the twitching hand froze, his eyes wide at the speed of their draw.

"I don't want to kill anyone," Jessica announced, "but I've got no problem doing so if need be."

The man who had spoken looked at the eyes of both Jessica and Kit, noting their steely gaze and razor-sharp attentiveness. Their speed had bested his, so much so that none of his cohorts had even gotten their guns half-drawn.

Nathan sighed. *Same old Jessica*, he thought.

"Like I said, we're not looking for trouble. So why don't we all put our guns away."

A devilish smile crept onto Jessica's face. "I believe we've made our point," she said, holstering her weapon.

Kit followed suit, his eyes still darting from one man to the next.

"Then what *are* you looking for?" the leader of the group asked.

Nathan started down the ramp again. "We're checking in with all the settlements in the area, looking for work."

"What *kind* of work, the man asked, still eying them suspiciously.

Nathan reached the bottom of the ramp, turning his head back toward his ship momentarily. "Kind of obvious, don't you think? We're looking for anyone who needs cargo runs. Imports or exports. Don't care much what. Just looking to keep our tanks filled and our pantry stocked." Nathan offered his hand. "Connor Tuplo, captain of the Seiiki."

"Jorda Basque," the man replied, shaking Nathan's hand.

Nathan did his best to match the man's grip strength, not wanting to send the wrong signals. He had no idea who these people were, and whether or not they could be trusted. But one thing he had learned over the years was that you didn't want to appear weak nor too intimidating. "Pleasure to meet you. This is Jessica, Kit, and Marcus."

"Kind of a small crew, huh?"

"Three more inside," Nathan told him. "Figured it was best not to come on too strong."

Jorda eyed the Seiiki a bit. "She looks new. There aren't many of these old birds flying any longer."

"We try to take good care of her," Nathan lied.

"Pretty odd, you showing up here. We don't get many visitors this far out."

"That's why we're looking out here," Nathan explained. "Less competition."

Jorda chuckled. "You could've found less competition without traveling so far past the line." He looked at Nathan again, then at the others, sizing them up. "You got Alliance troubles?"

Nathan wasn't sure what to say.

"Isn't that why *you're* out here?" Jessica chimed in nonchalantly.

"We're out here to *avoid* the complications that come with the Alliance," Jorda clarified. "But that doesn't mean we're interested in hiring operators that are, shall we say, *less* than legal?"

"You have nothing to worry about with us," Nathan assured him.

"I don't know. This *is* an Alliance shuttle. An *old* one, to be sure, but still Alliance."

"They stopped using these long ago," Nathan told him. "Sold them off in public auctions, in fact. Most of them are being used by privateers like us but closer in to the line."

"Why would a privateer want to use an ancient shuttle?"

"These Navarro-class shuttles are quite versatile," Nathan defended. "Especially if you manage to get your hands on some of the different mission modules...which *we* did."

"What kind of modules?" Jorda wondered, intrigued.

"Let's just say we can carry a lot of cargo, a lot of people, or a mixture of both. We can even take her into the more dangerous systems, if the price is right."

"You have weapons modules?"

"We know a guy," Nathan replied.

"Then you must be based somewhere," Jorda surmised.

"Persa," Nathan told him.

"Never heard of it."

"Most haven't. Like you, that's the way they like it. Not far though. A few hundred light years at most."

"Then you've got full energy banks?" Jorda asked, surprised.

"Of course."

"That explains why you prefer to steer clear of the Alliance."

Nathan and Jessica exchanged a glance.

"So, are you in need?" Nathan asked.

"We're in need of a lot of things," Jorda replied. "And this ship is one of them."

Nathan didn't like the way Jorda had said that. "I can give you a fair price for hauling... cheaper than most."

"What's to stop me from takin' her?" Jorda asked, his tone becoming less friendly.

"Other than quick-draw, here?" Nathan replied, pointing over his shoulder at Jessica. "Josh? You listening?"

On the underside of the shuttle, on either side of the bow and either side of the aft cargo bay opening, small, single-barreled plasma cannons dropped down and immediately took aim at the locals, their plasma generators humming to life as the cannons darted back and forth, demonstrating how quickly they could change targets.

The locals moved back one or two steps.

Apparently, the demonstration had achieved its desired affect.

"Like I said, we're not looking for trouble, just work. But we're not about to let some backwater potentate make trouble for us. If you're not interested in hiring us, that's fine, we'll be on our way. But if just one of you draws down on this ship, or any of my crew, we'll melt your little town to the ground and not bat an eyelash." Nathan took a step forward, staring Jorda in the eyes, a look of unwavering confidence on his face. "Do I make myself clear?"

Jorda stared at him for a few more seconds, trying to appear as confident as Nathan. Finally, his expression began to change, quickly forming a broad smile. He laughed out loud, turning to his men, who also laughed, although not as heartily. "How about I buy you all a drink?" he offered, slapping Nathan on his shoulder.

Nathan also smiled. "I think I'd like that...a *lot*."

* * *

After the initial confrontation, Jorda's attitude had changed considerably. In fact, he had become downright hospitable, treating them to a light meal in addition to their local brew.

"You never said how you came upon our little world," Jorda commented as he poured them another round.

"A long story, actually," Nathan replied. "Suffice to say it was more by accident than by design."

"What did you call this stuff?" Jessica asked, taking a sniff of the pungent concoction.

"Coru," Jorda replied. "It's a mixture of grains and

dekka fat, cooked and fermented. It's a complicated process that takes some time."

"With a bit of a buzz as well," Nathan added.

"You build up a tolerance to its intoxicating effects after a while."

"You guys drink this stuff all day?" Kit wondered.

"The men do. The women not so much. Most have a hot mug of it first thing in the morning, then a few cold ones throughout the day."

"Works for me," Marcus commented, taking a big swig of his brew.

"It's quite filling," Jessica added.

"Helps get us through the day without having to eat."

"You don't eat all day?" Nathan asked.

"For the most part," Jorda confirmed. "Dinner is our one big meal."

"I could go all day without eating if I got to drink this stuff all day," Marcus commented.

"What's a dekka?" Nathan wondered.

"A big rodent. Lives in the brush, eats anything that's already dead," Jorda explained. "Disgusting buggers, not edible at all. Their fat is the only thing worth a damn. But the only way to consume it is in coru; otherwise, it'll make you sick as a dog."

"So how long have you lived here?" Nathan asked, hoping to get some more information out of Jorda without tipping him off to their situation.

"About forty years," Jorda replied. "I came over with my parents when I was a child."

"How long has this settlement existed?" Jessica asked.

"Gruner was originally an aramenium mining base, established about a hundred years ago. But the vein ran dry sooner than expected, and the mining company pulled out. Most of the families just decided to stay."

"Why?" Jessica wondered. "From what we've seen, this rock is pretty barren."

"It's an acquired taste, that's for sure," Jorda agreed. "But it keeps the undesirables out. Most who come to live here are looking to get as far away from the Alliance as possible."

"Yourself, included?" Jessica asked.

"I've never had any contact with the Alliance, myself, but I understand why people dislike them. Too many rules and restrictions. Most people don't like being told what they can and can't do." Jorda eyed his guests, thinking. "I take it none of *you* has had much contact with the Alliance, either?"

"We try to stay clear of them ourselves. Makes life less complicated," Nathan explained, trying to appear of similar ilk.

Jorda topped off his own mug. "It was rather good timing for us," he stated. "You appearing when you did."

"How so?" Nathan wondered.

"Well, we do some trade with nearby systems," Jorda explained. "You know, to get the odds and ends we can't produce ourselves."

"What do you offer in trade?" Jessica asked.

"You're drinking it," Jorda smiled. "Coru is popular on fringe worlds. Especially barren ones like Dencke."

"Dencke?"

"That's what we call our little world."

"And coru gets you what you need?" Nathan wondered.

"Usually. Sometimes we have to trade it for

something else and then trade that with another world to get what we're looking for."

"You said it was *good timing* that we showed up?" Nathan queried.

"Our usual transport, the Coralie, is several weeks overdue."

"You think they ran into trouble?" Jessica wondered.

"Don't really care," Jorda replied. "My concern is the batch of coru that was supposed to ship out. Coru doesn't have a long shelf life, and we can't drink it all ourselves. We were counting on the Coralie to pick it up and trade it with a guy on Hadria for medical supplies, which we're running low on. Maybe you can help us out?"

"I don't see why not," Nathan said.

"What's our cut?" Jessica asked.

"Will you take ten percent of the coru as payment?" Jorda replied.

"Make it twenty, and you have a deal," Jessica countered.

"Only because if I don't, we'll probably lose the entire batch," Jorda said. "Deal. How soon can you depart?"

"How quickly can you load us up?" Nathan replied, downing the last of his coru and smiling.

* * *

"Hadria?" Cameron said. "Never heard of it. Do you even know where it is?"

"*About thirty light years from here,*" Nathan replied over comms. "*We managed to squeeze a little extra info about the place from them, so I'm pretty sure we can locate it.*"

"Well, what are you hauling for them?"

"*Coru. Think protein shake mixed with dark beer.*"

"Sounds awful."

"*Marcus loved it.*"

"I'm not sure this is a good idea," Cameron told him.

"*I'll send word via jump comm-drone when we get there,*" Nathan promised.

"You didn't tell them about us, did you?"

"*Nope. Our cover held. I think the fact that they were desperate to get their stuff to market helped.*"

"If we don't hear from you in twenty-four hours, I'm sending Dragons out to find you."

"*Fair enough,*" Nathan agreed. "*How are things there?*"

"Vlad has the starboard ZPED back online, but only at thirty percent. It should be enough to run all the environmental systems and power the shields to keep out wildlife," Cameron reported. "We still don't have artificial gravity, so we're still dealing with a port lean, but at least it's only five degrees."

"*I take it you've moved everyone back inside?*" Nathan asked.

"We're working on it," Cameron assured him. "The sun's already setting here. We should have everyone inside before it gets totally dark."

"*Very good.*"

"You guys be careful," Cameron urged.

"*Don't worry,*" Nathan replied. "*I've got Jess watching over me.*"

"That doesn't help," Cameron replied.

"*Okay, I've got Neli to answer to as well.*"

"That's better."

"*I'll send an update in a few hours. Seiiki out.*"

"Aurora Base, out," Cameron replied.

"Is he always this reckless?" Laza asked. "Procedure dictates the captain should stay with the ship and send junior officers out on such details."

"Nathan is more *hands-on* than most captains," Cameron explained.

* * *

Nathan studied the navigation display at the center of the Seiiki's forward console between him and Josh, dumbfounded by what he was seeing. It was the first time that any of them had returned to space since the crash earlier that day. "This can't be," he muttered in disbelief.

"I'm telling you, *that*'s Sol."

"But that puts us in the *Perseus* arm." Nathan looked at him again, still unable to accept what he was saying. "That means we jumped more than *ten thousand* light years. Hell, we don't even have charts for this area."

"Well, we need to get some soon, or we're going to be wandering around like idiots every time we try to go somewhere, *just* like we're doing now."

"I'm doing the best I can," Nathan defended. "A 'big, blue planet close in to a red dwarf' is an awfully vague description. You know how many red dwarfs there are within thirty light years of Dencke?"

"No...because we don't have any star charts for this area," Josh reiterated.

Nathan sighed in frustration. They had jumped to more than twenty red dwarf systems lying between twenty-nine and thirty-one light years from Dencke, and not one of them had a habitable world orbiting them. "Try this one," Nathan decided, sending the course information to Josh's console.

Josh looked at the nav data. "That's thirty-two light years out."

"Well, I ran out of red dwarfs in the twenty-nine to thirty-one range. That one's the closest red dwarf to us that's even close to that."

"Still jumping in circles?" Jessica teased as she entered the Seiiki's cockpit.

"Not funny," Nathan snapped.

"Jumping in five," Josh announced.

"I really thought this would be easier," Nathan admitted. He turned to look at Jessica. "If Josh is right, we're in the Perseus arm."

"What?"

"Yeah, at least ten thousand light years from home."

"Jumping," Josh announced as the jump flash washed over the Seiiki's cockpit.

"How long will it take us to get there by shuttle?" Jessica wondered.

"At least a month," Nathan replied.

"Twice that without charts," Josh added.

"Enough about the charts, Josh," Nathan pleaded as he studied the sensor display. "Hey, I think we may have found something. I'm picking up a planet close in. One point one five Earth's mass, liquid water, breathable atmosphere." Nathan paused, a smile creeping across his face. "And *lots* of emissions, some I can't even identify."

"You think it's Hadria?" Jessica wondered.

"Even if it isn't, it's worth checking out. I'm picking up inbound and outbound ships, so they probably have an active spaceport."

"And star charts," Josh said under his breath.

"Unfortunately, they'll probably have fees as well," Nathan added.

"Let's hope they'll take coru as payment," Jessica commented.

Nathan punched in some commands. "I'm dispatching a jump comm-drone with an update to Cam."

"We don't even know if this is Hadria, yet," Josh reminded him.

"If it isn't, and they don't accept coru as payment, then we may need Cam to send the Mirai to bail us out," Nathan explained. "Besides, she worries."

"Bail us out with *what?*" Jessica wondered.

Nathan pressed the launch button, and then looked to the right, spotting the comm-drone as it sped away, turned sharply, then jumped.

"How far out are we?" Jessica asked.

"About one light hour. Josh, jump us to comms range."

"How close?"

"Thirty light seconds should do."

"You got it," Josh replied, dialing up another jump.

"Maybe we should recon a bit first?" Jessica suggested.

"That would just make us look suspicious," Nathan argued.

"Assuming they can even see us."

"It's a pretty safe bet they can," Nathan told her. "With that many ships coming and going, they probably have approach control, and maybe even some kind of security fleet."

"Jumping in five," Josh reported.

"Even more reason to recon, if you ask me," Jessica insisted. "Could we at least raise shields?"

"Again, we don't want to appear suspicious."

"I was thinking *cautious.*"

"Jumping."

Again the jump flash washed over the Seiiki's cockpit. Nathan looked out the forward windows, spotting the tiny blue dot. "That's it." He tapped some buttons on the comm-panel, then tapped his comm-set. "Approach, this is the Seiiki. We're inbound, thirty light seconds out, looking for permission to land."

"Good idea," Josh complimented.

"What's a good idea?" Jessica asked.

"He hailed them as just 'approach'. That way, if that ain't Hadria, we don't look like idiots, we just appear to have bad comm habits."

"*Hey, Seiiki,*" a voice called over comms. "*Hadria doesn't have approach control.*"

"Uh, thanks," Nathan replied over comms.

"*Your first trip to that shithole?*"

"Yeah. Who am I speaking to?"

"*This is Captain Bartus of the Senecka.*"

"Connor Tuplo, captain of the Seiiki. Thanks for the info, captain. Any advice on where we should set down?"

"*Depends on what you're carrying.*"

"A few thousand liters of coru," Nathan replied.

"*Then you'll be a popular guy,*" Captain Bartus chuckled. "*Keep your shields up while you're on the ground, or that cargo of yours will get stolen.*"

"Will do," Nathan replied. "I guess there's no security then."

"*On a fringe world like Hadria? Fat chance. Make sure you're strapping at all times, Tuplo.*"

"Always."

"*Safe travels. Senecka out.*"

"To you as well," Nathan answered. "Seiiki out."

"Sounds like my kind of place," Jessica mused.

"Well at least we found it," Nathan commented. "Take us in, Josh."

* * *

Cameron came back down the dirt hill serving as the boarding ramp to the downed Aurora's port main cargo hatch. With the amount of foot traffic going in and out of the ship all day long, the uneven path had been firmly tamped down. It was still uncomfortably steep, but it was definitely easier to navigate than it had been.

It was still narrow, meaning no two-way traffic, so moving everyone and everything back inside had gone more slowly than she'd hoped.

"How are we doing?" Cameron asked Robert, who was directing traffic at the base of the ramp.

"It's going to be close," he replied, looking up at the quickly darkening sky. "Temps are dropping fast. According to Ensign Soray, we're moving into the shadow of this moon's parent, and the moon's rotation rate creates an odd timing every few days that creates a longer night and a deep freeze. She estimated it will happen about once every ten local days."

"Great. A desert planet that turns into an ice planet overnight." Cameron cupped her hands and blew into them. The air had gotten crisp and cold in less than an hour. "The sun sets quickly here," she commented, looking at the sky.

"It's that unusual timing," Robert explained. "It's like an eclipse happening at sunset. Soray says *that* should only happen every four or five cycles though."

"You know that famous *Na-Tan* luck?" Cameron asked.

"Yeah."

"I think that got left in the past."

"We *are* alive," Robert pointed out. "And we have shelter *and* power."

"God, you're another optimist, aren't you," Cameron joked as Doctor Chen and two med-techs approached, carrying the Selles' chief engineer. "How's he doing?" Cameron asked the doctor.

"He's hanging on," Doctor Chen replied. "But all this commotion isn't helping."

"Hopefully, this will be the last time you have to move him," Cameron said as they passed.

Vladimir and three crewman carrying parkas came down the ramp next, stepping carefully to the side to make room for Doctor Chen's party to pass.

"I'm not sure we can keep the shields up," Vladimir reported as he came down the hill.

"What happened?"

"My original assessments were based on more reasonable temperatures," Vladimir explained as one of the crewmen handed Cameron and Robert parkas. "If we're looking at prolonged sub-zero temps, we'll be using more power to maintain internal temps."

"It's a spaceship, Vlad. It's always in sub-zero temps," Robert commented.

"We've got numerous hull breaches, so we're not airtight at the moment. We've even got flooding in the lower cargo deck from this damned swamp we ended up in. Besides, I barely got the starboard ZPED stabilized. Running the shields along with environmental would've put it too close to its current redline. If we lose that ZPED, it will get very cold inside."

"What about the fusion reactor?" Cameron asked.

"We had to shut that down. I had to use several

of its containment field emitters in the starboard ZPED."

"Why couldn't you use emitters from the port ZPED?" Robert wondered.

"They're all fried."

"Well, let's hope whatever creatures inhabit this world stay home when it gets cold," Cameron said as she donned her parka. "You're not cold?" she asked Vlad, who was still wearing a standard uniform.

"This is like a nice, winter evening back home for me," Vladimir laughed as he continued on.

"We should probably recall the Dragons and get them secured for the duration of this cold spell. If power is going to be rationed, we won't be able to cycle them in and out from the flight deck."

"Good idea," Cameron agreed, tapping her comm-set. "Aurora Base, XO. Recall the Dragons ASAP and have ground crews ready to secure their birds on the ground."

"*Aye, sir.*"

"Make sure everyone gets cold-weather gear," Cameron told Robert. "No one goes outside without it. Not even Vlad."

"You got it," Robert promised. "You hear anything else from the Seiiki?"

"We got a second comm-drone a few minutes ago. They found Hadria."

"You see, that *Na-Tan* luck is still there," Robert teased.

"Let's hope," Cameron replied as she headed for the comm-shack.

CHAPTER TWO

The four of them stood at the top of the Seiiki's cargo ramp, staring out at the dilapidated, dusty, broken-down city that was Hadria.

"Are you sure we're in the right place?" Jessica asked.

"This is the largest population center on the planet," Nathan assured her. "I figured it was as good a place as any to start."

A gruff-looking man with two sidearms strapped to his hip and a rifle slung over his shoulder walked by glaring at them as he passed.

"I'm not sure we're carrying enough firepower," Kit commented.

"Never thought I'd see a place worse than Haven," Marcus grumbled.

"Neli, you, Sima, and Josh stay with the ship," Nathan instructed.

"Gladly," Neli agreed, appalled by the conditions outside.

"Why do I have to stay?" Josh complained.

"In case we need you to fly in and rescue us," Nathan replied.

Josh gazed out at the dusty streets, spotting two young women in suggestive attire looking his way and smiling as they passed. "Too bad," he sighed. "This place looks like fun."

Marcus just glared at him.

"Not sure this is the best place for R and R," Nathan said. "Shall we?" he added, heading down the ramp with Jessica, Kit, and Marcus following. "Keep the shields up," Nathan called back to Josh as they reached the bottom of the ramp and stepped onto the surface.

Josh walked over to the control panel at the left of the ramp, waiting until Nathan and the others were a few meters away before he activated the shields, setting them to glow a pale yellow.

"Does it always do that?" Ensign Dass wondered.

"Ever walk into a shield by mistake?" Josh replied. "Fucking hurts. Besides, it advertises that we don't want any visitors."

"Or that we have something on board to protect," Neli commented.

"Hey, I'm just following orders," Josh replied, activating the retraction cycle to raise the ramp back up before heading forward.

Ensign Dass sighed as Josh walked by. "I don't even know why I'm here. So far, everyone seems to speak English."

"Nathan just wants to be prepared," Neli assured her. She looked at the young ensign, noticing her uneasiness. "First time away from Earth?"

"That obvious?"

"Don't worry, you get used to it," Neli said, heading forward.

"It would be easier if I had something to do."

"You could help keep me from smackin' Josh."

Sima followed Neli, a confused look on her face. "Isn't Josh your son?"

"Oh *God* no," Neli laughed. "He's Marcus's stepson...sort of. Long story."

"He *is* irritating," Sima agreed.

"And today is one of his good days."

* * *

"We may have a problem," Vladimir announced as he entered the captain's ready room.

"We have *lots* of problems, Vlad," Cameron replied.

"This is a new one. The water is freezing up."

"What water?"

"Outside."

"Yes, we expected that," Cameron reminded him. "We're entering this planet's long night cycle."

"The front half of the ship is *in* the water," Vladimir explained. "The lower decks are flooded from hull breaches. Especially the forward weapons bay. If the water *inside* freezes as well, it will expand and create all kinds of damage."

"Can't we just heat it?"

"We only have one ZPED online..."

"And only at thirty percent," Cameron remembered.

"The only way I can keep the water *inside* the flooded areas of the ship is to keep those spaces abnormally warm, which means that *other* spaces will have to be kept at lower temperatures to compensate."

"Can you use the backup fusion reactor?" Cameron asked.

"I already am. If you want normal temperatures in the habitable spaces, we're going to have to move everyone from decks four and five up to deck three, and have everyone double or triple bunk. And we're going to have to shut down the heat in both the hangar bay *and* the entire Dragon system."

"So no flight ops until this is over," Cameron surmised.

"You could still launch a shuttle, as long as the crew wore cold-weather gear and moved quickly."

"Did you include the shields in your power calculations?" Cameron asked, fearing his answer.

"No shields," Vladimir told her.

"Of course not." Cameron leaned back in her chair. "Well let's hope the cold keeps whatever wildlife this planet has *inside* whatever they live in."

* * *

At the center of Hadria was a massive, open-air marketplace, nicknamed 'the pit' by the locals. If you wanted to sell something...*anything*...this was the place.

The pit was the wild west. There were *regulators* roaming about, wearing something slightly reminiscent of uniforms and carrying rather large blasters on both hips. In fact, everyone in the pit carried some sort of firearm. Even women with babies had short-barreled boomers mounted on their stroller handles.

"This place looks like fun," Marcus commented as they stood at the edge of the pit, looking across the marketplace.

"*Everyone* is packing. I wonder how many people die in there per day," Jessica wondered.

"You've been living in the Gamaze for too long," Kit chuckled.

"Yeah, it took me a while to get used to *not* carrying," she said, patting her sidearm affectionately.

"I'd be careful about touching that thing when we go down there," Marcus warned. "Places like this are full of itchy trigger fingers."

"I haven't been out of practice for *that* long," Jessica insisted.

"How the hell are we gonna find this Chiqua lady in *that*?" Marcus wondered, pointing to the vast marketplace.

Nathan took a deep breath, thinking the problem over. "Well, Jorda said she specializes in medical supplies, so I guess we start there."

"I don't suppose there's some kind of directory to this place?" Jessica asked.

Nathan eyed the chaos below, then looked back at Jessica. "I doubt that."

"Should we split up?" Marcus suggested.

"Oh hell no," Jessica snapped. "Four point movement. Nathan takes point, Kit and I will take left and right, and Marcus watches our six."

"You don't think that's being overly cautious?" Marcus grumbled.

Jessica paid him no mind. "Lead the way," she told Nathan, gesturing toward the market below.

* * *

Vladimir and several technicians entered the forward weapons bay, which was flooded with at least half a meter of muddy, smelly swamp water.

"God, it's even worse in here," Dixon commented as they entered.

"This breach is the most forward and the largest," Vladimir explained. "More crap came in here than anywhere else."

"Jesus, my legs are cramping up," Sergeant Ryu complained as they slogged through the thigh-deep water, carrying the portable heating elements.

"Are you sure these are going to work?" Vladimir asked.

"They're basically just water heater coils without a tank around them," the sergeant replied. "They'll take a while to warm up this much water, but they will keep the water from freezing without having to blast the air systems."

"You did the math?"

"I did the math," the sergeant promised. "But we need to spread them out evenly and put the two larger ones closer to where the water comes in."

Vladimir turned around. "Give me the large ones," he told the sergeant. "The ship is at a two-degree down angle, so the water will get deeper as we go forward, and I'm taller than both of you."

"Gladly," Sergeant Ryu agreed, handing him the two makeshift heaters. "I can't feel anything below my knees."

Vladimir took the heaters and continued pushing forward through the frigid water, which was now up to his crotch. The deeper the water got, the fouler the smell. By the time he got to the forward end of the bay, the water was up to his chest, and the smell was so bad that he could hardly breathe.

Vladimir set the heaters down, both of them disappearing beneath the swirling brown water. Once he felt them touch the deck, he raised the left one back up, leaving the other under the surface. He pulled the vegetation from the heater and then activated it with his right hand before submerging it, picking up the right heater, and continuing to the starboard side.

Now it was Vladimir who couldn't feel his legs. He used his left hand to hold onto each of the stored weapons turrets and pull himself along, the force of the current rushing in from the nearby breach threatening to knock his feet out from under him.

Two minutes later, he was on the starboard side, as close to the breach as he dared get. The water was even colder here than in the rest of the bay, and it seemed to change direction at will. Just as he had gotten accustomed to its pull, it would reverse, causing him to stumble.

Vladimir activated the second heater and placed it into the water, making sure that it was settled evenly on the deck under the water. He could already feel the heat from the unit with his right hand, but his legs were almost numb.

Something brushed against Vladimir's leg. His expression changed, and he looked around, uncertain of what it had been.

"What is it?" Sergeant Ryu yelled from the opposite corner. "Are they not working?"

"Something just touched my leg!" Vladimir yelled back.

"Probably just debris!" Dixon insisted. "There's all kinds of crap in here!"

Vladimir felt it again, this time on his right leg, and it wasn't debris. Whatever it was, it turned as it passed, partially wrapping around his right leg before passing between both legs. And it was large. "It isn't debris!" Vladimir yelled back as he hurried back across as best as he could.

Dixon's eyes suddenly became huge as he spotted the wake of something very big moving toward Vladimir as he splashed his way across the bay. "Oh my God! Get out of there!"

Vladimir continued on, but his legs felt like logs as he lumbered along. He felt something again, this time on his left calf. But it wasn't a brush like before. This time, it was a solid thump, as if something had purposefully hit him head on. Vladimir stumbled, falling to his left into the water, nearly going under.

Dixon and Sergeant Ryu watched in horror as

another wake headed toward Vladimir from the port side.

"There are two of them!" Sergeant Ryu cried out.

Vladimir suddenly went under, as if pulled down from below the belly-deep water. Something long and slithery raised up, its long body forming a hump above the surface before driving back down. Whatever it was that had taken the commander down, it intended to keep him there.

The water splashed and surged, with Vladimir's hands and feet occasionally coming up out of the water as he struggled to get free. Finally, he stopped coming up, and the water began to smooth out, with only the ripples from the two creatures causing any disturbance to the foul muddy water.

Dixon and the sergeant both scanned back and forth in a panic, desperate to find Vladimir. Finally, Dixon tapped his comm-set. "Bridge! Forward weapons bay! Man down in the water! Man down!"

"*Forward weapons bay, XO,*" Cameron called back over comm-sets. "Report."

"Something pulled the cheng under!" Dixon replied.

The loudspeakers crackled to life as an alert klaxon sounded, followed by Cameron's voice. "*Med-rescue to the forward weapons bay. Man down in the water. Repeat, man down in the water!*"

* * *

The deeper they ventured into the pit, the more crowded it became. It was becoming impossible to move about without brushing up against strangers with nearly every step. So often were they brushing up against others that Jessica found herself keeping her right hand on the butt of her sidearm at all times, fearing that someone might grab it.

Nathan did his best to blaze a path forward, but eventually had to veer to the left just to avoid the more densely packed core of the market.

"Where are you going?" Jessica asked, yelling to be heard above the increased noise of the dense crowd and the music blaring from the center of the market.

"I'm guessing that's live entertainment up ahead," Nathan called back. "That's why it's so packed! If we're going to find anything, it's not going to be near the core. We'll have to circle around, working our way further out with each loop until we find this Kimbro person!"

Nathan felt someone grab his arm.

"Hey!" the man who grabbed him yelled.

Jessica and Kit both drew their weapons instinctively, taking immediate aim at the stranger.

"Relax," the stranger said, holding both hands up so they could see that he was no threat.

Jessica glanced around, checking if the brandishing of her own blaster hadn't caused others to do the same. Many around her had their hands on their sidearms and their eyes on Jessica and Kit, ready to defend themselves, but none of them had actually drawn their weapons.

Jessica raised her left hand as she slowly placed her blaster back in its holster, eyeing all those around her as their hands eased off of their own weapons.

"First time in the pit?" the stranger surmised.

"What gave it away?" Nathan replied. "How can I help you?"

"I heard you say you're looking for Kimbro."

"That's right," Nathan replied. "You know her?"

"Not personally, but she's the biggest dealer of medical supplies on Hadria. Probably in the whole damn sector."

"Do you know where we can find her?" Jessica asked.

"Not down here in the crush," the man laughed. "She's got a hard shell on the east side, about two rows in from the rim. A big red cross on it. You can't miss it."

"Thanks," Nathan replied, turning to the east and pushing on. "At least we're getting somewhere!" he declared as he continued pushing through the crowd of people.

"I'm gonna need a shower after this," Jessica declared.

* * *

The water was still, with only the slightest of ripples caused by the undercurrent of the water as it moved in and out of the bay.

Mori and Jokay burst into the forward weapons bay, followed by two med-techs.

"What's the situation?" Mori demanded.

"Something took the cheng under," Dixon explained, pointing to the forward end of the flooded bay. "Over there."

"Something?" Jokay demanded.

"Some kind of huge water-snake," Sergeant Ryu said.

"How huge?" Jokay asked as he entered the water.

"He could be anywhere," Mori said as he also entered the muddy water.

"He's been under for more than a minute," the sergeant warned. "And that water is freezing."

"You take port, I'll take starboard," Mori instructed Jokay.

"Let's do it," Jokay agreed.

Both Ghatazhak ran into the water without concern for their own safety. Within seconds, they were both waist deep and getting deeper with each step as they splashed their way forward.

Mori felt around in the water with his hands, hoping to find something...anything. With each passing moment, he worried that they were too late.

"Look out!" Dixon yelled, pointing at the wave moving toward Jokay on the port side.

Jokay spun to his right, spotting the rise in the water and immediately pulled his combat knife. He felt something brush by his left side, and he turned in that direction, driving down with his blade. He felt the tip of his knife plunge into something semi-solid, like a large muscle.

There was a shudder in the water, as if something had let out a scream under water that shook the entire bay.

Mori spun around to look at Jokay, surprised by the vibrations. "What the hell was that?"

"I think I injured..." Jokay never finished his sentence, being pulled under in the blink of an eye.

"Jokay!" Mori yelled, rushing toward him.

Two more Ghatazhak arrived, immediately jumping into the water with knives in hand.

"What the fuck?" Chief Anson said as he pushed through the frigid water.

"Two under!" Mori yelled back as he searched for his comrades. "The cheng and Jokay! Something's got them! Something big!"

Corporal Teece leapt forward, practically diving in and driving his knife into the passing creature. Only he didn't let go, instead letting himself be dragged across the bay by the giant serpent.

Both Mori and Derel charged toward the corporal just as part of the creature rose up out of the water, and the short tentacle clutching Jokay released its hold on him.

Jokay splashed back to his feet, sputtering, his now bloody knife still in hand.

"You okay?" Mori asked.

"That thing is *strong!*" Jokay exclaimed.

"I've got him!" Chief Anson yelled, pulling Vladimir's lifeless body up from the water.

"Teece! Get out!" Mori ordered as he moved over to help Derel drag the big engineer out of the water.

The two med-techs didn't wait for the Ghatazhak to get the commander all the way out of the water, splashing in, with Cameron only a step behind.

"He's got a huge wound on his left side!" Derel reported as the med-techs reached them.

"Hold him here," the first med-tech instructed as he opened up an auto-tube kit. "Hold his head back," he added.

Mori did as instructed, leaning Vladimir's head back as the med-tech inserted the device into Vladimir's mouth and pressed the button on top. A second later, a breathing tube extended down through the commander's larynx and into his trachea, and tiny pumps began pushing pressurized oxygen into his lungs.

A green light appeared on the top of the auto-tube.

"Good tube! Get him out!" the med-tech ordered as he attached some tubing to the device, then to the small portable oxygen tank slung over his shoulder. "Prep a large dressing!" he barked at the sergeant waiting at the back end of the bay with the medical gear.

"I'll get the pacer ready," the other med-tech announced as they made their way across the bay, dragging the commander through the water.

When they reached the aft end of the bay, they pulled Vladimir's body up onto the landing and immediately began connecting him to the pacer.

"Is he alive?" Cameron asked.

"No pulse. His lungs are full of water," the first med-tech reported. "But he's ice cold, so there's still hope," he added as he worked frantically to get the commander ready to move.

"Pacer has captured," the second med-tech reported.

The first med-tech reached for Vladimir's neck. "Faint carotid. Push two loads of adrozine while I suction the water out of his lungs. Then we'll move him to medical." He tapped his comm-set. "Doc, Baris. Be ready for a traumatic, cold-water drowning."

* * *

It took the group more than an hour to push their way out of the densely populated core and back out to the edges of the pit. After that, they spent another hour zigzagging back and forth amongst the outer four rows of sellers. They circled to the East, making sure they didn't accidentally miss Chiqua's establishment.

"I think we're getting close," Jessica said. "That's the third medical supply seller we've seen in the last ten minutes."

Nathan stopped in his tracks. Ahead of them was a seller's station that was much larger than all the others around. It was also more permanent, composed of several smaller buildings joined together by covered breezeways. There were at least a dozen people working the complex, some handling sales and others providing security. There was even a two-story structure at the heart of the complex with windows overlooking the entire area.

"That's gotta be it," Nathan announced, pointing.

"If it isn't, then this Chiqua lady's got some serious competition," Marcus commented.

Nathan wasted no time, heading toward the complex.

"What's the plan?" Jessica asked, following.

"We ask to speak with Chiqua."

"Don't you think we should scope things out first?"

"I'd rather get right to it," Nathan insisted.

"Not a good idea," Jessica warned.

"I'm with her," Kit agreed.

"You two can *scope* all you want. Jorda said he had an arrangement with Chiqua. I intend to utilize that. The sooner I talk to her, the sooner we can get off this rock and back to the Aurora."

Jessica shared a glance with Kit. Both of them knew that Nathan could be quite stubborn when his mind was set on a plan of action. All they could do was to make the best of it. "On a swivel," she told Kit.

"Always."

Nathan walked up to the nearest salesperson, calling over the display table to him. "I need to speak to Chiqua."

"Nobody speaks to Chiqua," the man replied almost reflexively, turning his attention to the next potential customer.

"I'm here on behalf of Jorda of Gruner," Nathan continued.

The man looked back at Nathan. "You're from the Coralie?"

"No. I'm Connor Tuplo, captain of the Seiiki. I've got a few thousand liters of coru that Chiqua has agreed to accept as trade for medical supplies for the Grunites."

"The *Seiiki*? What happened to the Coralie?"

"I have no idea," Nathan replied. "Now, are you going to tell Chiqua that I'm here, or do I have to give the contact credit to someone else?"

The man eyed Nathan a moment, then acquiesced. "Wait here," he said, turning to depart.

Nathan watched as the man headed toward the center structure, stopping and whispering to one of the security guards along the way. The guard immediately said something into his comm-set as the man continued on his way.

"That got them interested in us," Jessica commented, noticing that every security guard in the area now had their eyes on the four of them.

"Not sure that's a good thing," Kit said.

Marcus glanced backward, spotting three more men moving in behind them. "They're surrounding us," he warned.

"No one touches their sidearm," Nathan instructed.

"Yeah, that would be a bad move right now," Kit agreed, noticing two more armed men moving into position on his right.

"I told you this was a bad idea," Jessica mumbled.

Nathan looked up at the second-floor windows of the center building. A young woman of small stature stepped up to the window, gazing down at them.

Nathan locked eyes with her, smiling. The woman did not react, turning away and disappearing from view.

A minute later, the woman came out of the center building, accompanied by the salesman and two bodyguards. Nathan looked around, noting the number of armed men focused on him. Regardless, he moved toward Chiqua, keeping his hands a little further away from his sides than normal, just to be safe.

Chiqua Kimbro was a diminutive woman who looked far younger than her true age, which no one really knew. Nathan's first reaction was one of surprise. Had he first spotted her under different circumstances, he would not have guessed her to be the largest supplier of medical supplies in the sector.

"Captain Tuplo," Chiqua greeted, coming to stand a meter away from Nathan. "What happened to the Coralie?"

"Jorda was hoping that you might know."

"I haven't heard anything...not that I care much. Portensa was a pig. Always trying to pad his cut at the expense of others. What did you say the name of your ship was?"

"The Seiiki."

"Never heard of her."

"We're new to these parts," Nathan told her.

"What kind of ship?" Chiqua wondered.

"Does it matter?"

"It might."

"An old Navarro-class shuttle...in *mint* condition, I might add."

"That's an *Alliance* shuttle. A risky choice for operations in the fringe. Some might mistake you *as* Alliance."

"Unlikely," Nathan disagreed. "The class was retired *long* ago. You can't even get parts for them anymore. We had to custom fabricate thousands of parts to get her space-worthy."

"Then why'd you buy her?" Chiqua questioned.

"She was cheap," Nathan said, smiling. "And I have a thing for classic spaceships. Plus I like her flexibility."

"You have some of her modules as well?"

"*All* of them," Nathan boasted. "Although, most of the time, we run her fitted for general cargo."

"You have the weapons modules?"

Nathan had not yet familiarized himself with every aspect of the Navarro-class shuttles, nor with the inventory of modules that the Aurora had launched with. He looked at Marcus, who nodded. "We do," he said, looking back at Chiqua. "Any reason you're showing such interest?"

"Just gathering information," Chiqua told him. "I understand you've got a load of coru for me?"

"Four thousand seven hundred liters, after our cut."

"Jorda usually sends me over six thousand liters."

"We took a larger cut, seeing as how the job was last minute," Nathan explained.

"I'll have to scale back my offer in trade," Chiqua warned.

"I'm not here to haggle with you, Miss Kimbro. The trade is between you and Jorda. We're just doing the hauling. Jorda seemed to trust you, so I'm sure what you offer will seem fair to him."

Chiqua looked Nathan over first, then Jessica, Kit, and Marcus. "There is something *off* about you," she told him. "I just can't put my finger on it."

"I'm sorry, are we not dirty enough for Hadria?" Nathan joked.

"Where are you parked?" she asked.

"Edge of town, due south," Nathan replied. "You can't miss us. We're probably the cleanest ship on this dusty rock."

"We'll be there after the market closes for the day," Chiqua told him.

"And when might that be?" Nathan wondered.

Chiqua cast a puzzled look his way.

"Like I said, we're new to these parts."

"The market runs from sunup to sundown," Chiqua said as she turned and walked away. "Have the coru ready to move."

Nathan turned around to face his team. "You see, that wasn't so hard."

"You do realize she's planning to double-cross us, right?" Jessica said.

"At the very least," Nathan agreed as he headed out.

* * *

Cameron stood outside the trauma bay, watching silently through the windows as Doctor Chen, Martina, and the med-techs tended to Vladimir. She had known Vladimir for fifteen years and had been his commanding officer on the old Aurora for seven. Although he often irritated her, there were few whom she trusted more than the commander. No one could diagnose and fix a problem like Vlad. Not even the engineering droids that SilTek had provided. He had a gift, there was no denying that. Without him, she doubted that the new Aurora would ever fly again.

Cameron cursed herself for even thinking about

their ship while her friend lay on the medical bed, with tubes and machines keeping him alive. She hated the fact that her own medical training was so limited. She felt useless standing outside looking in. Even the Ghatazhak were helping, as they had considerable medical training themselves.

Cameron noticed that the fervent pace of activity in the trauma bay had decreased. At first, she became concerned. But the machines keeping her friend alive were still running, and Martina was injecting something into one of the many tubes connected to him, so there still had to be hope.

When Doctor Chen turned to look at Cameron, the doctor's expression said otherwise, and Cameron's hopes faded again. Even more so as the doctor headed toward her.

Doctor Chen exited the trauma bay, a grim expression on her face. Cameron said nothing, simply waiting for the report she knew the doctor was about to give her.

Doctor Chen took a breath to gather herself before speaking. She had spent the last hour struggling to save the commander, and the strain showed on her face. "He's alive," she began, wanting to start on a positive note. "But barely."

"Did he drown?"

"I wish," Doctor Chen replied. "*That* would be easy to deal with, especially since the water was so cold. Even the wound to his side is pretty straight forward."

"Then what is it?" Cameron asked, sensing there was more.

"The creature, whatever it was, injected some kind of venom into him. As best I can tell, it's similar to a paralytic, but it affects *everything*. Skeletal muscles, smooth muscle, everything. If it moves, it's paralyzed."

"Can you create an antidote?" Cameron wondered.

"I haven't even begun to try to analyze the venom. At this point, I'm just trying to keep his body viable. *Technically,* he's dead. We've got him on full life support, but that can only work for so long. Eventually, various systems will begin to fail. Liver, kidneys, all of them."

"What about medical stasis?" Cameron asked. "Won't that buy us some time?"

"Even medical stasis doesn't completely stop the metabolism, it just drastically slows it down. It would probably buy us some time, but it would also slow down our ability to try any treatments on him to reverse the effects of this venom. So I'd recommend saving that option as a last resort."

"How long until we reach that point?" Cameron asked.

"Assuming the effects of the venom don't change, a few days maybe."

Cameron took a deep breath, letting it out slowly.

"Are you going to contact the captain?" Doctor Chen asked.

"Not yet," Cameron replied. "He has his own mission to worry about. Besides, he should be back in a day or two."

"Well, if things change for the worse, I may need a decision rather quickly," the doctor warned.

"If it comes to that, it's your call," Cameron instructed. "You're the doctor."

Doctor Chen placed her hand on Cameron's shoulder in sympathy, then headed out.

Cameron stepped up to the windows of the trauma

bay, gazing at her friend's lifeless body. "Hang in there, Vlad," she murmured to herself.

* * *

"That's the last one," Marcus announced as he placed the last keg of coru on the stack just outside the Seiiki. He straightened up, placing his hands on his lower back as he stretched and grimaced. "If running cargo is going to become a regular thing, we're going to need to carry some grav-lift movers. I'm getting too old for physical labor."

"What are you now, like six hundred?" Kit joked.

"Feels like it."

"You'd think they'd be here by now," Jessica commented as she came down the ramp.

"I guess it takes time to set up an ambush," Nathan replied.

"*I'm picking up movement,*" Josh reported over comm-sets. "*Looks like about twenty, moving in pairs.*"

"What direction?" Jessica asked.

"*All sides,*" Josh replied. "*Six coming in from aft.*"

"Don't deploy the ventral guns unless they start shooting," Nathan reminded him.

"It could be too late by then," Kit commented, "depending on how accurate their shooters are."

"There's still a chance we're wrong," Nathan insisted.

"She's gonna test us," Jessica warned. "She has to."

Nathan looked at her. "Why?"

"We've seen this before," Jessica explained. "Barter systems are all the same. The stronger person has the most bargaining power. You're an unknown, and Chiqua needs to know how far you're willing to bend if she's going to be dealing with you in the future."

"I was kind of hoping this would be a one-time thing, myself," Nathan said, turning to face the approaching vehicles.

"Left-right wide," Jessica told Kit, just before she began slowly moving to the left. Kit followed her lead, moving right at a casual pace as he thumbed his sidearm, setting it active.

Marcus realized what was about to happen and chose to step back a few paces, moving behind the stack of coru kegs.

"Really?" Nathan asked Marcus.

"I still got your back, Cap'n. I just prefer to have it from cover."

Nathan turned back toward the three approaching flatbed haulers coming down the road. He reached up and scratched his head, turning on his comm-set as he did so. "You ready?"

"*Seiiki is already selecting targets,*" Josh replied. "*She can fire within two seconds of your order. Shields can be up in five.*"

"Will they cover the coru?"

"*Yes, but extending them that far weakens them.*"

"That's okay," Nathan assured him. "I'm pretty sure they're not going to be packing much firepower."

"*I sure hope you're right,*" Josh commented.

So do I, Nathan thought.

The flatbed haulers, like everything else they had seen in this part of the galaxy thus far, were of an old design and looked as if they were barely holding together. They bounced along, suspension creaking with every bump due to their age and lack of adequate maintenance.

Nathan had to admit, they did look out of place. Their shiny new shuttle, their clean, mint-condition ancient sidearms, and their mostly clean clothing were all in stark contrast to the jalopies approaching and the men driving them. From Chiqua's perspective, Nathan and his crew had to look like an easy mark. Perhaps some rich kid who had bought himself a classic spaceship in order to have some adventures out in the fringe.

These were all assumptions, of course. Nathan had no clue what the state of the galaxy was at this point. He didn't even know exactly how far into the future relativity had taken them. The one thing he did know was that people in this part of the galaxy did not like the Alliance. Unfortunately, everything about the Seiiki screamed Alliance, right down to the emblem on her side.

The three haulers came to a stop, with two men climbing out of each, along with their boss, Chiqua.

"I'm surprised that you conduct such transactions yourself," Nathan commented as Chiqua and her two bodyguards approached.

"First-time transactions require my personal attention," Chiqua replied. "Especially when there is something *off* about the other party."

"What is it that you think is off about us?" Nathan asked.

"An ancient Navarro-class shuttle in *mint* condition? A charming young captain flanked by two mercs? And of course, there's grandpa back there," she added, pointing to Marcus standing behind the stacks of coru kegs. "If *that* guy isn't out of place, who is?"

"Call me grandpa again and I'll put *you* out of place," Marcus threatened.

Nathan glanced back at Marcus, smiling. "Wait until you meet the rest of my crew," Nathan joked. He leaned to the side, looking past her at the haulers, each of which carried several crates of what Nathan assumed to be the medical supplies Jorda had ordered. "Those for us?"

"You want to inspect them?" Chiqua asked.

"No need. We know where to find you if something's amiss."

Chiqua nodded. "Unfortunately, I don't have that luxury."

"Marcus," Nathan called. "Pull her a taste."

"I'm a bartender now?" Marcus grumbled as he pulled a cup out of his pocket and filled it. He handed it to Nathan, then stepped back behind the kegs.

Nathan offered the cup to Chiqua.

"I never touch the stuff," Chiqua insisted, glancing at the bodyguard to her right.

The man stepped forward, taking the cup from Nathan and tossing the contents down his throat. He licked his lips, then looked at his boss. "It's legit."

Nathan glanced around, noting the men on either side pretending to hide in the shadows, but purposefully being seen. "Security?" He asked Chiqua, tipping his head toward the distant men. "Or are they here to help with the grunt work?"

"I figured it would be rude to ask you to load the coru yourself, seeing as how I'm not planning on paying you for it," Chiqua told him. She was smiling, confident that she had the upper hand.

Nathan was also smiling. "That would be a mistake," he told her.

"Surely you had to see this coming," Chiqua replied. "Or are you really that naive?"

"Oh I saw it coming," Nathan assured her. "I was just hoping that I was wrong."

Chiqua shook her head. "Guys like you are all the same."

"Guys like me?"

"Money, charm, good looks. You think it puts you above everyone else. People like you expect to get your way."

Nathan sighed. "You know, I'm getting really tired of people misjudging me." With surprising speed, Nathan drew his sidearm, flipping the arming switch as he aimed the barrel at Chiqua's head.

At the same time, Jessica and Kit also drew. The difference was that *they* fired: six shots each, dropping the men hiding in the partial shadows to either side of the ship.

Chiqua's two bodyguards also drew, taking aim at Nathan's head. But Chiqua raised her hand, signaling them to hold their fire. "You're still out-gunned, Captain Tuplo. Three to one, by my count."

"Count again," Nathan replied.

On the underside of the Seiiki, doors slid open on either side of the stern and on the forward fuselage, and four double-barreled plasma cannons dropped down, swung out, and took aim on Chiqua's men.

Chiqua eyed the cannons, then looked back at Nathan. "You're *still* out-gunned."

"Maybe, but those guns are AI-controlled, and she's got orders to keep firing until all aggressors are eliminated. Including you."

Chiqua thought for a moment, weighing her options. Finally she said, "Just feeling you out, Captain. No hard feelings?"

"Not as long as we conclude this transaction

amicably," Nathan told her. "Minus one keg as a fine for your unwarranted aggression."

"Says the man with a gun to my head," Chiqua replied.

Nathan held his hand rock-steady for a moment before angling his barrel upward and returning it to his holster. "*Your* men do the loading."

* * *

"I've thrown everything I have at this to try to slow it down," Doctor Chen told Cameron. "I've never seen anything like it. If I hadn't put him in stasis, he'd probably be dead."

"How long will stasis give him?" Cameron asked.

"A few weeks, but that's only a guess," the doctor admitted. "We need to get him to a *real* hospital, preferably back on Earth."

"That's not an option at the moment," Cameron told her. "At least not in the next few days."

"Then we need to kill one of these creatures and analyze it. Maybe I can come up with a cure."

"You think that will work?"

"To be honest, I'm grasping at straws here," the doctor admitted.

CHAPTER THREE

Nathan and Jessica stood by, watching as the Grunites unloaded their new medical supplies from the Seiiki's cargo bay.

"Am I crazy, or isn't it supposed to be morning here?"

"You're not crazy," Nathan assured her. "I think this is some kind of extended night, due to that gas giant," he explained, pointing to the giant, blue planet looming low on the horizon.

"It's too damned cold," she complained, blowing on her fingers.

"We have cold-weather gear aboard, you know."

"Can't fight in those."

"You expecting to fight someone?"

"You never know," Jessica insisted. "We don't know these people that well yet."

"You know, everyone thought I was crazy to trust you," Jorda said as he came up the ramp. "They were all certain you'd fly off and keep all the coru for yourselves. Glad to see they were wrong."

"Reputation is what gets you jobs," Nathan said.

"Very true. Out here in the fringe, a bad rep is the quickest way to get pushed out into the badlands."

"The *badlands*?" Nathan asked.

"You haven't heard of the badlands?"

"Can't say that I have," Nathan admitted.

"Let's just say it ain't a nice place to operate," Jorda said.

"Where's it at?" Jessica wondered.

"Well, there's not really a border or anything," Jorda explained. "Basically, the further out you get, the wilder things become. Most colonies in the fringe have local rules, and most adhere to the basic rules of trade."

"I'm guessing Hadria wasn't one of them," Nathan opined. "Thanks for the warning, by the way."

"Yeah, Hadria's kinda on the border. Figured you knew that."

"We do now."

"We don't normally trade there," Jorda insisted, "but Chiqua's about the only trader of medical supplies nearby, and the further out we trade, the more it costs us."

"Then most worlds around here *aren't* like Hadria," Nathan assumed.

"You really *are* new to these parts, aren't you?"

"Yes, we are," Nathan confirmed.

"Where the hell did you come from? Hadria's pretty well known for at *least* a hundred light years."

"Further than that," Nathan replied, not wanting to give away any more information than necessary.

Jorda smiled. "You're fresh outta Alliance space, aren't you? I *knew* it."

"What gave us away?" Nathan asked.

"Well, this pretty little ship, for one. Ain't nothing this clean out here in the fringe. Hell, I'm surprised Chiqua didn't kill you just to take it."

Without warning, Nathan punched Jorda in the mouth, hard. "That's for not warning us."

Jorda put his hand up to his mouth, wiping away the blood from his lip, fighting back the urge to strike back. While he was pretty sure he could take Captain Tuplo, there was something about his crew that made him think twice. "I suppose I had that comin'," he decided, spitting some blood on the ground. "You might want to dirty her up a bit in the future. Maybe break a few things on the outside."

"I'll keep that in mind."

Jorda looked to Jessica, then over at Kit who was standing on the other side of the ramp, his eyes focused on Jorda. "Don't suppose you're interested in another run?"

"Not if it's to Hadria," Nathan stated firmly.

"We've got another batch of coru nearly ready to ship," Jorda told him. "Promised it to a settlement on Susberg."

"Is that in the badlands?" Jessica asked.

Jorda looked confused. "Do you people even have star charts for this area?"

"You just now figuring that out?" Jessica snapped back.

"How the hell did you end up out here, then?"

"I just pointed our nose outbound and jumped," Nathan replied. "I like to be spontaneous."

"Sounds more like being stupid to me," Jorda argued. "The main reason the Alliance doesn't expand into this part of space is because of all the gravitational anomalies out here. Surely you know that?"

"Of course we do," Nathan lied. "We just don't know where they are."

Jorda laughed again. "Then how the hell did you make it to Hadria and back?"

"Just lucky I guess."

"You people are crazy."

"Yeah, we've heard that before," Jessica commented.

"I don't suppose you have any local star charts you could share with us?" Nathan asked Jorda.

"Not hardly. If I were you, captain, I'd spend that twenty percent you kept on charts. Luck only lasts so long, especially out here."

"Any chance the people on Susberg would have charts?"

"Doubtful," Jorda replied. "But you could always go back to Hadria. With all the ships they have comin' and goin', I'm sure you could find someone willing to share some charts with you for a small fee."

Nathan looked at Jessica, sighing. "I guess we're headed back to Hadria."

* * *

Cameron was waiting in the corridor just outside of the hangar bay, where it was warmer.

Nathan and his crew came through the main hatch rather quickly, eager to get out of the cold.

"Jesus," Nathan exclaimed. "It's even colder here than it was in Gruner."

"We've been in the shadow of that gas giant for longer," Cameron stated.

Nathan noticed the dour expression on his executive officer's face. "What's wrong?"

"It's Vlad," Cameron replied.

"What did he do?" Nathan asked.

"He's in bad shape…"

Nathan didn't wait for further details, immediately heading to the nearby elevator.

Jessica and the others stepped up.

"How is he?" Jessica asked.

"Doctor Chen had to put him into medical stasis. It doesn't look good."

"What happened?" Neli wondered.

"They were setting up heaters in the forward weapons bay to keep the swamp water from freezing and damaging things. Vlad was pulled under by a large, aquatic snake. He was under for several minutes, and the creature injected some kind of venom into him."

"Christ," Kit exclaimed.

"Josh, we're going back to Gruner," Jessica said, turning back around.

"Why?" Josh wondered.

"Yes, why?" Cameron agreed.

"The Grunites might know about this creature. Maybe they have an antidote," Jessica explained.

"How are you going to explain what happened?" Cameron asked. "You can't tell them about this ship."

"If Vlad dies, it'll ruin Nathan," Jessica argued. "Not to mention we'll all be screwed. Without Vlad, this ship is never getting off the ground again."

"If we can make contact with the Alliance..."

"That's not an option," Jessica told her. "At least not any time soon."

"Why? What did you find out?"

"We're about ten thousand light years away from Earth," Josh told her. "We're all the way out in the Perseus arm."

Cameron was speechless.

"It could just be a local thing, but it doesn't look like everyone is happy with whatever the Alliance has become."

Cameron's mind was racing. "Did you figure out how far forward in time we've traveled?"

"Without accurate charts for this area, there's no way to calculate that," Josh explained. "I've already transmitted all our nav logs to Laza. Maybe she can figure it out."

"We're wasting time," Jessica argued. "We need to go *now*." She looked at Cameron. "Are you blessing this, or do I have to go rogue on you?"

"Go," Cameron agreed. "Do what you have to do. But don't leave this planet until you update me."

"We'll go there and back, nowhere else," Jessica promised. "Kit and Josh with me."

"No way you're leaving without me," Marcus insisted.

"Fine. Let's go."

* * *

Nathan stared through the clear cover on the medical stasis unit. He had never seen his friend so still. Vlad looked as if his eyes would pop open at any moment, and he would start laughing, having played a practical joke on him.

Memories of seeing his sister, Miri, lying in a similar unit nearly eight years ago, flooded his mind. He had been so scared then, had felt so alone. She was his only surviving family…her and her two children. That's when it hit him.

Nathan had been so busy taking care of his ship and crew that he hadn't even considered the fact that his sister, niece, and nephew were all long dead. He was truly alone, his only family being the people on this ship.

Vladimir was Nathan's oldest friend. When they first met fifteen years ago, they had instantly hit it off. There were very few people Nathan trusted as much as he trusted Vladimir. If it hadn't been for him, none of them would be alive today. Countless times, the burly Russian had managed to get things working just in time to save them all. When they had first met, Vladimir had boasted that he could 'fix anything.' Over the years, he had proven that to be true on numerous occasions.

"I'm sorry, sir," a voice said from behind.

Nathan turned to see a young crewman.

"It's my fault," Sergeant Ryu said. "It was my job to install the heaters. He just took them from me... insisted on doing it himself."

"No offense, Sarge, but that thing would've swallowed you whole," Dixon said.

"We got him out as quick as we could," Mori assured Nathan.

"Any idea what it was?" Nathan wondered.

"A giant snake," Mori replied.

"With a lot of stubby, little legs," Jokay added. "Like a giant zonatee."

"A what?"

"A tiny bug with hundreds of legs," Mori explained.

"How did it get inside the ship?"

"Through the breach in the bow. The entire forward weapons bay is flooded," Dixon explained. "The forwardmost portion is nearly chest deep. The commander insisted on taking the heaters there himself since he was the tallest. The creatures must live in the swamp. They were probably attracted to the warmer waters inside."

"Why were you trying to heat the water?" Nathan asked.

"The commander was afraid the water would freeze and damage equipment inside the bay, especially the gun turret trolleys. But cranking up the heat in the bay to warm the water would use too much power, so we rigged up some portable heating coils that used far less power."

"Did anyone consider just deploying the guns to get them out of the water?" Nathan suggested.

"The doors are damaged," Dixon defended. "And using the transfer tubes to get them to the upper tracks would take too much power, so the commander nixed that idea."

Nathan looked back at Vladimir. "We could survive *without* the guns."

Cameron entered, subtly signaling the others to clear the room. After they were gone, she spoke. "Doctor Chen is doing everything she can," she told Nathan.

"Maybe Jorda knows something about these creatures," Nathan commented, still staring at his friend.

"Jessica is already on her way there."

Nathan looked at Cameron, a bit surprised. Then again, Jessica had always been one to take matters into her own hands. It usually irritated him, but this time, it made him feel a bit better.

"How's the ship?" he asked Cameron. "Are we going to survive this long night?"

"Temps are holding. As long as it doesn't get much colder, we should be okay. Vlad's people are working on getting the other ZPED back online."

"He should have been working on *that* instead of trying to protect gun trolleys."

"He was trying to protect *everything*," Cameron told him, "*and* everyone. You know how protective he can be. It's even worse with *this* ship, since he supervised both her design and build."

"That's always been his biggest weakness," Nathan commented. "He gets too emotionally attached to his ship."

"He's an *engineer.*"

"He's also a *commander,*" Nathan replied. "He should have delegated."

"Like you do?" Cameron retorted.

Nathan glared at her.

"That's not who he is, just like it's not who *you* are."

Nathan turned back to Vladimir. He knew she was right. Delegation had always been difficult for him. During his first command, he had sent far too many people into harm's way. In his second command, he managed to do more himself, despite Cameron's objections at the time.

His time as Connor Tuplo hadn't made it any easier. Those years flying cargo as a privateer were always with him, even though they still felt like memories belonging to someone else. Commanding the Voss, with only a crew of seven, had also contributed to the problem.

Nathan doubted he would ever be able to delegate the more dangerous tasks to others. And he was fine with that. But he wasn't fine with his chief engineer doing the same. Especially under the current circumstances. "We have to save him," he said.

"We will," Cameron assured him.

* * *

Jessica and Kit were halfway down the ramp before the Seiiki's landing gear even touched the ground on the edge of Gruner.

"Where's Jorda?" she barked at one of the surprised locals.

"Maybe he's at that tavern?" Kit suggested when the local simply shrugged at them and continued on his way.

"It was that way, right?" Jessica said, heading off down one of the streets toward the center of the settlement.

"Ease up, Jess," Kit warned, keeping up with

her abnormally brisk pace. "You're gonna spook the locals."

"I don't give a shit."

"They are *armed*, you know."

"My friend is *dying*, Kit."

"And getting into an unnecessary firefight with these people isn't going to help him. You need to check your emotions."

"My emotions are fine."

"No they're not. You've been away from training for too long, and you were always easily triggered to begin with."

"You're about to see how easily I'm triggered."

Kit grabbed her arm, spinning her around. "I'm not kidding, Jess. You either get it under control, or I'm going to knock you out, tie you up, and leave you back in the ship and handle this on my own."

Jessica glared at him, fighting back the urge to punch him in the mouth. Unfortunately, as much as Kit liked to joke around, she knew he wasn't kidding. She also knew she couldn't take him in a fight. He had far more training and experience, and was one of the fiercest Ghatazhak she had ever known.

"You know I'm right," Kit told her. "You've always had this problem. That's why Telles brought you into our ranks to begin with. You need to get that focus back, if not for yourself, for Vlad."

She took a long, deep breath, waiting for the urge to punch him to subside. "Maybe you're right," she finally admitted.

"I am?" Kit replied, shocked that she had conceded so easily.

"Yeah, I have been away too long," she added, turning to continue.

A vehicle came down the road, loaded with four men, all of them armed.

"You see," Kit said as the vehicle pulled to a stop a few meters away from them.

Jorda climbed out of the vehicle. "That was quick," he said as he headed toward them. "You couldn't possibly have gotten star charts already. You decide to push your luck after all?"

"We need to talk," Jessica told him.

"Where's your captain?"

"Do you know anything about some kind of big-ass water snakes living in the swamps of this rock?"

"Boka snakes, yeah," Jorda confirmed. "Nasty things. It's why we stay away from the marshes. Why do you ask?"

"One of our people was bitten by one."

"What, just now? Was it Tuplo? Why the hell did you go into a marsh?"

"Long story," Jessica replied. "Is there an antidote for that thing's venom?"

"Effra root helps, but you gotta know how to prepare it."

"Do *you* know how to prepare it?"

"Me? No, but I know someone who does."

"Get him."

"She's a *her*." Jorda turned to one of his men. "Fetch Sina," he instructed one of his men. "Bring her to the Seiiki, and make sure she brings plenty of effra root."

"This stuff will cure him?"

"Sometimes yes, sometimes no. Every case is different. Take me to him."

"To who?"

"The patient, who else?"

"That's complicated."

"I can see your ship from here," Jorda pointed out.

"The patient isn't *on* the Seiiki."

Jorda looked at her and Kit. "I'm confused. You guys have a camp somewhere?"

"Something like that." Jessica looked at Kit.

"Might as well tell him while we're waiting for this Sina lady," Kit suggested.

"Tell me what?" Jorda wondered.

"Walk with me, Jorda," Jessica said, turning to head back to the Seiiki.

* * *

Jorda and Sina stood staring out the windows of the Seiiki's cockpit as it rose off the ground and began its departure from Gruner.

"First time?" Jessica asked, seeing their fascination.

"No, but it has been a while," Jorda admitted.

The ship pitched upward and began to accelerate toward the sky. Moments later, the pale, blue light spilled out across the stubby nose of the shuttle, then flashed brightly as the ship transitioned to orbit over Dencke.

"My God," Sina exclaimed, seeing her world from orbit. "First time for me," Sina said. "I was a baby when our family moved here."

"Why the jump?" Jorda wondered. "I thought your injured man was on Dencke?"

"He is," Jessica replied. "Jumps are faster."

"You're not worried about jumping too much?" Sina asked.

"Why would I be?" Jessica wondered.

Jorda and Sina exchanged glances. "You haven't heard?" Jorda wondered.

"Heard what?"

"The Alliance claims that standard jump drives disrupt the barrier that separates dimensions, and that they are the cause of all the rogue gravity wells plaguing the badlands."

"Doesn't the Alliance use jump drives?" Josh wondered.

Jorda looked at him oddly. "Who are you people?"

Jessica cast Josh a stern look, causing him to turn back to his console and begin pitching down for the descent jump.

Another jump field formed, again filling the cockpit with a flash of blue-white light. The ship was no longer in orbit, but instead was descending rapidly toward a long, gray object at the end of some kind of valley.

"What is that?" Jorda wondered, peering out the forward windows.

"*That* is our ship," Jessica told him.

Jorda looked at her in disbelief, then turned back to the windows, trying to make out the details of the distant object. "Impossible," he said, half to himself. But as they grew closer, more and more details became visible, and soon he had no choice but to accept it. "It's *huge*."

"And this one's only a third the size of her predecessor," Jessica told him.

Again, Jorda looked bewildered. He didn't blink as they approached, passing over the tail end of the ship and descending to the flight deck nestled between the two drive nacelles.

The ship touched down, the whine of its grav-lift generators immediately beginning to lessen as they began rolling toward the open hangar bay ahead.

"Incredible," Sina gasped.

"Surely there are bigger ships than this out there," Jessica said.

"Not out here," Jorda replied. "At least not that I've ever heard of. The largest ship I've ever seen in person was the Coralie, and she was about twice this shuttle's size." He looked at her as they rolled inside. "Where did you come from?"

Jessica thought for a moment. "I think I'd better let the captain explain that one."

"He's *here?* Captain Tuplo?"

"In a manner of speaking," Jessica replied.

* * *

Jessica led Jorda and Sina into the trauma bay, with Kit following behind. "Captain, this is Sina," she announced. "She may have something that can help."

"A pleasure to meet you," Nathan greeted. He cast a sidelong glance at Jessica. "You and I are going to have words," he told her.

"What have you got?" Doctor Chen asked.

"Sina, this is Doctor Chen, our chief medical officer."

"An honor," Sina greeted, holding out her satchel. "Effra root. It has many properties, but mostly it is used to absorb the toxic compounds found in many of the venomous creatures of Dencke."

"And you think it will cure the commander?"

"The venom of the boka is one of the most lethal, so it depends on how much of it was absorbed by the victim's liver, and how much of it has reached his brain."

"Boka?" Nathan wondered.

"That's what they call that thing," Jessica explained.

Nathan looked at Doctor Chen. "What do you think?"

"I'd like to run it through our analyzer first," Doctor Chen replied.

"How long ago was the patient bitten?" Sina asked.

Doctor Chen looked at the clock on the wall. "About two hours ago."

"Then there is very little time," Sina warned. "You must give it to him *immediately*. It may already be too late."

Doctor Chen looked at Nathan.

"How long does it take to prepare it?"

"Maybe ten minutes," Sina replied.

"Doc, you have ten minutes to analyze that stuff," Nathan decided.

Doctor Chen led Sina off to get started.

"I haven't thanked you yet for coming," Nathan said to Jorda.

"You can thank me by answering some questions," Jorda replied. "With this one, every answer raises more questions."

Jessica shrugged.

"Very well," Nathan replied. "But first, let me ask *you* a question. What *year* is it?"

Jorda looked confused. "Forty twenty-one, give or take. It's hard to keep track of out here."

Nathan's eyes widened, as did Jessica's.

"Why? What year did you *think* it was?" Jorda wondered.

Nathan took in a breath, taking a moment to wrap his head around the information. "Two days ago, we were attacked by battle cruisers of the Ilyan Gamaze."

"Never heard of them," Jorda said.

Nathan exchanged a glance with Jessica before continuing. "They launched a singularity weapon, trapping us in its gravity well."

"What? Singularity weapons were outlawed after the great war of thirty-six ninety," Jorda insisted. "Besides, if you were caught in one, you'd all be dead."

"In order to escape, we had to jump *through* the singularity," Nathan explained.

"Through it?" Jorda asked in disbelief.

"Through it."

"Captain, I'm no physicist, but I'm pretty sure that's about as impossible as it sounds."

"Maybe so, but here we are."

Jorda's brow furrowed, deep in thought. "If you were caught by a singularity, then you would have experienced some sort of time dilation, right?"

"That is correct."

"Well, what year was it when you were attacked?"

"Thirty-four eighty-six," Nathan replied.

Jorda's mouth dropped open. "You're joking, right?" He looked at Jessica, who looked just as serious as her captain. "That's like five hundred and something *years*."

"Five hundred and thirty-five," Nathan replied.

Jorda had to take a moment to let the information sink in. "I've heard stories of cargo ships that get pushed forward a few years by flying too close to a rogue gravity well, but nothing like this." After shaking his head, he added, "I guess that explains your *classic* shuttle." Then it hit him. "Are you people...I mean, *were* you people...*Alliance?*"

"Does it matter now?" Nathan asked.

"I don't know, does it?" Jorda wondered.

"I think we need to talk," Nathan decided. "I believe I have a lot of questions to ask you."

"I'm bettin' not half as many as I've got to ask *you*," Jorda insisted.

* * *

"I've never seen anything like this," Doctor Chen said as she studied the analysis of the effra root on the medical display. "It's like they're *feeding* on the proteins in the venom."

"The bacteria feed on effra root," Sina confirmed. "They also feed on boka venom, and by doing so, they prevent it from being absorbed by the victim. The problem is that effra root *itself* is toxic to humans. It is not deadly, but when introduced in too large of quantities into a patient who is already weakened by boka venom, it can result in severe neurological impairment, and even death."

"So, giving this to the commander, even in smaller doses, could cause brain damage?"

"It is a possibility."

"How often does this occur?"

"I have never seen it myself," Sina admitted. "However, the few cases of boka attacks I have treated received the effra root serum within minutes of being bitten."

"Any chance they aren't slowed by suspended animation?" Doctor Chen asked.

"I do not know. I know nothing about that technology."

"You've never heard of SA?"

"I've heard of it," Sina replied, "I just have no knowledge of how it works."

* * *

"History is of little importance on Dencke or any other fringe world for that matter," Jorda replied.

"Can you at least tell us about the *state* of the Alliance?" Nathan asked from across the conference table in the command briefing room.

"Anything I tell you will be rumor, nothing more," Jorda warned.

"Understood."

"This much I can tell you for certain," Jorda began. "There was a time when the Alliance was the protector of peace and prosperity throughout the galaxy. But a few hundred years ago, there was a great war."

"The one you referred to before? In thirty-six ninety?" Jessica assumed.

"Yes."

"Who did they fight?"

"The Jung."

Nathan and Jessica exchanged glances.

"Weren't the Jung *members* of the Alliance?" Kit pointed out.

"It was my understanding that they pulled out of the Alliance decades earlier. Why, I do not know."

"Any guesses?" Nathan asked.

"Perhaps they did not like the Alliance telling them how to run their empire?" Jorda speculated. "That is the main reason most people migrated to the fringe, after all."

"The Alliance charter specifically forbade such control," Nathan argued. "Every member retained the right to run their domains as they saw fit, as long as they did not prevent their citizens from leaving, and did not attack other members."

"I guess the Alliance changed the charter," Kit said.

"Why would they do that?" Nathan wondered.

"All I know is that it happened some time *after* the AIs took control," Jorda told them.

"The AIs? That's impossible," Nathan argued. "AIs have to take orders *from* humans."

"Perhaps *took control* is inaccurate," Jorda admitted. "Technically, the president is in control. The AIs just advise him."

"The *President* of the Confederated Systems Alliance takes advice from AIs?"

"AIs are the arbiters of all decisions," Jorda explained. "That's another reason people migrate out of the Alliance. They don't like machines telling them what to do."

"Then you don't use AIs?"

"In the *fringe*, no. At least not as far as I know. But I haven't been off-world in more than a decade, so things may have changed."

Jessica looked at Nathan. "I guess we aren't going to be looking to the Alliance for help."

Jorda looked confused. "But you *are* Alliance, aren't you?"

"We *were*," Nathan replied. "But if the Alliance is as you say, I'm not so sure we should be."

"But your commander. Surely the Alliance would be able to heal him."

"Are there any *real* medical facilities in the fringe?" Nathan asked Jorda.

"Not that I know of, but again, I'm not exactly an expert."

"Maybe *Chiqua* would know?" Kit suggested.

Nathan looked to Jorda for an opinion.

"She might," Jorda said.

"So we're going back to Hadria?" Jessica concluded.

"It appears so," Nathan replied.

"This time, we're taking more Ghatazhak," Jessica insisted. "*And* more *guns.*"

"Captain, if you have no objections, I'd like to go with you to Hadria," Jorda said.

Nathan looked to Jessica, who shrugged indifference. "Very well, but I can't promise you we'll be coming straight back. We may have to act on whatever leads Chiqua might give us."

"I understand."

"Assuming the bitch doesn't try to kill us again," Jessica remarked.

* * *

Nathan returned to medical on his way to the shuttle bay, checking in on his friend. Vladimir still looked terrible, lying pale and motionless in the medical SA tube.

"Captain," Doctor Chen greeted as she and Sina entered the compartment.

"Any change?" Nathan asked, fearing the answer.

"Yes, but not much. We've given him one dose of Sina's effra root formula, and I've reduced the amount of metabolic slow-down in the SA module to allow it to work. While I haven't seen any *actual* improvement yet, he hasn't gotten any worse since adjusting the level of SA. I'm hoping that's a good sign."

"When will you know for sure if the effra root is working?"

"Normally, I would administer an injection every four hours, and we would see improvement within a day," Sina explained.

"Because of the reduced metabolic state, I've put

him on a constant infusion of effra root," Doctor Chen added. "I've done the math, so we should be achieving the desired therapeutic levels."

"We're headed back to Hadria," Nathan told them. "We're hoping that Chiqua will know of a medical facility *outside* of Alliance space that can provide proper care."

"It seems unlikely," Sina warned.

"You don't think there are any hospitals in the area?"

"I have no idea," she admitted. "However, the boka is indigenous to *this* world and no others. It seems unlikely that another world would even know about it, let alone have an antidote."

"Worlds don't communicate about such things?"

"Not to my knowledge, which admittedly *is* limited."

"If we were back on Takara, the Ghatazhak could clone him," Kit said as he and Jessica entered.

"Maybe we should consider taking a shuttle to Takara?" Jessica suggested.

"We have absolutely no intel on the state of things within the Alliance," Nathan reminded them. "We could be flying into a nightmare. Besides, we don't even know if the Ghatazhak still exist."

"No way Telles would let the Ghatazhak cease to exist," Kit argued.

"I agree," Jessica added.

"I hope you're both right," Nathan replied. "But for now, we avoid the Alliance at all costs. I'm not going to risk everyone for one person, not even Vlad. That's what *got* us here, *five* centuries in the future," he added, looking at Jessica.

"Don't look at me," Jessica defended. "I didn't *ask* to be rescued."

CHAPTER FOUR

This time, Nathan and his party stayed on the outer edges of Hadria's pit, going directly to Chiqua's complex, escorted by four Ghatazhak, Jessica, *and* Jorda. Kit took the lead, parting the crowd with ease. As they were pushed aside, rough-looking shoppers, all of them armed, shot angry looks at Kit he passed. But when they saw the bravado on his face, the amount of firepower he was carrying, and that the others in his party were equally foreboding, their expressions quickly changed.

"People like Chiqua only care about money and power, and they don't care who they betray to get it," Jorda warned as he, Nathan, and Jessica followed in the Ghatazhak's wake.

"I've dealt with people like her before," Nathan assured the Grunite leader.

"I'm not sure you have. This display of power will not have the effect you are hoping for," Jorda added.

"Chiqua won't let *anyone* intimidate her," Jessica insisted. "She was *testing* us."

"And *we* are about to test *her*," Nathan stated confidently.

Jessica gave Nathan a curious glance. "Since when did you become so confrontational?"

"About five hundred and thirty-five years ago," Nathan replied, more to himself than to Jessica.

The approach of the Ghatazhak did not go unnoticed by Chiqua's men. Two smug-looking bodyguards stepped in front of Kit.

"Can I help you?" one of the men asked, stepping into Kit's path.

"Move or die," Kit stated in matter-of-fact fashion.

Four more men emerged from the crowd of shoppers, taking positions all around Kit.

"You were saying?" the man replied, grinning.

"You were warned," Kit said, his stride not breaking.

The man reached up and pulled the butt of the blaster rifle slung over his right shoulder, flipping it over to bring its double barrels to bear on Kit. To his surprise, Kit grabbed the barrel of the weapon with his left hand, twisting it clockwise to wrestle it from the man's hand. At the same time, he swept the man's legs from under him with his foot, sending him crashing onto his backside on the hard-packed ground.

Jessica and the rest of the Ghatazhak also went for their big guns, each taking aim at a different target. In a blink of an eye, every one of Chiqua's men also had a gun in their hand that was aimed at a member of Nathan's party. But the Ghatazhak had guns in both hands.

"KIT!" Nathan barked, not wanting him to pull the trigger.

Kit stood fast, finger on the trigger, his eyes locked on those of the man his weapon was aimed at. "Holster your heat, or this fuck will be the first to die," he warned Chiqua's men.

The man on his back grinned up at Kit. "We have you outnumbered."

"Think again," Nathan said.

The man looked toward his own feet, spotting Nathan's, his side arm aimed at his own crotch.

"In case he misses," Nathan told the man.

"Captain Tuplo," Chiqua greeted, stepping into view. "I didn't expect to see you again, let alone so soon," she commented as she walked over next to Kit.

She looked down at her man on the ground. "You're fired." She then looked at Kit. "You can kill him." To the rest of her men, she ordered, "Stand down."

"Are you sure you want to do that?" Nathan warned.

"If you wanted to kill us, you already would have," Chiqua stated confidently. "*You* are here for something else. A deal perhaps?"

"How do you know I'm not here for vengeance?" Nathan wondered.

"You brought the Grunite with you."

"Maybe I just wanted to demonstrate to him how we deal with betrayal."

"Again, you did not shoot," Chiqua reminded him. "That tells me everything I need to know about you."

"And what did you learn?" Nathan wondered.

"That although you are *willing* to kill, you have no *desire* to do so." Chiqua glanced over at the others in Nathan's party, including Jessica. "Your crew, however, I am not so sure of."

"My *crew* follows my orders," Nathan assured her. "Except for this one on occasion," he added, nodding toward Jessica.

Jessica just smiled at Chiqua.

"I'll keep that in mind," Chiqua replied. "Perhaps we should talk inside?" Chiqua offered, gesturing toward the central building.

"Out here will be fine," Nathan replied.

Chiqua eyed the Ghatazhak, all of whom still had their weapons drawn. "Can you at least stand your people down?"

Nathan looked around, checking that all of Chiqua's men had indeed holstered their weapons. He then turned his attention back to her. "Very well, but be warned. My men can drop any one of yours and have their guns back in their holsters before their victims hit the ground."

"Noted."

Nathan nodded to Kit, who in turn signaled his men with a nod, causing all of them to lower their weapons.

Once the tension had eased, Chiqua spoke up again. "So why *did* you return, Captain Tuplo?"

"One of my people was bitten by a..." he turned to Jorda.

"A *boka*," Jorda stated.

"I've heard of them," Chiqua said.

"We were hoping you had an antidote for the boka's venom," Nathan explained.

"Unfortunately, I do not," Chiqua replied. "Not much demand for boka antivenom. No one goes to Dencke, and the Grunite know better than to go into their swamps."

"A hospital, then," Nathan suggested. "One with the proper facilities to analyze and synthesize an antidote."

"Such facilities do not exist in the fringe," Chiqua replied. She looked to Jorda. "Don't your people have something?"

"We do, but its effectiveness is questionable," Jorda admitted.

Chiqua eyed Jorda, then Nathan and his party. There was something going on, something they were not telling her. "I'm afraid the nearest *real* medical facility is in the Pyru system, well *inside* Alliance space. I assume you have certification for operations within their space?"

"Why would you assume that?" Nathan wondered.

"Just a hunch."

"Assume that we do not," Nathan told her.

Chiqua sensed an opportunity. "Then you will need my help."

"Sorry, but we have all the medical supplies we need," Nathan told her.

"But you will need a fake certification to operate in Alliance space, and a properly encoded transponder...you know, to avoid being vaporized by the defense grids that surround all Alliance worlds."

Nathan thought for a moment. "I don't suppose you have up-to-date star charts for this area?"

"No, but I know where we can get some," Chiqua replied, a satisfied smirk forming on her face.

Nathan looked at Jessica. "What do you think?"

"I think she's full of shit," Jessica replied, staring at Chiqua.

"I like her," Chiqua said.

Jessica looked back to Nathan. "Unfortunately, she's the only lead we have at the moment."

"We can look elsewhere," Jorda told Nathan under his breath. "Surely there must be someone *else* on this world that can help us."

"Unfortunately, time is not on our side," Nathan said. He looked at Chiqua. "How soon can you depart?"

"Just give me a few minutes to get a team ready..."

"No team, just you," Jessica insisted.

"I don't go *anywhere* without my bodyguards," Chiqua stated firmly.

"But you've got *me*," Jessica quipped.

"That's a deal breaker," Chiqua insisted.

"Then I guess we'll look elsewhere," Nathan replied, turning to depart.

Chiqua wasn't sure what to think, but the opportunity was too rare for her to pass up. "Wait!"

Nathan stopped, turning back toward Chiqua.

"One guard," Chiqua suggested.

"*No* guards," Nathan countered, "and *that's* a deal breaker."

Chiqua sighed. "Promise you won't kill me?"

"As long as you don't kill any of us, we won't kill you."

"Fine. Just let me grab my coat."

"And leave your sidearm behind," Jessica called out as Chiqua walked away.

Jessica turned to Nathan. "Nicely done."

"Not my first negotiation," Nathan replied under his breath.

* * *

Nathan, Jessica, and Kit all waited at the bottom of the Seiiki's cargo ramp as Chiqua left her bodyguards at their vehicle and walked toward the ship. When she reached them, Jessica held out her hand to stop her, then stepped up to pat her down.

Chiqua held up her arms, looking annoyed. "I guess you don't trust me."

"Not in the slightest," Jessica replied.

"I'm hurt."

"*Trust* is earned, not bestowed," Nathan told her.

"She's clean," Jessica reported, finishing the pat-down and stepping aside.

"Welcome aboard the Seiiki," Nathan said, gesturing toward the ship.

"Thank you," Chiqua replied as she headed up the ramp.

Nathan turned and followed Chiqua. Jessica and Kit watched the two guards in the distance, also scanning the sides of the landing site for any potential threats. Once Nathan and Chiqua were inside, they headed up the ramp themselves, Kit walking backwards to keep his eyes on the two remaining guards.

Nathan led Chiqua up the short stepladder to the main deck landing, then through the hatch into the center bay, which was currently loaded with a long-duration flight module equipped with a lounge and a galley.

Chiqua appeared shocked.

"Something wrong?" Nathan asked.

"I just didn't expect it to be this nice."

"It's pretty much standard issue."

"It looks brand new. Restoring it must have cost a fortune."

"You have no idea," Nathan said as he tapped the intercom panel. "Josh, we're ready to lift off whenever you are."

"*Destination?*" Josh asked.

Nathan looked to Chiqua.

"Pangburn," Chiqua instructed.

"Never heard of it."

"About twenty-eight light years from here," Jorda said, coming down from the flight deck.

"I don't suppose you have coordinates for it," Nathan said.

"I expected *you* to already know of it," Chiqua admitted. "Steer right of Dencke and about ten degrees above her. Pangburn is a small, rocky world orbiting a trio of red dwarfs. The two inner stars orbit a shared axis, and the outer star circles the two inners. Pangburn orbits the outer star. It's the only such system in the area, so it should be easy to spot. It's also the only *habitable* planet in the entire system."

"You get all that, Josh?" Nathan asked over the intercom.

"*On our way*," Josh replied.

"And we can get accurate star charts on Pangburn?" Nathan asked as Jessica and Kit entered the compartment to join them.

"It's the nearest world with an *actual* spaceport. They get regular flights from border systems, so they should have the most up-to-date charts available." Chiqua eyed Nathan suspiciously. "Where did you say you people came from?"

"We didn't," Jessica commented as she passed by, headed forward.

The Seiiki's grav-lift systems began humming, their pitch rising.

"Let's just say it's a *long* way from here, and leave it at that," Nathan told her as his ship lifted off.

"Why?"

"Because I don't feel like explaining it."

"No, I meant *why* did you come here?" Chiqua corrected.

"That's also difficult to explain."

"No offense, Captain, but why exactly do we need her?" Kit asked.

Nathan looked at Chiqua. "Seems like a fair question," Nathan agreed. "Why do we need you?"

"You can't just *ask* for star charts," Chiqua told them. "That'll raise all kinds of questions."

"Like?"

"Like how you got here *without* them," Chiqua explained. "There's about a hundred rogue gravity wells between this sector and the border systems. I'm surprised you even made it through."

"I didn't realize you were a navigator," Nathan commented.

"I'm not," Chiqua admitted. "I just like to know things. *That's* why you need me."

"Because you *know* things?" Jessica scoffed.

"Information can be a very valuable commodity," Chiqua insisted. "It got me on this ship, didn't it?"

"Yeah, I'm still trying to figure out your angle in this," Jessica retorted.

"I don't have an *angle*. I just smell an *opportunity*."

"An opportunity to enrich yourself."

"Jess," Nathan scolded.

"An opportunity to learn more about the Seiiki, her captain, and her crew...and why they are jumping about the fringe without any star charts."

"Don't count on learning much," Jessica said.

"Why don't you go help Josh," Nathan strongly suggested.

Jessica held up her hands in resignation, then headed through the forward hatch.

"She speaks her mind, doesn't she," Chiqua said.

"More than you know," Nathan admitted as he filled a cup with water. "Thirsty?"

"No thank you."

"So why do you want to know so much about us?" Nathan wondered. "I mean, we're nobody. Just a small ship and crew, trying to set up shop in the fringe. Surely we can't be the first you've seen."

"Not by a long shot," Chiqua confirmed. "You're not even the first to show up in an antique ship. But one in *mint condition? That* is a first. And *that's* what I find most curious."

"Why is that?" Nathan asked, trying to keep her talking.

"There's no way you were able to restore this ship out in the fringe, which means you *came* from *Alliance* space. That's what doesn't add up. An antique like this in such perfect condition would surely be worth plenty back in the core. I'm sure there are hundreds of museums that would pay millions of credits for her."

"*That's* why you tried to steal her," Nathan realized.

"I never intended to *steal* your ship, Captain. I simply wanted to see how you'd react when faced with danger."

"And how did I handle it?"

"Like a man who has faced far worse," Chiqua replied. "Which has me even more puzzled."

"How so?" Nathan asked, wanting to keep the conversation going as long as possible, hoping to gather more information.

"Everything about you—your ship, your crew, the fact that you don't have any charts for this area—it just doesn't add up."

Nathan smiled. "Maybe your math is flawed?"

Chiqua smiled back.

"Truth is, we ended up here more by accident than by design," Nathan told her. It wasn't an outright lie, but it might be enough to satisfy her.

"That sounds like an interesting story. Perhaps you'll share it with me?"

"Perhaps, in time," Nathan replied.

"*Feet wet,*" Josh announced over the intercom. "*Jumping in five.*"

"Feet wet?" Chiqua wondered.

"An old term from Earth," Nathan explained. "Pilots would use it to report that they were now over the ocean."

"Never heard of it."

"It's *really* old," Nathan told her. "My pilot is a fan of ancient Earth vids."

"Hadria doesn't have any oceans."

"He uses it to announce when we have left the atmosphere and are back in space."

"Weird."

"Maybe, but he's a *really* good pilot," Nathan insisted. "So what can you tell me about Pangburn?"

"It's one of the larger colonies in the sector. Low gravity, which makes it ideal as a spaceport. Most of the traffic between border systems and this sector comes through Pangburn."

"Do they have landing fees?" Nathan asked.

"Don't all spaceports?"

"What kind of currency do they accept?"

Again, Chiqua looked puzzled. "We may not be *part* of the Alliance, but everyone out here still accepts Alliance credits. *Especially* spaceports serving as arrival ports for border system ships."

"So no barter then?"

"Probably not."

"That could be a problem. Is there anywhere on the surface we could land *without* having to pay?"

"You *could*, but the Pangburn government won't like it."

"We may not have a choice."

"Don't worry, Captain. I'll cover your landing fees," Chiqua promised.

"I'm not sure I like that idea," Nathan replied.

"Consider it an apology...for my previous transgression."

"*We found it,*" Josh reported over the intercom. "Jumping into the system in one minute."

"Does Pangburn have any kind of approach procedures we're supposed to follow?" Nathan asked Chiqua.

"Just jump in," she replied. "They'll call you."

* * *

"We just entered the Pangburn system," Jessica told Nathan as he entered the cockpit.

"How far out are we?" Nathan asked.

"Just over three million clicks," Josh replied.

"Any contacts?"

"Just a few ships coming and going near the planet," Jessica reported. "But those tracks are sixteen minutes old."

"Slow to orbital speed for the planet and jump us into RTC range," Nathan instructed.

"Already started the decel," Josh reported.

"There's supposed to be a full spaceport there, so after we jump, we'll hail them."

"Any idea what channel they're on?"

"Just hail across the spectrum and see which channel they answer on," Nathan told him.

"So we look like complete newbs," Josh grumbled.

"In *this* system, we are."

"Doesn't mean we have to *look* like it," Josh muttered as he punched in the next jump. "Jumping to comms range."

"Your comm-set's tied in," Jessica added as the jump flash washed over the cockpit.

"Pangburn, Seiiki," Nathan called over comms. "Inbound for landing. Requesting instructions."

"Seiiki, Pangburn approach," a voice replied over comms. "Your ship is unfamiliar to us. Do you wish to open an account?"

"We're ferrying a passenger in and out of Pangburn on business," Nathan explained. "We'll be using her account for this visit."

"Name of the account holder?"

"Chiqua Kimbro."

"Transmit authentication code."

"Uh..."

"Here," Chiqua's voice came from behind.

Jessica and Nathan both turned to look, seeing Chiqua and Kit standing at the hatchway to the cockpit.

"She said you'd need it," Kit explained.

Chiqua handed a small chip to Nathan. "Plug this into your comms and transmit on the data side band for the current channel."

"You might have mentioned this before we jumped," Nathan suggested, accepting the chip.

"Figured you knew."

Nathan didn't respond as he plugged the chip into the overhead comms panel and pressed the transmit button.

"From now on, just assume we know nothing. It'll be easier that way."

"And the mystery deepens," Chiqua commented.

"Authentication accepted. Transmitting arrival instructions. Pangburn does not allow AI-controlled landings."

"My kind of planet," Josh commented.

"Understood," Nathan replied. "Seiiki out." Nathan looked at Josh. "You get it?"

"It's coming in now," Josh reported, watching the instructions loading onto one of his flight displays. "Pretty standard stuff. Approach corridor, speed limits, pad assignment...oh, and they don't allow jump-downs. Between decel, transition, and descent, it's gonna be about half an hour until we touch down."

"Upper atmo looks pretty rough," Jessica warned, examining the weather forecast for the approach. "It's going to be bumpy."

Nathan pressed the button on the overhead, activating the ship-wide intercom. "All hands, buckle up for descent. No jump-down on this one. ETA to touchdown is thirty." Nathan turned to Chiqua. "How about you stay in here with us, just in case," he instructed, pointing to the starboard auxiliary console directly behind the copilot's seat where Jessica was sitting. "And don't touch anything."

Chiqua held up both hands as she took her seat, indicating that she understood.

"Jess," Nathan said. "Take the port seat and keep an eye on her."

Jessica climbed out of the copilot's seat, vacating it for Nathan and going to the port auxiliary station. "See that everyone is buckled in for descent," she told Kit. "We hit atmo in five minutes."

"You got it," Kit replied, turning to depart.

Jessica took her seat, faced Chiqua, and then pointed at her own eyes and then at Chiqua, warning her that she was being watched. "Has it occurred to you that she may be leading us into a trap?" she asked Nathan.

"I was more or less expecting it." Nathan admitted.

"I assure you that I have no such intentions," Chiqua assured her.

"Uh-huh," Jessica replied. "Let's hope so, because you'll be the first one I pop."

"Jess, be nice," Nathan urged.

"I *am* being nice."

Chiqua rolled her eyes and sighed. Gaining the trust of these people was not going to be easy.

* * *

As instructed, the Seiiki flew in over the inland

sea to the south of the spaceport, touching down on one of the many landing pads located along the rocky shoreline. After touching down, they rolled inland along the designated taxiway to one of the parking pads near the general-purpose terminal located at the middle of the sprawling complex.

"To be honest, I'm a little surprised by all of this," Nathan admitted as he stared out the forward windows. "I didn't expect anything this organized out here."

"Pangburn is a bit of an anomaly," Chiqua explained. "It's one of the few true spaceports *not* located closer to the Alliance border. You won't see many ships here that actually came directly from a border port. Most come from ports closer in."

"Then Pangburn is a shipping hub for this sector?" Nathan surmised.

"It's the *only* major port for a hundred light years."

"The city itself didn't appear large enough to support a port this size," Jessica commented.

"People on Pangburn don't live in cities. What you saw were just businesses that service visiting crews and port workers. Residents live on homesteads spread all over the continent. They only come into the city every few weeks for resupply."

"What about the people who work in the local businesses?" Nathan wondered.

"They live on homesteads as well, although usually closer in."

"I guess they love long commutes," Josh decided.

"Everyone on Pangburn owns a skimmer," Chiqua told them.

"A skimmer?" Nathan wondered.

"You're kidding, right?" Chiqua studied their faces, quickly realizing they were serious. "Aircars?

Hover sleds? Speeders?" She noticed a service sled cruising along the taxiway and pointed. "Like that, but for people."

Nathan stared at the service sled as it passed. "Everyone drives one of *those?*"

"Pretty much."

"How fast do they go?" Josh wondered.

"A few hundred kilometers an hour, at least, but they can't climb more than a hundred meters above the surface. Their grav-lifts are too weak. But they scoot around pretty fast."

Josh looked at Nathan. "We need to get one of those."

"First things first," Nathan told him. "I assume they sell updated navigation charts here?" he asked Chiqua.

"At the crew services desk in the general terminal," she replied. "Get whatever you need. They'll charge it to my account."

"Not sure I like the direction this is going," Jessica told Nathan, just loud enough to make sure Chiqua heard her.

"Josh, once you get the ship secured, head over to crew services and see about those charts."

"Where will you guys be going?" Josh asked as the shuttle came to a stop at the center of their parking pad.

"I'm guessing Chiqua has a destination in mind for us," Nathan said, looking at Chiqua.

"Kit, you and Abs are with us," Jessica told him. "Brill and Deeks will babysit Josh."

"*Babysit?*" Josh protested. "I'm nearly *thirty!* Give or take a few years."

* * *

While still a bit on the dusty side, Kitsi at least had a somewhat logical layout. Buildings were clustered together, from three to six, all sharing the same service module. It was all neat and tidy, but odd in the sense that there were very few residences. Most of the clusters appeared to be businesses. Restaurants, taverns, shops, professional services, even a few small hotels.

Skimming along just above the buildings, Nathan and the others had an excellent view of the small city. Beyond the city limits, they could see more clusters of buildings, most of which were residences. But the further out they got, the fewer the buildings until finally, in the distance, they were all single residences, separated by anywhere from meters to kilometers.

Everywhere they looked, there were skimmers moving along in varying directions and at multiple altitudes. It seemed a wonder that they were able to ply the skies of Kitsi without colliding. Nathan felt certain there was some level of automation involved.

"How many people live here?" Nathan asked Chiqua.

"I don't know. Maybe a few million on the entire planet. It was one of the first colonies established *outside* of Alliance space during the war."

"The war against the Jung?" Jessica wondered.

"The Collective, yes."

"The *Collective?*" Nathan asked.

"Of course," Chiqua replied, a puzzled look on her face that vanished a moment later.

"Seems like a nice place to live," Jorda commented as he scanned the vista.

"Don't be fooled," Chiqua warned. "The residents

may be spread out, but they reached carrying capacity decades ago. Pangburn's a closed world."

"So they don't allow immigrants?" Kit surmised.

"I heard they allow a few on occasion. If they have a skillset their population is lacking, or if their population falls precipitously low. They had an outbreak of dexa fever a few years back. Killed about three hundred thousand, I believe. They allowed about a thousand to immigrate to replace key positions, but that barely made a dent in the waiting list. Everyone wanting out of the Alliance wants to migrate to worlds like Pangburn. I suppose they don't have what it takes to survive in more rustic settlements."

"Are there still new settlements being established?" Nathan asked.

"Probably," Chiqua replied. "Though not as frequently as before. They'd have to go pretty far out, beyond the badlands in fact. There just aren't any hospitable worlds left in the fringe, and nobody in their right *mind* would settle in the badlands."

"Except for people like you," Jessica commented.

The slander caused Kit to smile, but it had no effect on Chiqua, the insult rolling off her shoulders. "Hadria is about as wild as I'm willing to tolerate. Truth be told, if I could move to a world like this, I probably would."

"And give up your little empire?" Jessica said, continuing to try to get a rise from her.

"Sometimes it's better to be a *little* fish in a *big* pond," Chiqua replied.

"So who's this Basava guy we're going to meet?" Kit asked. "Another criminal mastermind?"

"Just an old engineer. Three-time retread, I hear.

Supplements his retirement selling spoofed Alliance transponders and forged certs."

"And you trust him?" Nathan wondered.

"I've never met him," Chiqua admitted.

"Then why are we going to him?"

"Because, from what I hear, he's the best in the sector."

* * *

Josh entered the crew services department along with Mori and Jokay. "Wow," he exclaimed, looking around the well-appointed lobby. "Are we in the right place?"

"May I help you?" a young woman in a business uniform asked from behind the counter.

"Uh, yeah," Josh replied. "I was looking for up-to-date nav charts for this region?"

"Are yours expired?"

"Just a bit," Josh admitted.

"Just this sector?" the woman inquired.

"How many sectors you got?"

The woman looked puzzled. "All of them, of course."

Josh looked at Mori. "Jackpot."

"Josh…"

"We'll take 'em all," Josh told her.

"That's *quite* expensive," she warned.

"That's okay."

"What ship?"

"The Seiiki."

"Are you her captain?"

"Nope. Just her pilot," Josh replied.

"Maybe you want to check with your captain before making such a large purchase?"

"That sounds like a good idea," Jokay agreed.

"Captain's orders were to get nav charts," Josh insisted. "I'm pretty sure he meant *all* of them."

Mori looked at Jokay. "Makes sense."

"I'll need your current version numbers in order to send you the proper upgrade files."

"Just assume we don't have any nav charts," Josh told her.

"If you don't have *any* charts, then how did you get here?"

"Just lucky I guess."

"I see." The woman punched some commands into her terminal, then replied. "Well, your purchase was approved. However, I seem to be unable to connect to your navigation computer in order to send the updates to your ship."

"We've got a pretty old nav-com," Josh told her. "Antique, actually. Any chance I could just get a hard copy for a fresh install?"

"That will cost extra," she warned.

"Gotta do what we gotta do, right?" Josh said with a wink.

"I'll need to get some data cards. I'll be back in a moment."

"Take your time," Josh told her.

"Chiqua's not going to like this," Mori warned once the woman had left.

"What's she gonna do, shoot me?"

"The captain might," Mori replied.

"Hey, we *need* those charts if we're going to avoid those rogue gravity wells, not to mention flying approaches into controlled space...as in *Alliance* space."

"Can't you just wing it like we've done so far?"

"Not without raising suspicion," Josh explained.

"Trust me, it's an aviation thing. Lots of BS rules and plenty of jerks who'd love to write us up for a controlled-space procedure violation."

"Is that really a concern given our current circumstances?" Mori wondered.

"Trust me, nothing draws attention like a CSPV. I've heard of people getting their ships locked down over them."

"But that was five hundred years ago, Josh," Mori argued. "Maybe things have changed since then?"

"Governments never give up power once they have it. We *need* those charts."

"I hope you're right," Mori said. "This purchase will likely put us in Chiqua's debt."

"I didn't think of that," Josh admitted. "Eh...I'm sure the captain can work something out," he added with a wave of his hand.

* * *

After passing over the entire city, their skimmer ride took them into open country, where they picked up considerable speed. Gone were the clusters of homes, giving way to single residences and the occasional co-op farm complex.

"These people live pretty far out, don't they?" Nathan commented.

"They prefer it," Chiqua assured him. "This is actually considered *close in* by Pangburn standards."

"What are we, about twenty minutes out?" Jessica said.

"At least."

"How far out does Basava live?" Kit asked.

"We're almost there," Chiqua promised, glancing

at the skimmer's navigation display. "Should be just over the next hill."

Nathan turned and stared out the side windows, taking in the countryside as it streaked past below. Pangburn had its own unique beauty. It lacked the greenery of Earth, but its palette of reds, ambers, and yellows more than made up for it. For a moment, he almost forgot about the oddly pink sky. "Does anything even grow in this light?"

"Not much. Most of the farming here is done underground," Chiqua said. "That should be Dominic's place over there," she added, pointing to a single home nestled on the edge of a forest of yellow-leafed trees.

"Pretty isolated," Kit warned.

"Just what I was thinking," Jessica agreed.

The skimmer descended smoothly, kicking up dust as it settled twenty meters from the building. After a moment, its gull-wing doors opened, and its occupants emerged.

Jessica was the first one out, with Kit climbing out from the opposite side. Each of them quickly scanned the area, checking for threats, more out of habit than necessity. This far out, the residences were easily several kilometers apart, if not further, and they had not detected another skimmer for the last ten minutes of their flight.

Kit pulled a device out of his pocket and began scanning the area. "I'm only picking up a single life sign," he reported.

"You brought a tac-pad?"

"You didn't?"

"Any automated weapons systems?" Jessica wondered.

"None that this thing can detect," Kit replied. "Then again, it is five-hundred-year-old technology."

Chiqua headed toward the building, not waiting for permission. Nathan, of course, followed, as did Jorda.

Jessica glanced at Kit, rolling her eyes before falling in behind the others. "Keep an eye on our ride," she told Kit. "It's a *long* walk home."

The comm-link on Chiqua's wrist beeped three times. She raised her left wrist and tapped the device, causing the holo-display to activate, displaying the message. "It appears that your pilot has acquired the navigation charts you desired."

"That's great," Nathan replied.

"You may not think so when you see the price." She angled her wrist so that Nathan could see the holographic display.

Nathan's eyes widened, and his mouth dropped open. "Five hundred thousand credits? For a nav chart?"

"Not *a* nav chart," Chiqua corrected, "*all* of them."

"What do you mean...*all?*"

"All charted space. All four hundred and twenty-seven sectors, including the unsettled frontiers. An area more than twenty thousand light years across."

"How the hell did he pay..." Nathan looked at Chiqua, realizing the answer to his question.

"It seems you are now indebted to me, Captain."

Nathan wasn't sure how he felt about that. On the one hand, he needed more information about the current state of the galaxy, and those charts would prove invaluable. But on the other hand, being indebted to Chiqua carried unknown risks, the magnitude of which he couldn't begin to imagine.

One thing was certain, he and Josh were going to have words.

"Don't worry, Captain, I'm sure we can negotiate an amicable way to resolve your debt."

The smile on Chiqua's face wasn't comforting.

Chiqua stepped up onto the front porch of Dominic's home and rang the bell. Immediately, several devices dropped out of the porch ceiling, swinging about to point at Chiqua, Nathan, and Jorda, who was two steps behind them, just off the porch.

"Should we be worried?" Nathan wondered.

"I'm not sure," Chiqua replied.

Four shots rang out, tiny bolts of red plasma energy zipping from behind them and slamming into each of the devices hanging from the porch ceiling.

"Jesus, Jess!" Nathan exclaimed without even turning around.

An energy shield suddenly materialized around Nathan and Chiqua, trapping them where they stood. Jorda stepped back from the barrier.

Nathan turned to look at Jessica. "Are you happy now?"

"Shit," Jessica cursed.

"*Identify yourselves,*" a man's voice demanded over a speaker in the ceiling.

"I'm Chiqua Kimbro of Hadria. I've brought you a customer."

"*Identify yourself,*" the man said again.

"I'm Connor Tuplo, captain of the Seiiki."

"*Why did you disable my security measures?*"

"My apologies," Nathan offered. "My subordinate acted on instinct. She was only trying to protect me."

"*As was I.*"

"Again, I offer apologies. We are more than happy

to compensate you for the damage," Nathan offered. After getting no response for more than a minute, he added, "Mister Basava?"

"*You and Miss Kimbro may enter,*" the voice announced. "*All others will remain outside.*"

"No way," Jessica argued.

"This is getting kind of old, Jess," Nathan told her.

"Nathan," Jessica began to object.

"I'm a big boy, Jess. I can take care of myself." He could tell by the look on her face that she wasn't happy. "That's an order," he added, leaving her no choice.

"You think that makes me feel better?" Jessica questioned.

"It wasn't meant to," Nathan replied, his expression conveying his intent.

Jessica's expression was equally communicative, though she did acquiesce.

The lock clicked, and the front door swung open.

"After you," Nathan told Chiqua.

Chiqua shot him a look, then entered the building.

The entryway was a separate room, with a closed door inside. Once they had both entered, the front door closed, trapping them inside. A flat plane of orange light came down from above, passing over them from head to toe.

"*Leave your sidearm in the storage locker in the entryway,*" the voice instructed.

A small panel on the side wall popped open. Nathan removed his weapon and placed it in the compartment, pushing the door closed. As soon as the small door clicked closed, the entryway's inner door opened.

Chiqua entered the house, followed by Nathan.

The entryway opened into a modest living room, furnished with a couch and several sitting chairs, all of which faced an oversized fireplace. The room reminded Nathan of his grandfather's mountain retreat back on Earth, which he had not visited since he was a lad.

"Welcome," the voice called.

Nathan and Chiqua turned to see a man in his early thirties come into the room.

"Are you Dominic Basava?" Chiqua asked.

"The one and only."

Chiqua didn't look convinced. "It was my understanding that you were much older."

"Chronologically yes, but I prefer to recycle every ten years and stay forever thirty-something," Dominic explained. "I rather liked my thirties. Old enough that people don't automatically assume you are naive, yet young enough to be without the aches and pains of aging."

"How old are you?" Chiqua wondered.

"Not as old as Mister Tuplo, here." Dominic looked at Nathan. "Connor Tuplo, born November twelve, thirty-four forty-seven, son of Ella and Robson. Acquired the Seiiki as compensation in a liable suit. Operated her as a privateer in the Pentaurus sector for five years before suddenly vanishing from all records and presumed lost." He paused, examining Nathan more closely. "How many bodies have you been through? Seven? Eight?"

"Three that I'm consciously aware of," Nathan replied.

"*Three?* Then you must have been in stasis for quite a while."

"Something like that," Nathan replied, not wanting to get into details.

"According to records, the Seiiki did not have SA pods."

"It's not the *same* Seiiki," Nathan explained. "My current ship was only *recently* acquired."

"I see." Dominic headed across the room for the wet bar. "And what services do you require?"

"He wishes to operate within Alliance space."

"How *deep* into Alliance space?"

"Does it matter?" Nathan wondered.

"Indeed it does," Dominic replied. "I assume the *current* Seiiki has a working jump drive?"

"It does."

"Then you must shield it from detection," Dominic warned as he filled three glasses with a red beverage. "While the Alliance does allow jump traffic between certain border worlds and the fringe, all traffic further in must use the trans-gate network."

Nathan almost asked what the trans-gate network was but then realized that it had to be the jump-gate concept that Abby had been working on. "Of course."

Chiqua wasn't fooled. She could tell that this was the first time Nathan had heard the term 'trans-gate network'.

"What kind of ship is the *current* Seiiki?" Dominic wondered. "And more importantly, why does it not show as an operational vessel in the current registry?"

"Are *all* ships, even the ones in the fringe, in the registry?" Nathan asked.

"No, they are not," Dominic admitted. "What kind of ship did you say you flew?"

"A Navarro-class shuttle," Nathan replied somewhat reluctantly.

"Navarro-class shuttles were retired centuries ago. Which version?" Dominic asked as he picked up the drinks and headed back toward Nathan and Chiqua.

"Version One, I guess. The original."

Dominic stopped in his tracks. "You're flying a five-hundred-year-old shuttle?"

"I assure you, she's in excellent shape."

"He's not kidding," Chiqua confirmed. "It looks like it just rolled off the assembly line."

Dominic continued toward them, a new gleam in his eyes. "You seem to be surrounded by mysteries, Captain Tuplo," he said as he handed Nathan, then Chiqua, their drinks. "I did not mention the second Seiiki on record. The one assigned to the Aurora, which disappeared only days after going into service."

"Coincidence," Nathan stated in stride.

"Unlikely." Dominic thought for a moment. "You'll need papers as well. Certification to operate in Alliance space, a valid trans-gate account, registry papers, proof of ownership, the whole lot."

"Is all of that really necessary?" Nathan wondered.

"The Alliance maintains strict control of all space travel within their territory. Impromptu inspections are not uncommon, both in port *and* in space."

"He'll need the whole package," Chiqua insisted. "And it's a rush job."

"What's the hurry?"

"I have a sick friend who needs a hospital," Nathan explained.

"Rush jobs cost extra," Dominic warned. "And an entire package is already expensive."

"Cost is not an issue," Chiqua assured him.

"The hell it's not," Nathan objected.

"I'm covering his costs," Chiqua assured Dominic.

Nathan pulled Chiqua aside, speaking in hushed

tones. "We haven't discussed this," he said. "How are we going to repay you?"

"How about you start by telling us the truth about who you are, and why you're here," Chiqua suggested. "Maybe then we can create an arrangement that benefits us all."

* * *

"Is it working yet?" Mori asked as he joined Josh in the Seiiki's cockpit.

"Most of it...I think."

"You think?" Mori said as he took the copilot's seat.

"I'm just loading the last data card now," Josh explained. "I was hoping it would have the missing routes, but it looks like it's just the outer frontiers."

"What missing routes?"

"The ones in Alliance space."

"There are routes missing in Alliance space?"

"They're *all* missing!" Josh exclaimed.

"Maybe she didn't sell you the complete set?"

"No, it's the complete set, alright," Josh insisted, "there just aren't any nav-routes. Just a network of jump gates that connect *all* the inhabited worlds *within* Alliance space."

"Jump gates?"

"Some kind of gate you fly through, and it *jumps* you to the destination world...*I think*."

"What do you mean, you *think*?"

"I'm just making assumptions here," Josh defended. "But what else can they be?" He touched the navigation display, selecting one of the gates. "This is a list of worlds that this particular gate can reach. However, some of them can only reach *one* world." Josh touched another gate. "Like this one. It only connects to a world called Jentlen...way the fuck over here," he said, zooming out and sliding the map over, and then zooming back in. "Eighteen thousand and five light years away."

"In a *single jump?*" Mori couldn't believe it. "Can all the gates reach that far?"

"It doesn't appear so," Josh replied. "But again, I'm making a *lot* of assumptions here. Best I can tell, most gates operate over much shorter distances, like maybe a few hundred to a few thousand light years. A lot of them are part of a chain. So, for example, if you're going from system A to system F, you'd have to go through the gates at B, C, D, and E to get there."

"How many gates are there?" Mori wondered.

"Fucking thousands," Josh replied. "And it looks like every one of them has a fee code."

"So you have to *pay* to use a gate," Mori surmised.

"Yup, and it probably ain't cheap. Someone is making a fortune, that's for sure."

"Something like this isn't about wealth, Josh, it's about control and the power that it creates."

* * *

"You might want to choose a lie that is a little easier to believe," Chiqua suggested.

"Everything I've told you is true," Nathan assured her.

"You want us to believe you jumped *through* a singularity." Dominic scratched his head. "You do realize how impossible that is? I mean, from a physics perspective alone..."

"I offer no explanation as to *how*," Nathan stated.

"Were I you, I wouldn't believe me either. But the fact is, I'm here, alive, in the year forty twenty-one, when just a few days ago it was thirty-four eighty-six."

Chiqua looked over at Dominic. "That would explain the condition of his shuttle."

"What's wrong with his shuttle?" Dominic wondered.

"Nothing. It's like new. Like it just rolled off the assembly line."

Dominic shook his head. "The Aurora was destroyed at the battle of Gamaze. All hands were lost, including the life of her notorious captain."

"Notorious?" Nathan didn't like the sound of that.

"I'm afraid history has judged you rather harshly, Captain," Dominic told him. "Assuming you *are* who you claim to be."

"I am," Nathan assured him. "How harshly?"

"It is said that *your* actions in the Gamaze system were the spark that led to the great war, in which trillions of lives were lost."

"Not to mention the reformation of the Alliance," Chiqua stated with obvious disdain.

"I was following orders," Nathan defended.

"Said nearly every scapegoat in history," Dominic commented. "In fact, some believe that the Alliance *wanted* that war, and that they knew what would happen if they sent the Aurora into the Ilyan."

"Why would the Alliance *want* a war that would kill trillions?" Nathan asked.

"The same reason every war has been fought," Chiqua stated. "To gain power."

"But the Confederated Systems Alliance was formed to *prevent* war."

"And they have," Dominic agreed. "But only *after*

the great war and at the cost of individual liberty. That's why people like myself migrated to the fringe."

"You might want to stick to your Connor Tuplo identity out here," Chiqua suggested. "Again, assuming that you *are* Nathan Scott."

Nathan had a feeling he already knew the answer, but felt compelled to ask the question nonetheless. "Why?"

"If the Alliance finds out that you are alive, they are likely to put a bounty on your head."

"One that someone like *you* would want to collect?"

"It would resolve your debt and then some," Chiqua admitted. "But don't worry, Captain. I suspect there is more of an advantage to being your ally than your enemy." Chiqua smiled. "At least for the time being."

"If the Alliance is so big and powerful, why would they care about me?" Nathan asked.

"Because *you* were *there*," Dominic replied. "*You* know the *truth* about that battle, and I suspect it contradicts history's official accounts."

"You'd be a big hit with the conspiracy-theory nuts," Chiqua chuckled.

"Captain, if you hope to take your shuttle into Alliance space, you're going to need transponder codes, fake registration files, flight logs, the works. You're even going to need financial accounts in order to use the gate network."

"Can you do all of that?"

"Not the financial accounts."

"Can they use mine?" Chiqua asked.

"Only if you are the registered owner," Dominic replied. "And we'll have to create a back history for the shuttle, as well as a bill of sale to you."

Chiqua smiled. "I've always wanted my own shuttle."

"I'm not selling you the Seiiki," Nathan insisted.

"You could *lease* it to her," Dominic suggested.

Nathan didn't much care for that idea either.

"It *is* the only way you're going to get your friend to a hospital within Alliance space," Dominic insisted.

"Fine," Nathan sighed. "How long will it take to get everything ready?"

"A few minutes, but I will need to make alterations directly to your shuttle's transponder to utilize current authorization codes."

"How much is all of this going to cost?" Nathan wondered.

"I'll cover it," Chiqua assured him.

"I'm already deep in hock to you," Nathan objected.

"Do you have any other choice?"

"I'll do it for free," Dominic offered. "In exchange for *seeing* the Aurora."

* * *

The front door to Dominic's house suddenly swung open, the shield in front of it dissipating. Nathan was the first one out, followed closely by Chiqua, and then a man Jessica assumed was Dominic.

"Jess, meet Dominic," Nathan said as he walked past her toward the skimmer.

"Where are you going?" Jessica asked, a bit surprised by their sudden emergence from the house.

"Back to the Seiiki," Nathan replied as he passed.

"Why?" Jessica asked, falling into line behind them.

"We're leaving."

"Well where are we going?" Jessica wondered.

"Ask her," Nathan replied, pointing over his shoulder back at Chiqua. "It's her ship."

"What?"

CHAPTER FIVE

"Nathan, this is a *huge* fucking mistake," Jessica argued as she followed Nathan into the Seiiki's cockpit.

"What's a mistake?" Josh wondered.

"Get us off the ground," Nathan instructed.

"Chiqua's already proven she'd have no problem killing us in cold blood, and you just *met* this Dominic guy," Jessica continued.

"Where are we going?" Josh asked.

"Back to the Aurora."

"You can't take them there," Jessica insisted. "It's a *gigantic* security risk, and as your chief of security..."

"Which you're not," Nathan reminded her.

"Who are we taking to the Aurora?" Josh wondered.

"Just get us in the damned air, Josh," Nathan reiterated.

"Sorry! Just asking!"

"I just assumed I would be..."

"And you probably will be," Nathan agreed.

"Then you should *listen* to me..."

"Are you still an officer in the Alliance?" Nathan asked her.

"Of course I am."

"And what rank are you?"

Jessica rolled her eyes.

"Yeah, that's what I thought," Nathan said. "Now go back and keep an eye on those two security risks you're yapping about."

Jessica looked as if she would explode. "This isn't over," she insisted.

"Actually, it is," Nathan replied as he took the

copilot's seat. He began strapping himself in, then glanced back over his shoulder. "In case you weren't sure, that *was* an order."

Jessica stormed off in a huff, disappearing through the hatch.

After a tense moment of silence, Josh asked, "Why do you let her get away with that?"

"Because she's Jess," Nathan replied.

"You wouldn't let any of *us* argue with you like that."

Nathan just looked at him. "You have a very short memory."

Josh shut up, knowing that he had argued with Nathan on countless occasions, both during his time on the Aurora and on the original Seiiki. "We already have automated departure clearance," he reported.

Nathan glanced at the status board, checking that all the external hatches were closed and sealed, and that the ship was ready for takeoff. "Let's get going."

Josh activated the departure sequencer, and the ship's grav-lift systems began to hum as the shuttle lifted slowly off the pad.

"We don't need to taxi out first?" Nathan asked.

"Nope. Automated departures just go straight up off the parking pad. Only the big ships have to taxi out for departures."

"Great."

Josh thought for a moment as the Seiiki continued to climb straight up, wondering if he should speak. Of course, being Josh, there was never really any question. "She's got a point."

"I know."

"Then why *are* we bringing them?"

Nathan sighed.

"I'm not challenging your decision, Cap'n. I'm just asking so that *I* understand."

The ship began to accelerate forward as it continued to climb, its automated systems following the instructions transmitted by the Pangburn spaceport.

"We're five hundred years in the future, and it looks like our *Alliance* is not what it was originally *intended* to be."

"So we're *not* part of the Alliance?"

"I honestly don't know," Nathan admitted. "But one thing I *do* know is that I've learned a *lot* about the current state of things from those two, and I want to learn more."

"Why don't you just tell Jess that?"

"Because once Jessica gets her mind set on something, she won't give up. You have to just say no and then wait for her to come around…which she will once she cools down."

"So you're just bringing them along to interrogate them?"

"Chiqua's got connections all over this sector. She can probably help us out. Besides, we currently have a huge debt to repay," he added pointedly, looking over at Josh.

"Hey, you said to get us nav charts, and I did," Josh defended.

"And this Dominic guy is an engineer with at least two centuries of experience. He can probably help us understand and apply whatever new technologies are available."

"Has he agreed to that?"

"Not in so many words," Nathan admitted. "But I saw the curiosity in his eyes. He *wants* to see the Aurora with his own eyes."

"And what does *Chiqua* want?" Josh wondered.

"That's the part that worries me."

* * *

"Incredible," Dominic gasped at his first sight of the Aurora, lying battered on the surface of Dencke, her nose partially submerged in the frozen swamp.

"I must apologize, Captain Tuplo...I mean Scott," Chiqua said. "I did *not* believe you."

"Then why did you come along?" Nathan wondered.

"More curiosity than anything else. I guess I just wanted to see how far you'd take this."

"Putting the fact that you survived a blind jump *through* a singularity aside," Dominic continued, "the fact that you came *out* of that jump on a collision course with a planet *and* without main power, and then survived an uncontrolled crash-landing? I mean, the odds of any of these things happening must be astronomical...but all of them *together?*"

"I try not to think about those things," Nathan admitted.

"History did say you had incredible luck," Dominic added. "Right up until your luck ran out."

"I'm hoping that it hasn't."

"Of course."

"She appears to be structurally intact," Dominic observed as they passed over the Aurora's stern and descended toward the flight deck nestled between her nacelles. "Have you completed a damage assessment?"

"My chief engineer had, right before he was bitten," Nathan replied as the Seiiki touched down and began her roll into the hangar bay.

"We'll be doors down in five," Josh reported.

"Stay here and keep the systems hot," Nathan instructed as he rose from the copilot's seat. "I want to be wheels up again as soon as possible."

"You got it."

"We need to don cold-weather gear to disembark," Nathan informed Dominic and Chiqua. "We've got a bit of a power problem on the Aurora at the moment, and this world's long night isn't helping."

"Perhaps I can be of assistance?" Dominic offered. "I am an engineer after all."

Nathan cast a dubious look at Dominic. "What's it going to cost me?"

"It's on the house," Dominic assured him. "I'd do anything to get a look at an original Expedition-class ship up close."

"Thank you," Nathan replied.

"Just to be clear," Chiqua said. "*My* services will *not* be on the house."

* * *

Nathan and the others entered the main corridor from the hangar bay, clad in cold-weather gear.

"Cam, this is Chiqua and Dominic," Nathan told Cameron. "This is Captain Taylor, my executive officer."

"A pleasure to meet you, Captain," Dominic greeted, pulling his gloves off to shake her hand.

"Jess, escort Dominic to power gen and see what he can do to get our power levels up."

Jessica did not look happy, and the look she shared with Cameron communicated that fact quite well.

Nathan turned to Jessica, wondering why she hadn't responded.

"Follow me", Jessica told Dominic, all the while glaring at Nathan. "Kit, you shadow the dragon lady."

"She means me," Chiqua said, offering her hand to Cameron.

"A pleasure," Cameron told Chiqua as she shook her hand. "Captain, a moment?"

"How's Vlad?" Nathan asked as he followed Cameron a few steps down the corridor to get out of earshot of Chiqua and Jorda.

"No change," Cameron replied. "What are they doing here? First the Grunites, and now these two? I thought you wanted to keep our existence a secret until we figured things out?"

"All of that changed when Vlad got injured," Nathan insisted. "We no longer have the luxury of being cautious."

"Is that the same Chiqua?"

"Who tried to hijack the Seiiki? Yes."

Cameron stared at him.

"I know, but I had no choice. She was our only real source of intelligence, and she hooked us up with Dominic."

"Who is my second question."

"He's an engineer with more than two hundred years of experience. He's going to update the Seiiki's transponder to allow us to operate in Alliance space. We need that in order to get Vlad to a *real* hospital."

"And he's going to do that from power gen?" Cameron questioned.

"He offered to help us get our power levels up."

Cameron sighed. "You don't think you're putting too much trust in these people?"

"Let's hope not," Nathan replied. "Tell Doctor Chen to get Vlad ready to move," he added as he turned to leave. "I want to depart as soon as possible."

"Where are you going?"

"Power gen."

* * *

"She doesn't like my being here," Chiqua stated as she and Nathan headed into the elevator.

"She just questions my decision to share the truth with you and Dominic."

"She is your second in command, right? Does she regularly question your decisions?"

"It's kind of her thing."

"And you allow that?"

"I depend on it," Nathan admitted.

"I envy you."

As the elevator doors opened, Nathan cast a curious look her way.

"In my line of work, you have to lead with an iron fist."

"Difficult way to live," Nathan stated as he stepped out of the elevator onto the Aurora's main deck.

Chiqua looked around as she stepped out, taken aback by the height and width of the corridor as compared to the one they had just been in.

Nathan turned left toward the intersection a few meters away. "We call this the 'main deck'," Nathan explained, noticing her surprise. "It's the only deck that runs the full length of the ship, stem to stern." Nathan pointed aft down the central corridor. "Power gen is this way."

"I'm surprised you allowed Dominic to inspect your power issues," Chiqua admitted. "I thought you wanted to get your friend to a hospital as soon as possible."

"I do, but as long as we are at minimal power,

my ship and crew are at increased risk," Nathan explained as they walked down the main corridor. "Besides, I expect it will take some time for Doctor Chen to prepare him for transport."

"I see."

"Mind if I ask you a direct question?" Nathan asked.

"Please."

"What's your angle here?"

"Honestly, I don't know yet," Chiqua admitted. "Just a gut feeling, I suppose." After a short silence, she asked, "May I ask *you* a question?"

"Of course."

"Are you hoping to get this ship flying again?"

"That is the plan."

"And then what?" she wondered. "Do you plan on returning to the Alliance?"

"I haven't decided," Nathan replied.

"Didn't you swear some kind of oath or something?"

"That's why I haven't decided," Nathan explained. "My oath was to the *principles* of the Alliance charter, not to the Alliance itself. If the Alliance has strayed from those principles, it would be my sworn duty to try to correct that error."

Chiqua had to fight back a laugh. "You might want to rethink that," she warned.

"Why do you say that?" Nathan wondered.

"Things have changed in the last five hundred years," she explained. "Yes, the Alliance *has* strayed from its founding principles. Hell, they've practically *abandoned* them. But you are one man with one ship, and the Alliance is the largest, most powerful entity in human history."

"So were the Jung," Nathan stated.

"You're proving my point," Chiqua replied.

"I suppose you have an idea as to what I should do?"

"I do." Chiqua stopped in her tracks, Nathan following suit. "Live, Captain...*live*."

"For some, just *surviving* is not enough."

"Then find some other cause to fight for," she argued. "The Alliance is here to stay." Chiqua noticed the sign on the wall over the doorway. "I assume this is our destination?"

Nathan gestured for her to go in first, contemplating her words as he followed her inside.

"Captain," Chief Avelles greeted, caught by surprise by Nathan's arrival.

"I see you've met our guest," Nathan commented. "Find anything?" he then asked Dominic.

"I didn't need to," Dominic admitted. "Chief Avelles and Specialist Tompra have already determined the problem, and quite accurately I might add."

"It's still just a matter of containment field emitters, sir," Chief Avelles stated. "And we already used all our spares to get the power that we have."

"How long to fabricate new ones?" Nathan inquired.

"About a week to fabricate all the ones we need to get one ZPED back to full power," Melisha reported.

"The problem is, as long as we're trying to keep the ship from completely freezing over, we don't have the power to fabricate *anything*," Chief Avelles added.

"My understanding is that it will pass soon," Nathan told them.

"I take it you haven't spoken with Ensign Soray," Chief Avelles said. "She said there is another moon to consider."

"The endless night," Jorda stated.

"That doesn't sound good," Nathan decided.

"It's just an expression," Jorda assured him. "It occurs every few years. The moon Lorent blocks the sun from reaching Dencke, making the long night four days *longer*."

"So this cold spell is going to last an additional *four days?*"

"More like six," Jorda replied. "The sun will start to peak out from behind Lorent on the fourth day, but it will take two *more* days for it to become fully revealed."

"Jesus," Jessica swore to herself. "Six days of night, followed by a two-day long sunrise? Why do you people live here?" she asked Jorda.

"It's not that big a deal if you're prepared for it," Jorda defended.

"Are we going to make it through this?" Nathan asked the chief.

"As long as nothing else goes wrong, we should."

"There is no need to wait," Dominic stated, catching Nathan's attention. "You should be able to purchase used containment field emitters on Pyru."

"Five-hundred-year-old emitters?" Chief Avelles asked.

"No, but it should be easy to adapt them to fit your ZPED, at least temporarily."

"What about just getting a portable fusion reactor powerful enough to run our fabricators?" Chief Avelles asked. "Then we could fabricate exactly what we need."

"Get two or three of them, and we could get minimal standard power back to the entire ship," Melisha commented.

"What do you suggest we *buy* them with?" Jessica pointed out.

Chiqua cleared her throat.

Nathan looked over at Chiqua, then to Dominic. "Any idea how much that would cost?"

"Fusion reactors are fairly common in the fringe," Dominic stated. "However, they *are* expensive, because they are always in demand."

"What about using the reactors from one of our shuttles?" Jessica suggested.

"We've only got two," Nathan reminded. "And we can't risk one of them being down."

"We already considered that," Chief Avelles told them. "They'd help, but their ZPEDs are low-gen/high-peak, so they're not powerful enough to run our fabricators."

"What about the Dragons?"

"Their ZPEDs are even *less* powerful," the chief replied.

Nathan looked at Chiqua again, sighing. "How good is our credit?" he asked.

"At this point, unlimited."

"Fuck that," Jessica objected. "I vote we freeze our asses off for another week. Better than owing *her* even *more.*"

"It may take us months to be able to pay you back," Nathan told Chiqua.

"You have Dragon fighters?" Chiqua inquired, her face lit up with curiosity.

* * *

"*No can do, Cap'n,*" Josh replied over Nathan's comm-set. "*The data is copy protected. You have to buy a separate copy for each installation.*"

"We hacked the license of an AI for Christ's sake," Nathan replied.

"*That was Vlad and princess smart-ass.*"

"Something wrong?" Chiqua asked as they stepped out of the elevator back onto deck three.

"Apparently the nav-charts we bought are only good for one installation."

"They're all that way," Dominic explained.

"Any chance *you* can hack them?" Nathan asked.

"I suppose, if given time."

"How much time?"

"On my *own*, months, at least."

"What if you had an AI to assist you?"

"Much less, I'm sure," Dominic confirmed. "However, we don't *have* AIs in the fringe."

"This ship *has* an AI," Nathan told him.

"I wouldn't advertise that fact too broadly," Jorda warned.

"Well, it's offline at the moment," Nathan admitted.

"Why not just buy the charts you need?" Chiqua suggested.

"We're already deep in debt," Nathan objected.

"There are many ways for a man with your resources to obtain funds," Chiqua told him.

"I'm not turning the Aurora into a pirate ship," Nathan warned her as the group paused at the entrance to the medical department.

"I wasn't suggesting you do so," Chiqua assured him.

"How long to get the Seiiki ready to operate in Alliance space?" Nathan asked Dominic.

"It shouldn't take me more than an hour."

"Jess."

"Whatever he needs. I've got it," Jessica assured him.

Nathan turned and headed into the medical department, Jorda, Chiqua, and Kit in tow.

"This is a bad idea," Doctor Chen objected when she saw Nathan approaching.

"Maybe, but it's all we've got," Nathan replied. "How long until he's ready to move?"

"I'd like to get another round of effra into him first."

"How long?" Nathan repeated.

"A couple hours."

"We're wheels up and headed for an Alliance hospital in *one* hour...*with* Commander Kamenetskiy on board."

"Captain..."

"Is the effra root helping?" Nathan challenged.

"At best, it's keeping his condition from deteriorating," Doctor Chen admitted.

"The same as medical SA?"

"More or less."

"One hour," Nathan repeated.

"Then I'm going with him," Doctor Chen insisted. "And I want the Seiiki fitted with a medical module."

Nathan tapped his comm-set. "Marcus, switch out the Seiiki's center bay with a medical module."

"*Got it,*" Marcus replied. "*Where's she goin'?*"

"Into Alliance space."

"*Then I'm comin' with.*"

"Josh? You listening?" Nathan asked.

"*Always.*"

"Plot a jump course to Pyru, then hand copy it and punch it into the Mirai's nav-com," Nathan instructed.

"*Why?*"

"In case they have to come rescue us," Nathan replied.

"*Good reason.*"

"I'll need a couple med-techs, in case he crashes en route," Doctor Chen said.

"We'll have four Ghatazhak on board," Nathan stated, looking at Kit.

"We've all got med-tech training, Doc."

"What about your patients here?" Nathan asked.

"They're all stable, and I assume we won't be gone for more than a day or two."

"Let's hope," Nathan agreed.

"What about us?" Jorda asked.

"If I'm financing this expedition, I'm going with you," Chiqua insisted.

"I figured as much," Nathan replied. "Jorda, we'll drop you and Sina back at Gruner before jumping to Pyru, unless you *want* to visit Pyru."

"In Alliance space, no thank you."

Nathan turned back to Doctor Chen. "One hour, Doc."

* * *

"Nathan," Robert called from behind as Nathan walked down the corridor. "Got a minute?"

"As long as you don't mind walking and talking," Nathan answered.

"Where ya headed?"

"Mess. Thought I'd get a bite before we departed again."

"You may regret that," Robert joked. "Everything Neli's serving is cold. I heard you're headed into Alliance space?"

"News travels fast."

"I also heard that the Alliance isn't exactly what it was when we left."

Nathan looked at him, slightly surprised.

"Like you said, news travels fast," Robert added. "I'm guessing it would be a waste of time to suggest that you be careful."

Nathan didn't respond.

"Have you thought much about the future?" Robert asked.

"As in?"

"As in what your future plans are."

"Right now, I'm just concentrating on saving our chief engineer."

"And after that?"

"You want to get to the point, Robert?" Nathan asked, growing impatient.

"I know you want to get the Aurora back in the air, but have you thought about what your *crew* wants?"

"I'm pretty sure they want to get *off* this rock."

"I'd agree, but fixing the Aurora isn't the only way to get them *off* this world," Robert pointed out.

"Our first responsibility is to *this ship*," Nathan insisted.

"Actually, it's to your *crew*. The ship is just a thing."

"It's the *thing* keeping us all alive at the moment."

"Yes, I know, and by taking care of the *ship*, you're taking care of the crew as well. But that only applies for so long."

"The crew took an oath, just like you and I did."

"Not everyone on this ship took that oath," Robert pointed out. "More than a third of them are civilian contractors, which means they have the *right* to decide their own futures."

"And they will," Nathan promised. "But don't you think they'd like to have a clear idea of what their options *are* before they decide?"

"Of course," Robert agreed as they entered the mess.

"Where is this coming from?" Nathan wondered as they headed for the serving counter. "Are you hearing things?"

"No, I just know you."

"What does *that* mean?"

"You tend to get a little single-minded at times like this."

"That's why I have Cam and Jess," Nathan replied as he scooped up a serving of cold stew. "Is this all we've got?" Nathan asked the crewman on the other side of the line.

"That's about it at the moment."

Nathan took his bowl of stew and headed for a table. "This isn't coming from the crew, is it?"

"Not exactly," Robert admitted. "However, I'm certain that many of them are thinking the same way."

"From our guests, then," Nathan surmised.

"That's where it started, yes," Robert confirmed. "Mostly from Hanna. Martina is keeping busy helping out in medical, and I've got Erica in the flight simulator, training as a backup pilot. But Hanna doesn't have a *purpose*. She helps out where she can, but you can see it in her eyes. She's lost."

"Any suggestions?"

"One, but you might not like it."

"I'm not liking most things these days," Nathan admitted.

"Take her with you."

Nathan wasn't expecting that. "Why?"

"She's a journalist. She needs to be out in the world, seeing what's going on."

"She's a *reporter*, Robert. "What is she going to *report* on?"

"Us."

"Us?"

"Hanna has a singularly unique perspective. She has seen humanity at its original peak and has seen its fall. And now, she has the opportunity to see its future, with people who are from its *middle*. It would be a shame if she didn't chronicle all of it for posterity's sake. As a student of history, you should understand that better than anyone."

"We don't know what we're flying into," Nathan objected as he sat down and began eating.

"I'm pretty sure she's been through worse."

"I'm not sure now is a good time," Nathan told him.

"I'm pretty sure it's *never* going to be a *good* time."

Nathan thought for a moment, chewing his cold chow. "Have you talked to her about this?"

"Not yet. I wanted to run it by you first."

"I appreciate that."

"I *did* tell Jess about the idea though," Robert admitted. "I figured if *she* was okay with it, you might feel more inclined."

"And *Jess* didn't have any objections?"

"Oh, she had plenty," Robert chuckled. "But she *didn't* say no way, which in Jess-speak means she doesn't care one way or the other."

Nathan stared at Robert a moment. "I'm not sure I'm seeing an immediate plus side with this."

"She'd be able to report on the condition of the galaxy to the rest of your crew, so that they'd be able to make an informed decision about their own futures when the time came."

Nathan sighed, not terribly happy about the idea. "She'd have to agree to follow orders without argument."

"Of course."

"And she can't report *anything* until it's been reviewed by Jessica."

"Yeah, Jess already insisted on that."

"I'll think about it," Nathan told him.

"This trip into Alliance space would be the perfect time for her to start," Robert pushed.

"I've got a pretty full ship already."

"One more won't hurt," Robert argued. "Navarro-class shuttles are *huge*. They shouldn't even be *called* shuttles."

"She wouldn't have much privacy," Nathan warned.

"Come on, Nathan. You're grasping at straws now."

"Fine," Nathan sighed. "But she has to be ready to go in half an hour."

"She will be," Robert assured him, pushing his stew aside and rising from his seat to depart.

"You're not going to finish that?"

"Are you kidding? That stuff is terrible," Robert objected.

"Beats the hell out of emergency rations," Nathan said, taking Robert's unfinished portion. "Thirty minutes," he reiterated.

"She'll be there," Robert promised.

"Maybe you should consider changing careers," Nathan joked. "You should be in human resources."

* * *

Bundled up in cold-weather gear, Nathan moved quickly up the boarding steps built into the Seiiki's deployed forward boarding hatch, through its airlock, and into the boarding compartment, where it was considerably warmer. "Everyone aboard?" Nathan asked Marcus, who was waiting for him inside.

"Four Ghatazhak, Jess, the doc and Vlad, and our four guests. And of course, the dumbass is in the cockpit."

"You really have to stop calling him that," Nathan said as he removed his coat. "He's not a kid anymore."

"He'll always be a kid in my eyes. And he'll always be a dumbass."

"What about Miss Bohl?"

"Who?"

"The reporter."

At that very moment, Hanna came up the boarding steps and into the airlock. "Do I need to ask for permission to come aboard?" she asked before stepping into the boarding compartment.

"Just get your ass in here so we can shut the outer door," Marcus barked.

"That's his way of saying 'welcome aboard'," Nathan assured her as she stepped inside.

Marcus just growled as he slipped past her, activating the controls and causing the clamshell outer doors to begin folding up and back into the ship.

"Robert told you the rules?"

"Follow orders without question and stay out of the way," Hanna replied as she took off her coat. "Oh, and everything I report has to be cleared by Jessica."

"Correct," Nathan replied, taking her coat and hanging it in the locker with the rest of the cold-weather gear.

"Where do you want me?" Hanna asked.

"Aft cargo bay for now. I want you checked out on sidearms."

"I've never been much for guns."

"I wasn't asking," Nathan reminded her.

"Of course. Aft cargo bay." Hanna paused a moment, looking around. "How do I get there?"

"Through the hatch behind you, follow the corridor to the end. Can't miss it."

"Got it," Hanna assured him. "Thank you for letting me come along, Captain."

"Don't thank me yet," Nathan replied. "You may regret it."

Hanna departed without another word.

"Oh, she'll definitely regret it," Marcus grumbled as he closed the inner hatch.

"Any time you're ready, Josh!" Nathan said into the intercom panel.

"*Gruner first?*"

"I'll join you after we drop Jorda and Sina off."

"*Got it,* " Josh replied. "*Starting our rollout now.*"

"I'm gonna check on Vlad," Nathan told Marcus.

"I'll keep an eye on things up here," Marcus assured him.

* * *

The medical module currently installed in the Seiiki's midship bay was not as roomy as the size of the bay might lead one to expect. Its walls were lined with cabinets, counters, and equipment lockers, and the overhead was littered with adjustable lighting and medical scanners on adjustable arms. Normally there were two patient beds in the middle, but currently there was just Vladimir's medical SA pod.

"How's he doing?" Nathan asked Doctor Chen as he entered.

"So far, so good," she replied. "When do we depart?"

"We've already started our rollout," Nathan told her. "We should be airborne in a few minutes."

"How long will it take to get to the hospital?"

"I honestly don't know," Nathan admitted as he approached Vladimir's SA tube. "We can't just jump directly *to* Pyru," he explained, peering down at

Vladimir's unmoving face through the tube's window. "We have to start at a border world and then use the Alliance gate network to get there."

"I'm not even going to ask what that is," Doctor Chen decided. "Just promise me we won't take any side trips until *after* we get him to a proper medical facility."

"As soon as we drop off Jorda and Sina, we'll be on our way. I promise we'll take the most direct route possible."

"How do we know they'll take him?"

"Well, Chiqua seems certain that they will."

"Do you trust her?"

"Not at all," Nathan admitted. "Worst case, we take the entire hospital hostage and force them to treat him at gunpoint."

"You *are* kidding, right?"

"Let's hope we don't have to find out," Nathan said as he headed back for the exit. "Let me know if you need anything."

* * *

"You got it?" Jessica asked Hanna.

"I got it," Hanna replied, studying the blaster in her hands. "This one turns it on and off, and this one adjusts the power level, and I should keep it on stun at all times."

"And?"

"And the safety automatically turns off when I pull it from its holster."

"Excellent," Jessica said. "Give it back to me."

"Is that it?"

"That's it," Jessica replied, holstering the weapon and handing the gun belt to Kit to store.

"You don't want me to wear it?"

"If you need to wear it, we'll give it to you."

"Oh thank God," Hanna said, a wave of relief washing over her. "I really didn't want to carry that thing around."

"You may change your mind, depending on how things play out," Jessica warned.

"What do I do now?" Hanna wondered.

"Find a place to park. We should be touching down in Gruner shortly, then we'll be on our way to Pyru."

Hanna stood there a moment as Jessica headed forward, disappearing through the forward hatch, joking with the four armed men gathered at the forward end of the Seiiki's cargo bay. She turned around to face aft. On one side, two men and a woman were seated and talking, and on the other side was one young woman, seated alone.

Hanna went over to the lone woman. "Hi. Mind if I sit here?"

"Be my guest," Sina replied.

"I'm Hanna."

"Sina."

"I haven't seen you around. Are you a member of the Aurora's crew?" Hanna asked.

"Oh no. I'm a Grunite."

"What's a Grunite?"

"People who live in Gruner. It's the name of our colony."

"Where is Gruner located?" Hanna asked.

"On Dencke."

"This is probably going to sound stupid, but where is Dencke?"

Sina looked at Hanna. "It's the world the Aurora crash-landed on."

"Oh of course."

"I take it *you're* not a member of the Aurora's crew, either," Sina surmised.

"Not exactly," Hanna confirmed. "I was rescued just before the whole singularity thing happened."

"Then you're from the past as well?"

"Yup."

"It must be difficult for you."

"You have no idea," Hanna told her.

"I didn't mean..."

"It's all right. What do you do...in Gruner?"

"I'm an apothecary."

"*Really?* I didn't realize there was such a thing anymore. At least not in the future."

"I don't understand."

"Well, apothecaries sort of fizzled out a *long* time ago. Probably about the time that big pharma began."

"Of course. Pharmaceutical companies still exist, but in small colonies out in the fringe, apothecaries are quite common. You see, we don't get regular shipments of pharmaceuticals. We have to make our own using local resources, or plants and herbs that we brought with us and cultivated here."

"You don't have medical care in Gruner?"

"We have some basic diagnostic scanners and lab equipment. We used to have a doctor, but she died a few years ago."

"It must be rough."

"We do okay," Sina insisted. "We may not have all the conveniences of the more populous worlds, but we have the basics. Food, shelter, power, and just enough trade to keep ourselves going."

"I don't know that I could live that way," Hanna admitted.

"You get used to it I suppose."

"How long have you lived there?"

"Since I was very young."

"I don't think I could get used to it," Hanna admitted.

"You might be surprised."

"I'm pretty sure I'm right about this," Hanna insisted. "When the Aurora rescued us, we had been marooned for months... Six or seven at least. But it was more than enough for me to realize that I *need* civilization."

"I don't mean to say that Gruner isn't civilized. I mean, we have buildings and running water, power, businesses. It's just very small. Everyone knows each other. At least, that's how it feels at times."

"I guess that doesn't sound so bad."

"Where are you from?" Sina wondered. "I mean before you were marooned."

"San Diego."

"I've never heard of that world."

"It's a city actually. On Earth."

Sina looked confused. "The Aurora's from Earth. If you're from Earth, how did you end up marooned?"

"It's a *really* long story," Hanna replied.

"I'd love to hear it," Sina said.

"*Jumping down to Gruner,*" Josh announced over the intercom as Nathan entered the cargo bay. "*Prepare for landing.*"

"Maybe another time."

* * *

Nathan escorted Jorda and Sina down the ramp at the landing site on the edge of Gruner. "I wanted to personally thank you for your help," Nathan told Jorda.

Jorda nodded to Sina. "I'll join you shortly."

"It was a pleasure to meet you, Captain," Sina said.

"Thank you for your help," Nathan told her.

Jorda waited long enough for Sina to get out of earshot before continuing. He looked back up the ramp, checking that Chiqua was nowhere near the cargo door. "Use caution when dealing with Chiqua," he warned Nathan. "I am not certain she can be trusted."

"You've dealt with her before though?"

"Yes, but always through an intermediary. This was the first time I've seen her in person, and I find myself wishing I did not have to trade with her."

"Why is that?"

"I worry about who she wronged to get the goods she trades in," Jorda explained. "I do not believe she cares about anyone other than herself."

"Most people are that way I'm afraid."

"Just be careful. Do not become *too* indebted to her, or you may be forced to do things *you* find distasteful."

"No one forces me to do something I don't *want* to do," Nathan assured him. "But I will remember your advice."

Jorda nodded. "I trust you will keep me advised of your progress? We are, after all, neighbors, at least for the time being."

"I shall," Nathan promised, offering his hand.

"Good luck to you, my friend," Jorda said, shaking Nathan's hand.

"I will see you soon," Nathan promised.

Jorda turned and headed toward Gruner, joining up with Sina. Nathan watched them for a moment before heading back up the ramp, tapping his comm-set on the way. "Get us back in the air, Josh."

CHAPTER SIX

Nathan was the last one up the ladder leading to the Seiiki's flight deck, joining Jessica, Dominic, and Chiqua in the small crew cabin directly behind the cockpit.

"What's our status?" Nathan asked Josh, leaning in the cockpit door.

"*Feet wet, waiting for a destination,*" Josh called back.

Nathan reached up for the overhead control panel, activating the holographic projector and calling up a star map for the area of space that they were currently in. "This is where we're at, and these are the closest border worlds with jump gates. The question is, which one should we use to reach Pyru?"

"I would recommend Kathrion," Dominic suggested. "It has the smallest garrison, and its population is less supportive of the Alliance than any of the other border worlds in this sector."

"Does that matter?" Jessica wondered.

"It does if your papers are questioned."

"*Will* they be questioned?"

"None of the work I have provided others has ever come into question to the best of my knowledge," Dominic stated. "However, it is always wise to use caution, especially the first time the fake credentials are used."

Jessica looked at Nathan. "Makes sense I suppose."

"Do you make that recommendation to all your clients?" Nathan wondered.

"No, only the ones I'm riding along with," Dominic replied.

"How many have you ridden along with?" Nathan wondered.

"You would be my first."

"Not very inspiring," Jessica quipped.

Nathan swung the holographic map over with a swipe of his hand then used another gesture to zoom in. "To get from Kathrion to Pyru, we'd have to go through six gates. That seems like a lot of exposure to risk."

"All that matters is the first port at which you enter the trans-gate network," Dominic explained. "Your clearance is forwarded to your destination before you even enter the gate. As long as the destination controllers receive it, and your transponder codes match those in the clearance—which they will—you won't be given a second glance."

"Unless they flag you," Chiqua added.

"Flag us?" Nathan didn't like the sound of that.

"That almost never happens," Dominic insisted.

"I don't know," Chiqua disagreed. "I've heard a few stories."

"Not from any of *my* customers."

"That's why I came along," Chiqua reminded Nathan. "Having your client on board lends credence to your clearance profile. That and because I'm the one paying for this little adventure."

"If you're worried about the additional travel time, I assure you it will be minimal," Dominic assured him.

"What do you define as *minimal*," Nathan asked.

"A few hours at the most," Dominic replied. "It depends on how many ships are in the queue at each gate."

"I'd prefer less delay," Nathan stated.

Dominic stepped up to the holographic map and

adjusted it, picking out a series of gates to create an alternate route from Kathrion to Pyru. "*This* would be the fastest route to Pyru."

"Looks more like the long way to me," Jessica opined.

"I admit it is not the most direct, but all but two of the gates in this route are dedicated gates, which means the jump queues move much quicker."

"What's a *dedicated gate?*" Jessica wondered.

"One that has only a single destination. Routes using such gates are faster because you don't have to wait for them to re-point the gate between each jump."

"They have lower fees as well," Chiqua added. "Not that there is any limit on your credit."

"And Pyru is the *closest* hospital?" Nathan questioned. "It's pretty far inside Alliance space. None of these worlds along our route have one?"

"Every world has clinics providing basic care," Dominic explained. "But their expertise is limited. Unless the creature exists on their world, it is doubtful they would have a cure for the venom that threatens your friend's life. You need a level one medical facility, and the nearest one is on Pyru."

Nathan sighed. "How long do you think this route will take?"

"A couple hours at the most," Dominic assured him.

Nathan zoomed the map back out, studying it for a moment. "And you're sure there's not a better route?"

"Better as in *safer* or better as in *faster?*"

"Both actually."

"There are, but considering that your client's registered banking address is on Hadria, starting at a border gate *outside* the sector might raise questions," Dominic warned.

"Kathrion it is," Nathan decided after a moment. "Sending a route to you now, Josh!" he called out as he reached up for the overhead panel and sent the navigation data back to Josh.

"Got it!" Josh yelled back. "We'll be on our way in a minute!"

Nathan moved over to the small kitchenette area on the opposite side of the cramped compartment, pulling a bottle of water out of the fridge before turning back toward Dominic and Chiqua. "Before we jump to Kathrion, I have to ask each of you the same question, and that is: what is in this for you?"

"I'm just trying to help," Dominic assured Nathan. "You'd be surprised how bored you can get after living a few hundred years."

"You, I believe," Nathan said. He looked at Chiqua.

"I'm just trying to help as well," Chiqua assured him.

"Bullshit," Jessica commented.

"Exactly," Nathan agreed, pointing at Jessica. "Altruism doesn't fit you," he told Chiqua.

"I believe I'm offended," Chiqua asserted.

"Bullshit," Jessica said again.

"You either come clean, or I'm locking you up for the duration."

"You need my credit authorization codes," Chiqua reminded him.

"I've already got them," Nathan pointed out, "from the purchase of the nav-charts."

"But you don't have my personal POI chip."

"POI?"

"Proof of identity," Dominic explained. "A small

transponder embedded in one's forearm. It's used throughout Alliance space."

"Can't we just cut it out of her?" Jessica suggested. "We've got a doc on board after all."

"The device is bio-linked to her physiology to prevent theft," Dominic explained.

"Do you have one too?" Nathan asked.

"I do, but I suspect I don't have nearly the funds that Miss Kimbro has."

Nathan sighed. "What happens if I just jump my way directly to Pyru?"

"You and your crew would be arrested, and your ship would be impounded," Dominic explained.

Chiqua just sat there, smiling.

"I say we take our chances," Jessica opined.

"I'm waiting," Nathan told Chiqua.

"Fine," Chiqua acquiesced. "The truth is, I've been trying to gain a foothold in the badlands for years. There's a huge demand for medical supplies there, but the damned Korsan always hijack my cargo."

"Who are the Korsan?" Nathan wondered.

"An organized crime ring that rules a large chunk of the badlands and some of the fringe," Dominic explained.

"Calling them *organized* is too gracious," Chiqua insisted. "They're fucking pirates."

"Each ship, or group of ships, operates independently, but they have to turn over fifty percent of everything they acquire to the Korsan."

"So, space pirates overseen by extortionists," Jessica surmised. "Nice."

"What does this have to do with us?" Nathan asked Chiqua.

"You have a ship...an *Expedition-class* ship. The Korsan wouldn't have a chance against you."

"My *Expedition-class ship* is grounded for God knows how long," Nathan reminded her.

"But you also have shuttles, and more importantly, *Dragon fighters*. The Korsan generally fly junk fighters and broken-down cargo ships fitted with whatever weapons they could bolt to their hulls. *You could get my shipments through to the people who need them.*"

"Oh *pa-leeze*," Jessica groaned. "You don't give a shit about those people."

"Does that make their need for what I sell any less real?" Chiqua questioned.

"So you want us to run cargo through the badlands for you," Nathan surmised. "And you think that getting us indebted to you will leave us with no choice."

"Other than tossing her out the airlock as soon as Vlad is okay," Jessica suggested.

"Not a bad idea," Nathan agreed.

"That's not your style," Chiqua stated confidently. "Besides, you need me for more than just saving your chief engineer's life. You need me to help repair your ship."

"We can repair our ship *without* your help," Jessica insisted.

"You will need resources," Chiqua insisted. "More than you can find on Dencke. I can help you acquire those resources. You'll also want to upgrade some of your systems. A lot has changed over the last five hundred years, and as advanced as the Aurora might have been at the time she was launched, she's an antique compared to the top warships of today. Again, I can help you find such things. More importantly, I can help you acquire the funds to *pay* for them."

Although Nathan was pretty sure he already knew the answer, he had to ask the question. "How?"

"We become partners," Chiqua suggested. "With your shuttles and Dragons *alone*, we can make a fortune running goods into the badlands. And once you get the Aurora up and upgraded, we could *rule* the badlands."

"There it is," Jessica groaned.

"I wasn't surprised," Nathan said, "right up until that last part about ruling the badlands."

"I don't mean *literally*," Chiqua defended. "I'm just talking about interstellar trade. The Korsan have kept the badlands practically isolated from the fringe. Less than half of what is shipped into the fringe actually reaches its intended destination. And the only reason the Korsan allow *that* much to get through is so that privateers keep trying, hoping that they'll get through with full holds and make a killing."

Jessica laughed. "Interesting choice of words."

"I have no intention of starting a war with the Korsan," Nathan declared in no uncertain terms. "Nor in cornering interstellar trade in the badlands. All I want to do is save my friend and fix my ship."

"To do what though?" Chiqua pushed. "You can do a lot of good for the people in both the fringe and the badlands. You can bring hope to people who only know despair."

"Man, she really knows what you want to hear," Jessica chuckled.

Nathan glared at Jessica. "It's not going to work, Chiqua. It's not our job to police the badlands or the fringe."

"Then I guess you're Alliance after all."

"*We're ready for the jump to Kathrion,*" Josh reported from the cockpit.

Nathan studied Chiqua for a moment, pretty sure that they'd just been insulted. Then, without a word, he turned and disappeared through the doorway to the cockpit.

"I think you just screwed up," Jessica jeered as she got up to follow Nathan.

* * *

Nathan took the copilot's seat. "Jump whenever you're ready," he told Josh.

"Jumping," Josh replied, pressing the jump button.

The Seiiki's cockpit momentarily filled with blue-white light, the stars outside shifting slightly as the ship transitioned to a new location more than one hundred and sixty light years away.

"You should know that you are no longer the Seiiki," Dominic said from the doorway as he, Chiqua, and Jessica all entered the cockpit. "That name might have raised some questions."

"Then who are we?" Nathan wondered.

"We are now the Andrea Reynen," Josh announced.

Nathan looked at him in disbelief. "The girl who pretended to be in love with you and then robbed you blind back on Ursoot?"

"Yeah," Josh recalled fondly.

"She left you bound and naked on the balcony, in the rain."

"Yeah."

"You froze your ass off!" Nathan reminded him. "You were sick for a week!"

"So worth it."

"How close did you jump us in?" Nathan wondered.

"I put us right in the middle of the arrival area for our approach course. About five hundred thousand clicks out."

"That probably wasn't even her real name," Nathan said.

"It was the only name I could think of at the moment," Josh defended.

"You could've used your mom's name."

"Jesus, you want me to jump back out and we can pick another name?"

"I'm just messing with you, Josh," Nathan chuckled.

"You been taking lessons from Loki or what?"

"Will you two focus?" Jessica suggested.

"Are they always like this?" Chiqua wondered.

"Not always, but more often than I'd like," Jessica replied.

"This is the proper syntax for requesting a gate route booking through the network," Dominic said, passing his data pad forward.

Nathan studied the data pad a moment. "Did you enter all this into the nav-com?" he asked Josh.

"Yup."

Nathan activated the comms and began his hail. "Kathrion Approach, this is the Andrea Reynen, inbound from Dencke, approach area two five. Requesting transit to Pyru. Ready to transmit preferred routing." Nathan looked back at Dominic. "How was that?"

"I have no idea," Dominic admitted. "I've never been in the cockpit for something like this."

"*Andrea Reynen, Kathrion Approach,*" the controller responded over comms. "*No listing on your vessel. Hold course and speed, and transmit full registration data."*

"Andrea Reynen is holding course and speed, and transmitting reg data," Nathan replied.

"You almost sound like you know what you're doing," Jessica teased.

"Are you sure this will work?" Nathan asked Dominic as he prepared to transmit the forged data.

"Of course," Dominic assured him. After a moment, he added, "But you should probably have an escape jump ready, just in case."

Nathan looked at Josh.

"Already done," Josh assured him.

"Here goes nothing," Nathan murmured as he pressed the data transmit button.

"What do they do with the data?" Jessica wondered.

"First, they'll run it through the wanted ships list, then against the most recent copy of the ships already authorized to operate in Alliance space."

"Which we won't be on," Nathan surmised.

"Yes, but your certification date is only two days old, and they only get an update about twice a month. So they'll just check your pilot certificates and ownership record, and then create a new account for you."

"What if they got updated yesterday?" Josh asked.

"They'll assume your application approval hasn't been processed yet and clear you through. They just want to get paid. The local government gets a percentage of every gate fee collected, in order to fund gate operations. Out here, they don't get much traffic, so they need all the transits they can get in order to keep their gate. The Alliance will pull a gate that isn't at least breaking even, and these border worlds depend on that gate to keep trade flowing."

"*Andrea Reynen, Kathrion Approach. State the nature of your cargo.*"

"Kathrion, Reynen, no cargo. Just two passengers, one sick man bound for the hospital on Pyro, accompanied by his doctor, two med-techs, two bodyguards, and his wife, who is paying for the flight."

"*Nature of the illness?*"

"He was bit by a venomous water snake called a boka," Nathan replied.

"*Never heard of it.*"

"Neither had I."

There was no response.

Nathan turned to face the others behind him. "You think they bought it?"

"His *wife*?" Chiqua asked.

"Sounded more believable than an altruistic trader in medical supplies."

"*Andrea Reynen, Kathrion Approach. You're cleared as filed. Transmit account info.*"

"Kathrion, Reynen. We'd like to open an account on behalf of our client, Chiqua Kimbro."

"*Reynen, Kathrion. Transmit personal ID codes.*"

"How do we do that?" Nathan asked Dominic.

"That box on your left, just above the center console. It will scan her chip and relay the data automatically."

"So *that's* what that's for," Josh said.

"You didn't ask what a new device on your console was?" Nathan scolded.

"I figured you knew."

Chiqua stepped up and bared her left forearm. A moment later, a green light appeared on the device.

"Green is good, right?" Nathan asked.

"Green is good," Dominic confirmed.

"Reynen, Kathrion. Your client's new gate account codes are included in your clearance data. Just one more question...Is that really an original Navarro-class shuttle you're flying?"

"Uh, it is," Nathan replied.

"We don't see those around here very often. Any chance you've got some pics you could send us?"

"Sorry, no."

"No problem," the controller replied. "We'll just copy your transit pic. We like to post pics of rare ships that pass through here on the lobby wall. Have a good flight. Kathrion out."

"Thanks," Nathan replied. "Reynen out." He turned to look at Dominic. "*Pictures?*"

"Relax," Josh told him. "He already changed the name on the side."

"Not my first time," Dominic said.

"This must be our clearance," Josh said as data began scrolling down the comms display. "Jesus, at the speed they've assigned us, it will take *two hours* just to get to the first gate."

"It looks like there are two ships headed for the gate as well," Nathan said, pointing at the sensor screen in the center of the main console. "I'm guessing we're behind them in the queue."

"And it takes time to realign the gate after each jump," Dominic explained.

Nathan examined the route more closely. "If the second gate has the same delay, then we're going to be four hours just to get to the third gate."

"The dedicated gates cycle ships through much more quickly, I assure you," Dominic promised. "I doubt it will take more than a few hours to get the rest of them, *after* the first two gates, of course."

"Maybe you should take a nap, Cap'n," Josh suggested. "You've been up for two days."

"So have you," Nathan replied.

"Then take a short nap, and then relieve me."

Chiqua stepped up, noticing the list of gate fees. "Not exactly the cheapest route, is it."

Nathan looked at Chiqua as he rose from his seat, wondering if she was going to change her mind now that she saw the price of traversing the gate network all the way to Pyru.

"Relax, Captain. I'm sure we can work out a payment plan."

"That's what I'm afraid of," Nathan muttered to himself as he exited the cockpit.

* * *

Nathan woke to the sound of the intercom beeping. "Yeah?"

"*Ten minutes to the Kathrion gate,*" Josh reported over the intercom.

"On my way." Nathan sat up, swinging his legs off the side of his bunk. He had been asleep for more than an hour and a half but felt as if he had closed his eyes only a moment ago. Normally, a short nap would leave him refreshed, but the events of the last two days had taken their toll, both physically *and* mentally.

After visiting the head, Nathan headed forward, stopping by the medical module in the midship bay to check on Vladimir.

"How's he doing?" he asked Doctor Chen, who also looked like the last two days had taken its toll.

"Still declining, but at least it hasn't accelerated."

"Have you gotten any rest?" Nathan asked.

"Shows, huh?"

"On all of us."

"I take catnaps in between treatments," she told him. "An hour here, an hour there."

"Maybe you'll be able to get a full night's sleep once we get him to a hospital."

"I'll get a full night's sleep when his eyes are open and he's talking our ears off again."

Nathan smiled, exiting and heading forward through the starboard corridor toward the boarding compartment. Once in the compartment, he climbed up the access ladder just right of center to the flight deck above.

To his surprise, the crew cabin was empty. He stepped over and entered the cockpit, finding Josh and Jessica inside. "Where are Dominic and Chiqua?"

"I sent them to the starboard cabins for the duration," Jessica answered.

"And they agreed?"

"I didn't give them a choice."

"She's lying," Josh sneered. "Chiqua was all for some down time, and she got Dominic to cooperate by giving him access to our schematics."

"Only to the non-critical systems," Jessica insisted. "It was either that or make small talk with them for hours."

"Isn't that your favorite pastime?" Nathan joked as he took the copilot's seat. The first thing he did was look out the forward windows, spotting the approaching jump gate. After a glance at the navigation display, he realized just how massive the faraway object was. "Damn."

"Yeah, it's big," Josh confirmed. "Big enough to fit *two* Aurora's side by side."

"And the fixed gates are even bigger," Dominic commented from the hatch. "May I?"

Jessica gestured for him to take the starboard auxiliary station behind Nathan.

"How are we looking?" Nathan asked, noticing that the gate was growing rapidly as they approached.

"The gate appears to be lined up with Cano," Josh replied. "And we're on the proper course and speed."

"Good job," Nathan replied.

"AI's doing all the flying."

"And it will be for the rest of the flight," Dominic warned. "It's a requirement when flying in Alliance space."

"The AIs do *all* the flying?" Josh asked, shocked.

"That's correct," Dominic told him.

"Looks like you're out of a job, Josh," Nathan teased.

"Don't worry, son," Dominic told Josh. "Most ships still have a backup pilot on board, just in case. And there's always the fringe, where most worlds frown on the use of AIs."

"I think I prefer the fringe," Josh stated.

By now, the gate filled both forward windows and took on a cylindrical shape. Rather than a gate, it looked more like a tunnel enclosed within a massive lattice of trusses, with large structures on either side.

"It's weird," Nathan stated, gazing out the windows. "It was only a week ago that Abby told me she was working on the prototype for that."

"That's right," Dominic realized. "You *knew* Doctor Sorenson, didn't you?"

"We did."

"Amazing," Dominic said. "She was considered one of the greatest physicists of all time."

"Was?" Jessica wondered.

"She fell into disrepute when she contested the ASA's findings about rogue gravity well propagation."

"ASA?" Nathan wondered.

"Alliance Science Authority. They canceled all her funding, took away her position on the ASA council, basically ruining her."

"What happened to her?" Nathan asked.

"No one really knows," Dominic admitted. "She sort of fell off the map. Some say she changed after the loss of her oldest child. A son, if I remember correctly." Dominic looked at Nathan. "Wasn't he on your crew at the time..."

"He still is," Nathan assured him.

Dominic shook his head in disbelief. "Relativity plays some amazing tricks."

"Something is happening," Josh warned, pointing out the front window.

Nathan looked out the forward window again. The gate's emitter arrays were beginning to glow. First one array, then a second one interspersed within the first. But the color was off. It was still the familiar pale bluish white, but it was far less opaque than the jump fields they were accustomed to.

Dominic sensed the trepidation among them. "Once your ship has fully entered the gate, the first emitter array will fire, creating an inner jump field that will close in around you and encompass your hull. A second or two later, the second array will fire, creating an outer jump field that will also shrink toward you. The outer field will collide with your inner field *after* you exit the gate, and the jump will occur."

"So no big energy dump?" Nathan inquired.

"No, that's what the ASA claims causes damage to the dimensional barriers and leads to rogue gravity wells," Dominic explained. "The outer field created by a jump gate is *already* highly charged and therefore more stable...or so they claim."

"You don't believe them?" Nathan gathered.

"I don't really care," Dominic stated. "I moved to the fringe for *ethical* reasons, not *political* ones."

Nathan was captivated by the image of the glowing emitters and the formation of their open-ended jump field. "And this works?" he asked, still unconvinced.

"It works quite well," Dominic assured him.

The nose of the Seiiki entered the tunnel, the inner jump field now fully formed. Two seconds later, they were fully inside the tunnel, and the inner field quickly closed in around them on all sides, its front enveloping them as it closed around their hull, taking its shape.

The outer field was next. It was brighter than the inner field but was also shrinking down around them as they continued toward the exit end of the tunnel. Nathan's eyes kept darting between the collapsing outer field and the approaching exit, seeing that they would indeed exit the tunnel prior to the two fields colliding.

Their nose cleared the exit end of the tunnel, and they could again see the stars through the glowing blue-white haze of the jump fields. Two seconds later, the outer field made contact, and the jump flash occurred, illuminating the interior of their cockpit momentarily.

The fields disappeared, the stars outside having shifted slightly with their transition.

Josh studied the navigation computer's display.

"We're in the Cano system," he reported. "Smack dab in the middle of the Kathrion arrival area." He looked at Nathan. "I guess that crazy thing works."

"I have to admit, it's pretty impressive," Nathan stated.

"Wait until you see the *big* gates," Dominic told them.

"Looks like we'll make the next gate in just over an hour," Josh stated.

"Too bad for you," Nathan said.

"No problem," Josh replied. "Since the AI was doing all the flyin', I *slept* most of the way to the Kathrion gate."

"Looks like she's turning us toward the Cano gate," Josh announced. "Well, since the AI's got this, and I've already slept, I think I'll get some chow and stretch my legs a bit." Josh climbed out of his seat and headed aft. "Let me know if you need help flying this thing."

"I think I can handle watching the AI fly us to and through the next gate," Nathan assured him.

"I'll be back before we reach the next gate," Josh assured him. "I gotta earn my keep after all."

"I could use something to eat, myself," Dominic stated. "May I?" he asked, rising from his seat.

"Help yourself," Nathan told him.

"I'll give you a hand," Jessica offered, rising to follow him out. "You don't want to eat the wrong ration pack. Some of those things are nasty."

* * *

Monitoring the Seiiki's systems as her AI guided their ship across the Cano system to their departure gate had given Nathan time to investigate her flight deck displays and controls. It really was a fine ship, and her flight controls were perfectly designed, which was surprising considering that she was designed to be piloted by her AI rather than by a human.

It had also given him time to think about what had happened, about what the Alliance had become, and what their future might be. But one thought kept permeating all others. *What had gone wrong?* Had he been reckless? Had the cloaking system been faulty? Had the Ilyan been tipped off?

"I brought you a meat bar," Jessica announced as she entered the cockpit.

"Thanks," Nathan replied, accepting the offering. "Where's Dominic?"

"He went back to his cabin," Jessica said as she took the pilot's seat.

"What about Josh?"

"He's still eating."

"Of course."

Nathan opened his ration bar and took a bite.

"I don't know how you can eat those things," Jessica commented.

"They're not that bad."

"What have you been doing up here all alone?" Jessica asked. "Let me guess...second-guessing every decision you made over the last two days?"

"More like the last two weeks," Nathan admitted.

"When are you going to stop doing that?"

"It's my thing."

"You do realize it was all a trap, right?"

"Which part?" Nathan wondered.

"All of it. Sending me into the Ilyan. Taking out Robert's XK. Sending you and the Aurora in to rescue me. The whole thing had to have been orchestrated. That's just too much bad luck at one time."

"You do realize how crazy that sounds?"

"That's *my* thing," Jessica replied, smiling. "Think about it though."

"Why would someone want to start a war between the Ilyan and the Alliance?" Nathan challenged.

"Maybe a war wasn't the primary goal but rather an advantageous side effect," Jessica suggested.

"What are you suggesting, that *I* was the target?"

"It's possible. Or maybe discrediting you was part of another agenda. Like defeating Miri in the next election."

"Miri wasn't even planning on running again."

"Had she announced that?"

"Not that I know of," Nathan admitted.

"Maybe it wasn't about you. Maybe it was about profit. War is great for the economy of the winning side. It's also the catalyst for all kinds of agendas not possible during peacetime."

"Yeah, I thought of that," Nathan admitted.

"The Ilyan's anti-Alliance campaign was picking up steam," Jessica stated. "It was only a matter of time until we clashed."

"And you think someone decided to make it happen sooner rather than later?"

"Why not? SilTek would make a *huge* profit if the Alliance and the Ilyan went to war. It would also drive membership, especially along the Ilyan's borders."

"But according to Jorda, *trillions* died," Nathan said. "That seems like an extreme measure just to make a profit."

"Not to an AI," Jessica argued. "It's just numbers and probabilities to them."

"Perhaps."

"There's another possibility as well."

"The Jung," Nathan surmised.

"Then you *did* consider them."

"Only because of something Trever said to me when he introduced Laza. That she was one of the only Jung officers who wouldn't shoot me on sight."

"You think she was part of it?"

"If she somehow sabotaged the cloaking device, that would explain how the Gamazan ships detected us so easily."

"Then maybe we should lock her ass up when we get back," Jessica suggested.

"Not much she can do to us now that the Aurora is grounded."

"She could still kill you," Jessica argued.

"If her mission was to kill me, I'm pretty sure she would've done so by now."

"Well, if her mission was to start a war between the Alliance and the Ilyan so that we would destroy each other, it didn't work. It's my understanding that the Jung *sided* with the Ilyan, and that they *too* were conquered by the Alliance."

Nathan sighed. "Which leads me to my second hypothesis."

"That the *Alliance* set us up," Jessica surmised.

"The Alliance leadership council has, or should I say *had*, been pushing for a broader scope of control over member worlds, and for a more rapid buildup of forces," Nathan explained.

"And SilTek had no problems with that, I suppose."

"They didn't say anything publicly, but I'm pretty sure they were at least in favor of the buildup."

"And a war would give them an excuse."

"Get rid of me and the Aurora, then blame it on the Jung *and* the Ilyan colluding together," Nathan outlined. "It all adds up."

"Just because it adds up doesn't make it true," Jessica reminded him.

"An odd statement coming from you," Nathan said.

"Just because I'm always looking for conspiracies doesn't mean I buy into them without evidence," Jessica defended. "The thing is, does it really matter at this point? Whatever happened is past history. Discovering the truth isn't going to *change* anything. We're still going to be stuck here, five hundred and thirty-five years in the future."

"True, but it might have bearing on what we decide to do going forward," Nathan argued, "as well as who to trust," he added, looking at her.

"Soray?"

"The thought crossed my mind."

"Mine too," Jessica admitted. "Problem is, most saboteurs don't want to become victims of their own sabotage, and the Jung have never been known for their blind faith in their empire."

"More like blind faith in their right to dominate others," Nathan said. "So, do you think we can trust her?"

"No more than we have to," Jessica stated. "Same as Chiqua and Dominic."

"Sometimes it's better to keep your enemies close." Nathan surmised.

"At least until we figure out exactly *who* our enemies *are*."

"You think Chiqua and Dominic are our enemies?"

"I haven't decided yet," Jessica admitted. "They sure as hell aren't our friends."

"What about Jorda?" Nathan asked.

"His motivations are too local to be much of a threat at the moment. He's on the other side of the planet and doesn't have a shuttle. Even if he did, he doesn't have enough firepower to take us on. His best play is to remain friendly. But you already knew that."

"Just checking where your head's at," Nathan said, smiling.

"Same place it always is," Jessica assured him, "watching for bad guys behind every friendly face."

"Hard way to live."

"I kind of like it," Jessica replied. "Besides, someone has to offset your insane tendency to trust everyone."

"I don't trust *everyone*."

"Yes you do."

"I give them the benefit of the doubt so that they have a chance to *prove* they are trustworthy," Nathan insisted.

"Bullshit. You believe everyone is good until proven otherwise."

"And you believe everyone is up to something nefarious."

"That's what I'm talking about," Jessica declared. "Balance. It's why you need me."

Nathan was silent. The truth was he did need her, and at times he resented that fact.

"You see, I'm right."

"I *need* you to follow orders," Nathan stated firmly.

"I do...for the most part."

"The hell you do."

"I take action when action is needed instead of waiting for orders to do so. There's a difference."

"Not much of one," Nathan insisted.

"Yeah, it's a pretty fine line," she admitted. "But that's what I'm trained for, and that's why you need me."

"You suck," Nathan laughed.

* * *

Hanna peered up the ladder leading from the boarding compartment to the Seiiki's flight deck.

"No one's going to shoot you," Kit assured her.

His commented startled her.

"Sorry."

"No problem," Hanna told him. "I'm not much of a space traveler."

"Didn't you spend a thousand years in space?"

Hanna nodded. "Am I allowed to go up there?"

"Hold on," Kit told her, tapping his comm-set. "Jess, can Hanna come up?"

After a moment, Jessica replied, "*Send her up.*"

"You're all clear," Kit told Hanna.

Hanna put her hands on the ladder but didn't head up. Instead, she turned back to Kit. "You're one of those Gatazka?"

"Gha-ta-*zhak*," Kit corrected. "Yes."

"So you're some kind of soldier?"

"We prefer the term *operator*," Kit explained. "But, essentially, yes, we are soldiers."

"How long have you been a...*Gha-ta-zhak*?"

"My entire adult life."

"How old are you?"

"By whose calendar?" Kit joked.

"Right. Uh, whatever calendar you prefer, I guess."

"I'm just joking with you. I'm thirty-six in Earth years."

"So about sixteen years?"

"More like twenty-four."

"You've been a Ghatazhak for *twenty-four years?*

That would've made you *twelve years old* when you enlisted."

"Well, technically I've only been a Ghatazhak for fourteen of your years. It takes ten of your years for a Ghatazhak to complete their initial training."

"Ten years?" Hanna asked in disbelief.

"Yup."

"That's a lot of training."

"Yes, it is," Kit agreed. "You'd better get up there, or you're going to miss the next jump."

"Jump?"

"Trust me," Kit said, pointing up the ladder.

Hanna looked up the ladder, then back at Kit. "I'd like to know more about the Ghatazhak. Maybe I can interview you sometime?"

"I'll be around."

Hanna smiled and headed up the ladder, finding Jessica waiting for her in the crew cabin above.

"You get a front row seat," Jessica told her, pointing to the cockpit doorway.

Hanna stepped through the doorway, pausing to take it all in. The cockpit was smaller and more cramped than she had expected based on the size of the shuttle. Every square centimeter was covered with controls, displays, or small compartments. Two large windows sat above the forward console, with windows on either side. There were two side-facing consoles as well, one of which was occupied by Dominic.

Hanna nodded to Dominic, having already met him earlier. Then she bent down slightly to get a better view through the front windows. When she did so, her mouth fell open. "What the hell is that?" she asked.

Nathan turned back toward her, rotating slightly in his seat. "Welcome to the cockpit."

"*That* is a variable destination jump gate," Dominic told her. "Probably a GX seven by the looks of it."

"What does it do?"

"Just like it sounds," Dominic replied. "It jumps a ship to another star system light years away."

"How many light years?"

"If I remember correctly, the GX seven has a range of about one hundred light years at max passage size," Dominic explained. "So, for this size ship, probably closer to one hundred and fifty."

"What does it mean…jump?"

"You're about to see," Nathan told her from the copilot's seat.

Hanna realized what was about to happen. "We're going to fly *through* that thing?"

"That's how it works," Josh chuckled.

"It uses the same principal as the jump drive, but without the massive energy dump into the outer jump field," Dominic explained. "It allows any ship capable of interplanetary flight to travel to other star systems, without requiring its *own* jump drive."

"I don't understand anything you just said," Hanna admitted.

"Think of it as a way of removing the inconvenience of *time* from interstellar travel," Nathan told her.

"How is that possible?"

"That's a long story," Nathan replied.

"That's what I'm here for," Hanna reminded him.

"Thirty seconds to gate threshold," Josh warned.

"Maybe later," Nathan replied. "You might want to sit down for this. The first jump can be a bit… *shocking*."

Hanna took a seat at the starboard auxiliary station just behind Nathan, her eyes fixed on the massive tunnel they were about to fly into. "It's so big."

"This is one of the smaller gates," Dominic commented.

Hanna's eyes remained fixed on the forward windows as the primary array emitters inside the tunnel began to glow, quickly building in their intensity until their pale blue light seemed to pour out of them like water. The inside of the tunnel quickly became covered with the semi-transparent layer of light as another set of emitters also began to glow.

"Threshold," Josh reported.

Hanna's eyes glanced to the right and up, gazing out of the corner of the starboard window as the entrance to the tunnel passed over their bow. The first field of light began moving quickly toward them, hugging the hull of the ship.

"Are we accelerating?" Hanna asked, noticing that the trusses forming the massive tunnel seemed to be moving past them with increasing speed.

"It just seems that way now that we're inside," Nathan assured her.

"Ten seconds to exit," Josh reported, "twelve to the jump."

Hanna continued to stare out the forward windows in fascination as the second field of energy formed and began moving closer, surrounding them on all sides just like the first.

"Five seconds," Josh reported.

The second energy field continued to move toward them as their shuttle cleared the end of the tunnel.

"Clearing the tunnel," Josh added.

Hanna began to feel uneasy. "What's going to happen?" she wondered, her question barely audible.

"Three..." Josh began counting.

"You'll see," Nathan replied.

"Two..."

Hanna grasped the arms of her seat, bracing herself for the unknown.

"One..."

The second field reached the first, and the two fields flashed brightly, filling the cockpit with pale, blue-white light.

Hanna's eyes popped open, and she leaned back sharply at the sudden flash. Then it was gone. "What just happened?"

Josh glanced at his navigation display. "Welcome to the Caelo Delta system."

"The where?" Hanna asked. "What just happened?" she asked again.

"We just jumped from the Cano system to the Caelo Delta system, sixty-seven light years away," Nathan explained.

"Just like that?"

"Just like that."

Hanna looked at Dominic, then back at Nathan. "And you guys do this sort of thing all the time?"

"They do, I don't," Dominic said.

Hanna slumped back in her chair in shock. "My God."

* * *

"What's up?" Cameron asked Robert as she entered the power generation control compartment.

"Cori may have come up with a temporary solution for our power problem," Robert boasted.

"Really?"

"Well, not so much for the *whole* problem," Cori corrected. "But I think I can power our shields."

"How?" Cameron wondered.

"Using the Mirai's ZPEDs," Cori explained. "If we connect her to the Aurora's shield power grid and run them both at full power, it should be enough to get all her shields up to around twenty percent."

"Not enough to defend against an attack, but more than enough to keep boka snakes, and God knows what else, out of the ship," Robert commented.

"What's the catch?" Cameron wondered.

"The only way to hook into the shield power grid is from *outside*," Chief Avelles explained. He punched in some commands, and the display of the Aurora's power schematic shifted, zooming in on the dorsal aspect of her stern. "Here," he said, pointing at the display. "Just forward of the stern heat transfer array."

"It's minus fifty outside," Cameron reminded them. "Besides, I'm pretty sure we don't have a power cable long enough."

"We don't *need* one," Cori told her. "We just need to park the Mirai on top of the hull, just in front of the connection point. Then we just have to run eight short cables, four from each nacelle."

"Again, it's minus fifty."

"We can use the pressure shield rescue rigs to create a safe working environment," Cori explained.

"So it'll be what, only minus twenty?" Cameron stated.

"That's what I said," Chief Dixon agreed.

"Pressure shields hold air pressure within, not the other way around," Cameron reminded the young engineer.

"Not if we reverse them," Cori told her.

Cameron looked at Chief Dixon. "We can do that?"

"Theoretically, yes."

"It will work," Cori insisted.

"It will still be cold as hell though," the chief insisted.

"We'll throw some portable space heaters into the aft cargo bay. Once we extend the cargo bay pressure shield to include the ramp, we can overlap the rescue nets to be part of the same airspace, so the space heaters should raise the temperature up enough to work in, as long as we work quickly."

"How long will all this take?" Cameron asked.

"An hour or so to set up, and then another hour to make the connection once the Mirai's in place," Cori replied.

"Any risk?" Cameron asked. "To the Aurora *or* the Mirai?"

"I can put automatic cutoffs on the connections to the Mirai's ZPEDs," Cori suggested.

"The Aurora's shield power grid is completely separate from her internal grid, and every emitter has its own overload sensor on the input side. So there shouldn't be any risk at all," the chief confirmed. "The only real risk is hooking it all up. Those space heaters aren't going to do much."

"Work in shifts," Robert suggested. "Divide the process into tasks and rotate the teams in between each task."

"That'll slow things down," Cori warned.

"And we don't have a whole lot of engineers available at the moment," Chief Dixon added.

Cameron sighed. "It's too bad our AI is down. We could really use our tech-droids about now."

"This will work, sir," Cori insisted.

Cameron looked to Robert. "She's your engineer."

"If Cori says it will work, it will work," Robert insisted.

"I guess I can't ask for better than that," Cameron decided. "Get to work."

"Yes, sir," Chief Dixon replied.

Cameron looked to Robert as Cori and Chief Dixon headed out. "Sharp girl you've got there."

"Yes she is."

* * *

"We're sixth in line for the gate," Josh reported.

"*Sixth?*" Nathan groaned.

"ETA is only twelve minutes though."

"That's normal for fixed destination gates," Dominic assured them.

"So these gates are *everywhere*?" Hanna asked, still wrestling with the concept of instantaneous interstellar travel.

"Every Alliance member world is issued a gate," Dominic explained. "Assuming they *want* one."

"Why would they not?"

"Some worlds prefer isolation. However, even those worlds eventually find themselves with a gate, whether they wanted one or not."

"Why would the Alliance force a gate onto a world that didn't want one?" Josh wondered. "Those things have to be expensive."

"Control," Nathan surmised.

"Precisely. A gate gives the citizens of an otherwise isolated world access to healthcare, automation, better food, clothing, housing, you name it. The result is usually a dramatic increase in their quality of life, according to Alliance standards, which results in the growth of that world's population."

"The bigger the population, the more goods they need," Hanna stated.

"And the more ships that utilize that gate," Dominic said.

"Which means more money for whoever *owns* that gate," Nathan added.

"All the gates are *owned* by SilTek," Dominic explained. "But the Alliance gets forty percent of all profits from the gates. *That's* how the Alliance has become so powerful. They control all shipping throughout their territories."

"Is that why people move to the fringe?" Hanna asked.

"On the surface, yes, but most fringe worlds couldn't survive without a constant stream of goods coming from worlds *within* Alliance space. So, in essence, they're still dependent on the Alliance gate network. Even the worlds in the badlands depend on goods from Alliance worlds."

"But there is trading going between fringe worlds, right?"

"Yes, but most of it is exchanging things of value that they created for manufactured goods from Alliance worlds."

"Like coru," Nathan surmised.

"Yes, coru is very popular, especially on less populated worlds."

"How does coru get turned into credits?" Nathan wondered.

"Someone like Miss Kimbro sells it to buyers who can pay in Alliance credits, usually to importers on border worlds. With that, she can purchase the medical supplies—supplies that were manufactured on Alliance worlds—to be traded with fringe worlds."

"Seems like an equitable system," Hanna commented.

"It depends on your point of view, I suppose," Dominic remarked. "For example, the coru that Dencke trades is worth three times what Miss Kimbro offers them in trade."

"Do the Gruners know this?" Hanna wondered.

"They know it's worth more than they're getting, but not how *much* more. But they do not have the capability of shopping around or selling directly to border worlds. So trading with someone like Miss Kimbro is their only option."

"The more isolated the world, the less trading power they have," Hanna surmised.

"Not exactly," Nathan interjected. "It's also about what they have to trade."

"True. Aramenium is far more valuable than coru. That's why Gruner grew so quickly in the beginning. They believed the planet possessed massive deposits. Unfortunately for both the investors and those who migrated there, it turned out to be untrue. Some even say it was a hoax."

Hanna looked surprised. "You'd think in the future such things wouldn't be possible."

"They are quite common outside of Alliance space," Dominic assured her.

"But not within?" Nathan wondered.

"They happen, but the penalties are far more severe."

"Humans never change," Nathan commented.

"Some of us jokingly refer to that as the 'universal constant'," Dominic joked.

"That's why Chiqua wants to trade in the

badlands," Nathan realized. "She can charge a fortune."

"Especially if she is the only one able to get goods through."

"What are these *badlands* you keep referring to?" Hanna wondered.

"The furthest reaches of humanity," Dominic explained. "The *true* frontier."

"It sounds dangerous," Hanna decided.

"It is," Dominic confirmed. "Completely unregulated, completely unsupported by the Alliance, and completely controlled by organized gangs."

"There's more than one?" Nathan asked. "I thought it was just the Korsan."

"The Korsan are just the nearest, and one of the larger ones," Dominic explained. "The frontier is vast. It may only be a hundred light years deep, but it encircles all of human-colonized space. Not even the Alliance could regulate that much territory."

"How many colonies are there in the badlands?" Hanna asked.

"They're more like settlements," Dominic told her. "A few hundred people at the most. Some are just a few homesteads, perhaps no more than a couple dozen people total."

"People establish homesteads on *unexplored worlds?*" Hanna asked in disbelief. "Aren't they afraid of something going wrong?"

"It's a risk they are willing to take. Besides, every habitable world within twenty thousand light years of Sol has been remotely surveyed and cataloged by SilTek."

"*SilTek* surveyed them?" Nathan asked.

"They manufacture every level of homesteading kit imaginable," Dominic explained. "Everything from pop-up survival huts to self-assembling homesteads, complete with house, barn, power plant, water processing, skimmer, the works."

"Aren't they afraid of the gangs?" Hanna asked.

"The criminal element doesn't generally interfere with settler transports. The more people who move to the frontier, the more targets they have to extort or steal from. It's an odd balance."

"Why would people want to homestead if it's so dangerous?" Hanna wondered.

"Most would rather take the risk than continue living under Alliance rule," Dominic explained. "Of course, SilTek's marketing greatly downplays the risk, insisting that such criminal activity is rare. Of course, they also sell security systems, homestead shields, defense systems, you name it."

"Still, it seems insane," Hanna insisted.

"And the Alliance doesn't interfere with people seeking to leave their governance?" Nathan asked.

"They do not. In some ways, they encourage it. They claim they want everyone to be happy, even if that means living outside of their sphere of control."

"Well at least they kept that part," Nathan commented.

"Not really. SilTek makes plenty outfitting homesteaders, and the Alliance gets a more compliant population. They claim there are two kinds of people. Those who wish to be part of a structured, peaceful, and secure society, and are willing to give up certain freedoms toward that end, and those who prefer complete freedom despite its risks."

"Which are you?" Hanna asked.

"I'm kind of in the middle," Dominic admitted. "That's why I only migrated as far out as Pangburn.

That and because it was a good location to ply my trade."

Hanna thought for a moment. "I'm probably the type who would give up freedom in exchange for security."

"There's nothing wrong with that," Nathan assured Hanna.

"The majority of people believe just that," Dominic stated. "Until they are pushed too far. That's when they leave."

"So SilTek makes money from both sides of that coin," Nathan realized.

"They do. And when too large a majority of Alliance citizens are happy where they are, the Alliance changes society just enough to drive the centrists out. This is how they maintain a compliant population while maintaining the *appearance* of freedom."

"Interesting," Hanna commented.

"Frightening is the word I would use," Nathan insisted.

"Actually, it's not a bad system when you think about it," Dominic said. "In the end, everyone gets what they want. The freedom to choose the *type* of society they want to live in."

"Just how many worlds *are* there?" Hanna wondered.

"That's hard to say," Dominic admitted. "Last I heard, there were about thirty-five hundred inhabited worlds in the Alliance."

"What level of population?" Nathan wondered.

"Anywhere from tens of thousands to tens of billions, depending on their state of development."

"Are there any uncolonized worlds within Alliance space?" Hanna asked.

"There are, but their numbers are falling."

"Why don't people just settle on those worlds?"

"The Alliance controls *all* worlds within their boundaries."

"The worlds don't have a choice?" Nathan asked.

"They do not. That's why many head for the frontiers."

Nathan shared a look with Josh. The Alliance they had initially created had not turned out the way they had hoped.

* * *

"*This will be the shortest flight ever,*" Aiden announced over comm-sets as the Mirai rose slowly from the Aurora's flight deck.

Cori stood at the cargo deck ramp threshold, clad in cold-weather gear that included a full-face mask, as the Mirai began to back slowly toward the Aurora's stern, her flight deck sliding past under them.

The shuttle continued to rise until it was only a few meters above the height of the drive nacelles on either side, continuing to slide backwards as it leveled off.

Cori clutched the side of the cargo bay opening as the wind outside buffeted the shuttle. She could feel the cold radiating through the pressure shield, despite the fact that she was thoroughly covered, and the heating in the cargo bay was set to maximum.

She watched as the shuttle backed its way toward the raised aft section of the Aurora, slowing as it approached its destination. "I see it," she announced, pointing at the hull outside. "That's the connection panel right there."

The Mirai's backward motion slowed to a stop.

"Is that close enough?" Aiden asked.

"That's good," Cori answered.

"Setting down," Aiden announced as the shuttle began to descend toward the hull of the Aurora below.

Cori held on as the aft landing gear made contact with the Aurora's hull, then continued to pitch nose down until its forward gear touched the hull a few seconds later.

"All four down," Aiden reported.

Cori was now leaning slightly forward, the shuttle's nose now five degrees lower than her stern, due to the angle of the forward aspect of the Aurora's aft center hull section.

"Hang on a moment, while I try to level us a bit," Aiden warned.

Cori and the others braced themselves, the deck beginning to slowly level as Aiden transferred hydraulic pressure from the aft gear to the forward gear. After a minute, the angle change ceased. There was still a bit of a tilt, but less severe.

"That's about as level as we're going to get," Erica reported from the Mirai's copilot seat. "Aft gear is at zero pressure, and forward gear is fully extended."

"That'll have to do," Aiden told her. "That's it, people. You're clear to get started."

"Understood," Cori replied. *"Lowering the ramp to the hull."*

"Thanks for recommending me," Erica said.

"No problem," Aiden replied. "I figured you needed to get your feet wet. Sims can only teach you so much."

"And this was the shortest flight in history," Erica said.

Aiden smiled. "Baby steps, right? Besides, we're going to be stuck here until the long night passes, and none of us are critical to the Aurora's current operational state."

"I hope you realize that I'm going to be asking you a *lot* of questions while we're here," Erica warned. "Not only about flying, but also about everything else."

"Like what?"

"Like what's gone on since we left Earth? What's the current state of humanity? How many inhabited worlds are there?"

"Didn't Captain Nash answer those questions?"

"Some, but not all of them."

"Doesn't the Aurora have a historical database?"

"Probably, but they're not accessible while we're on emergency power," Erica reminded him.

"Oh yeah," Aiden replied. "Well I'll do my best, but I'm certainly no expert."

Cori was the first one out the door, heading down the Mirai's cargo ramp with a rescue kit in hand. "I'm going left," she announced over comm-sets.

"*I'm going right*," Hani replied.

The moment Cori stepped off the side of the cargo ramp, she was hit with a strong wind that knocked her against the back of the Mirai's port side. "Damn!" she exclaimed. "It's windier than I thought."

"*It's just you,*" Hani teased. "*What are you, like forty kilograms soaking wet?*"

"At least I'm not a sail like you," Cori joked back.

"*You want us to start running cable?*" Dino asked.

"Not until we get these rescue emitters up," Cori insisted as she reached the far edge of the port side and began opening up her kit. "Damn, it's cold!" she complained, already beginning to lose feeling in her fingers.

"*You want some help?*" Sori offered over comm-sets.

"I've got it," Cori insisted as she deployed the emitter tripod and placed it against the corner of the shuttle. She quickly secured it to an attachment point on the shuttle's hull, then pulled the cable reel out of the kit. After connecting the cable to the base of the emitter stand, she began walking backward toward the cargo ramp, paying out cable with each step. "Christ, I can't feel my fingers!" she realized.

Her back hit the side of the ramp, stopping her.

"*Hand it to me,*" Dino told her.

Cori turned to her left, handing the reel to Dino. She was quickly losing feeling in her arms as well. They felt as if they were becoming weaker, as did the rest of her body.

"*Give me your hand,*" Sori suggested.

Cori continued turning around, extending her arm to grab Sori's hand, but her fingers didn't seem to respond.

"*I've got you,*" Sori assured her as he pulled her onto the ramp and back inside the Mirai's pressure shield.

Cori was already shaking from the extreme cold, practically being dragged by Sori back into the cargo bay.

"Are you okay?" Sori asked as he eased her down to the deck along the forward bulkhead.

"I'm...fine."

Sori didn't ask twice, immediately following Dino back out onto the starboard side of the ramp to help Hani.

Cori watched, partly in shock, as Dino grabbed the other reel from Hani and laid the cable out across the cargo bay deck, plugging it into the connector on the starboard bulkhead.

Sori helped Hani to the deck next to Cori, who turned slowly to look at him. "You...okay?" she asked.

"*I'm...f...f...f...frozen,*" Sori replied.

"Let's just...sit here...for a while," she suggested.

Sori just nodded.

"*Rescue emitters are ready,*" Dino announced. "*Fire them up.*"

"*Charging rescue emitters and extending pressure shields,*" Erica replied.

Cori watched from her position on the deck along the forward bulkhead as the pressure shield over the back opening moved outward, creating extensions on either side out to the corners of the ship. Hopefully, it would give them a more tolerable working environment.

* * *

"Jesus, you could fly the Glendanon through that thing," Josh exclaimed as he stared at the approaching fixed destination gate in the Seiiki's forward windows.

"And there are even larger ones," Dominic commented. "Onori is only a Class C system. Class B systems have larger gates and usually more than one. Class A's have multiple gates and even super gates."

"What are super gates?" Hanna wondered.

"Just really big gates?" Josh surmised.

"Yes, they're bigger, but they're usually designed for a specific transport vessel. Usually a heavy cargo ship or a ferry."

"A ferry?" Nathan asked.

"Yes. Massive vessels. Not much to them, really. Just a big empty tube with simple drives and basic maneuvering. Other ships dock inside of them and then are ferried through a fixed gate. They're generally used in a dedicated loop route, where they go back and forth between two systems, usually completing the circuit every two or three hours."

"There are systems with that much traffic?" Nathan asked.

"Indeed. I once lived on Gelan Alpha Four but went to work every day on Prinitz in the Vega Ipsi system, two hundred light years away," Dominic explained.

"That's a hell of a commute," Hanna gasped.

"Actually, I had my own mini-shuttle, so door to door was about an hour each way if I timed it right. The flights were completely automated, so I usually ate my meals on the way there and back."

"Why didn't you just *live* on Prinitz?" Hanna wondered.

"If you'd ever *been* to Prinitz, you wouldn't be asking that question."

Hanna looked at Nathan and Josh. "Have either of you been there?"

"Never heard of it," Nathan admitted. Josh just shrugged.

"We're next up," Josh reported. "Two minutes to the entry threshold."

"I still can't get over all this," Nathan sighed. "I

mean, when Abby told me about the project, I knew it would be big, but…"

"I still can't get over that you *knew* Doctor Sorenson," Dominic exclaimed.

"Who is this Doctor Sorenson?" Hanna asked.

"Only the inventor of the jump drive, and one of the greatest theoretical physicists of all time," Dominic declared.

"Actually, Abby used to get angry when she was credited with the jump drive's invention," Nathan corrected.

"You called her *Abby?*" Dominic's mouth was agape.

"That was her name," Nathan replied. "It was her father's idea. He got the idea after analyzing some errant data from a thousand-year-old, multi-layered shield test. He realized that what had been interpreted as an incorrect position calculation was actually a micro-jump caused by a reactor overload and energy dump at the precise moment that the two fields collided. It took him ten years to figure out how to recreate that accident on purpose and in a controlled fashion."

"I had no idea," Dominic gasped. "Are you certain?"

"I *was* there for the first jump," Nathan assured him.

"That's right, I forgot."

"So the jump drive was created back in your time?" Hanna asked Nathan.

"It may have been invented, but the accident that sparked its creation occurred back in *your* time," Nathan told her.

"Incredible," Dominic gasped.

"This is getting really confusing," Hanna admitted as she scribbled notes on her data pad.

"What are you doing?" Dominic wondered.

"Making notes," Hanna replied, as if it were obvious.

"I meant, why are you using that archaic device?"

"The data pad?" Hanna asked.

Dominic removed the small pin from his lapel and handed it to her. "Try this."

"What is it?" Hanna asked, accepting the pin.

"Put it on, then tap it once to activate it."

Hanna did as instructed, mounting the pin on her lapel, then tapping it. A nearly transparent projection appeared in the air in front of her, with a list of available tasks and several icons along the top and bottom of the projection. "What is this?"

"It's the future's version of that data pad," Dominic explained.

"This is cool," Hanna said as she began touching the icons in the air and getting a feel for the interface hovering before her.

Josh looked back at the projection, then at Nathan. "Can we get some of those?"

"You're the pilot, remember?" Nathan chided.

"It's all automated, *remember?*" Josh snapped back.

* * *

"*Tell me again why we didn't use EVA suits for this?*" Hani asked over comm-sets.

"They're too bulky," Cori insisted as she struggled to connect the wires to the output bus on the Mirai's starboard drive nacelle. "There's no way we could get inside this thing with pressure gloves on."

"*Maybe, but at least we wouldn't be freezing our asses off.*"

"I'm almost done," Cori told him.

"*I am done*," Hani replied. "*Power up the port reactor.*"

Erica reached up to the overhead panel and pressed a switch, powering up the port reactor as requested. "Port reactor coming online," she reported.

"Keep an eye on it," Aiden told her. We don't want it to get above ten percent until *after* he gets clear."

"I set the limiters to ten percent per the checklist," Erica assured him.

"I know, but the shuttles use the same zero-point reactors that the XKs used, and their limiters don't always work. Sometimes you have to just keep your finger on the dial and readjust if they spike."

"Why isn't that in the ops manual?" Erica wondered.

"Not everything that *should* be in there *is* in there," Aiden explained. "That's why you have to get your feet wet. The simulators follow design specs, not real-world performance."

"It was the same way back in my time," Erica admitted.

"We call it the 'fudge factor'."

"So did we," Erica exclaimed. "It's amazing how some things are completely different now, yet others are exactly the same."

"Yeah, well, humanity hasn't changed much. It's just gotten bigger."

"That's not very reassuring," Erica stated.

"You were there for the whole *plague* thing, right?"

"Unfortunately yes."

"Nash told me you were actually *on* Earth during the outbreak."

"Sort of," Erica replied. "But I was just flying a shuttle around; I never even left the cockpit."

"Still, you must've seen some horrifying stuff, even from the cockpit."

"I try not to think about it."

"Sorry."

"I'm showing twelve percent on the port reactor," Erica reported, quickly responding and dialing it back a bit.

"*Don't worry,*" Hani reported. "*I'm all done here. You can take it to full power.*"

"Take it to full," Aiden instructed Erica.

"Bringing port reactor to full power," Erica acknowledged as she dialed the reactor up. "Port reactor shows full power."

Aiden flipped a switch, tying his comm-set into the external comms. "Aurora, Mirai. You can bring your shields up to ten percent."

"*I'm done here,*" Hani reported over comm-sets. "*How are you doing, Cori?*"

"I can't feel my fingers again, but I'm kind of getting used to it."

"*You want me to finish up for you?*"

"I thought you were freezing your ass off."

"*I exaggerated,*" Hani admitted.

"Get inside and warm up, just in case you have to go back out to make adjustments," Cori instructed. "I'll be done here in a minute."

"*Heading up the ramp now,*" Hani replied.

"Mirai reports they have connected the port reactor, and we can bring our shields up to ten percent," Ensign Dass announced from the Aurora's comm-station.

Cameron stepped up to the tactical console and activated the Aurora's shields. "Let's hope this works."

"You think there are more of those things aboard?" Sima asked.

"I expect so," Cameron admitted. "I think they're attracted to the warmth."

Sima shuddered at the thought.

"Let's just hope they stay in the water," Cameron said.

Cori stepped back from the open panel, inspecting her work. "Okay, I'm ready here," she reported over comms. "Power up the starboard reactor to ten percent."

"*Powering up the starboard reactor,*" Erica replied over comm-sets.

Cori stood there, shivering in the frigid night, struggling to remain standing in the errant winds as she examined the connections she had just made. The status lights on the external bus connection panel switched from red to green, indicating the bus was now charged and sending power across the line.

"Thank God," she said to herself.

"*Starboard reactor at ten percent,*" Erica reported over comm-sets.

"We're good here," Cori reported as she swung the cover plate closed and began turning the fasteners that held it in place. "I'll be in shortly."

"As soon as we get buttoned up, I'm going to make dinner for everyone," Hani announced.

"You can cook?" Dino asked.

"Of course."

"And by 'cook', he means heat up the stuff that Neli already prepared for us," Sori corrected.

"*Who cares as long as we eat?*" Cori said over comm-sets.

"What's taking you so long?" Dino asked.

"*I'm just locking down the cover plate.*"

"You're supposed to do that *before* powering up," Hani scolded.

"*It goes on easier if the bus is warm,*" Cori argued.

"*Says who?*"

"*Says someone who has done this before,*" Cori replied.

"So I guess we're going to be here a while?" Erica said, trying to make small talk while she monitored the reactor outputs.

"*For someone who has done this before, you sure are taking a long time,*" Hani teased over comm-sets.

"At least until the long night is over and things warm back up outside," Aiden replied.

The output indicator on the starboard reactor suddenly jumped.

"*Hey, this ship has showers, right?*" Cori asked.

"Starboard reactor output just jumped," Erica reported, noticing the change.

"*Yup,*" Hani replied.

"Dial it down a bit," Aiden told Erica. "They

usually settle down after they've been running a few minutes."

"*Hot ones?*" Cori asked.

Erica glanced back at the indicator. "It already settled back down."

"Just keep an eye on it then," Aiden suggested.

"*Three guesses where I'm going after th...*" Cori stopped mid-sentence.

The indicator jumped again, only this time it maxed out for a second before dropping back down to ten percent.

"*I was thinking the same thing,*" Hani said over comm-sets.

"Oh shit," Erica exclaimed.

"What?" Aiden asked.

"It just spiked to full power and then dropped back to ten percent."

"That shouldn't happen."

"Maybe it was damaged," Erica suggested. "A lot has happened the last few days."

"Cori, everything all right out there?" Aiden asked over comm-sets. "Cori?"

"*Hey, Cori, the captain's calling you,*" Hani said.

"Somebody go check on her," Aiden instructed. "The starboard reactor just spiked to full power for a moment."

"Oh shit!" Hani exclaimed, jumping to his feet. "She was still putting the cover on!" he added as he donned his face mask and headed for the cargo ramp. He was down the ramp before Dino and Sori could even get their jackets back on.

Hani jumped off the starboard side of the ramp,

already feeling the drastic drop in temperature just by leaving the cargo bay. It took him only ten steps to reach the starboard edge of the shuttle, but Cori wasn't there. "She's gone!"

"What the hell do you mean, gone?" Aiden snapped as he activated the ship's external cameras and lighting. "Eyeballs out the window," he told Erica. "She was on your side, and we're on a downhill slope. She might have rolled forward."

Erica immediately rose from her seat, straining to get a better viewing angle out the starboard and forward windows, just as the forward lights flickered to life. "There!" she reported, pointing out the forward window. "She's all the way down onto the flight deck! She's not moving!"

Hani made it around the starboard side of the shuttle and started forward but had to stop when the slope became too steep for him to safely navigate. "We need ropes!"

"*No!*" Aiden barked over comm-sets. "*It's too steep! You'll just end up injured as well!*"

Dino and Sori came running up next to Hani, peering over the edge with him. They could barely make out Cori's motionless form on the flight deck below.

"We gotta do something!" Dino insisted.

"*Get your asses back inside!*" Aiden barked. "*That's an order!*"

"Captain!" Sima exclaimed. "Captain Walsh is reporting an emergency. Cori has fallen. She's lying on the aft end of the flight deck, and she's not moving."

Cameron quickly tapped a button on the intercom panel on the tactical console before her. "Medical emergency, crewman down…hard!"

"*Master Sergeant Baris here, sir. Where's the patient located?*"

"On the flight deck, aft end," Cameron replied. "She fell from the top of the dorsal aft rise. She's not moving. Suggest you access from the aft cargo hatch to the flight deck, and you'll need cold-weather gear."

"*Understood.*"

"Captain, the Mirai is asking how long," Ensign Dass reported.

"Baris, what's your ETA?" Cameron asked.

"*At least ten minutes,*" the master sergeant replied. "*It's a long way to the aft end, and the transit system is offline because of power.*"

"*Bridge, Bravo Lead,*" Chief Anson called. "Teece and I are just aft of power gen. We can be there in five if we double-time it."

"You'll need cold-weather gear," Cameron warned.

"*We can handle it,*" the chief assured her.

"Then go!" Cameron agreed. "Baris, XO. Two Ghatazhak can be there in five."

"*Anson, Baris,*" the master sergeant called directly to the Ghatazhak. "*Drag the patient inside. I'll meet you in the aft cargo airlock.*"

"*Copy that,*" Chief Anson answered.

Cameron turned to her comms officer. "Tell the Mirai help is on the way, ETA five minutes."

CHAPTER SEVEN

"*Andrea Reynen, Pyru Approach. State your destination,*" the voice called over comms.

"The Tollis spaceport," Dominic suggested.

"Why not direct to the hospital?" Nathan wondered.

"The hospital will not have a landing pad large enough for this ship, and Tollis is the closest class E spaceport."

Nathan tapped his comm-set. "Pyru Approach, Andrea Reynen. Our destination is the Tollis spaceport."

"*Understood. Stand by to receive planet-fall procedures.*"

"Why Tollis?" Nathan asked, turning back toward Dominic.

"Class E spaceports have no control tower, which means they don't have AAA inspectors on site."

Nathan flashed him a quizzical look.

"Alliance Aerospace Authority," Dominic explained. "The last thing you want is for them to inspect your ship and discover your non-compliant jump drive."

"What would they do if they did?"

"At best, cite you and charge you a fine, along with a stern warning. At worst, impound your ship. In a place like Tollis, the most you'll get is a few curious looks from admirers of ancient spaceships."

"Tollis it is," Nathan decided.

"How do we get Vlad to the hospital?" Jessica asked.

"We hire a private medical transfer shuttle," Dominic replied. "It shouldn't be a problem."

"I hope your chief engineer is worth all the debt you're taking on," Chiqua said, failing to hide the satisfied smirk on her face.

"He is," Nathan assured her.

* * *

The aft section of the Aurora was so cold that it wasn't safe for anyone to spend much time there, even in cold-weather gear. But the Ghatazhak were not just anyone.

Chief Anson and Corporal Teece knew that it would be even colder outside, but when the outer airlock door opened, the blast of freezing air was worse than expected. But the Ghatazhak were trained to block out the effects of numbing cold. Cori, however, would not survive long in this environment, even with the cold-weather gear she was wearing.

The chief was the first one out the door, moving carefully across the frozen flight deck. Corporal Teece was right behind him. In half a minute, they reached Cori. The chief rolled her over onto her back. "She's not breathing," he told the corporal as he reached them. "We've got to get her inside."

"What about her injuries?" the corporal reminded the chief. "That had to be a nasty fall," he added, looking up the steep slope at the Mirai parked precariously above.

"No time," the Chief said, scooping up her limp body with both arms. "Jesus, this kid isn't forty kilograms soaking wet," he exclaimed as he started back for the large cargo airlock they had just come from.

A minute later, they were back inside the cargo airlock, the massive doors closing behind them as the chief set Cori carefully down on the floor. Corporal Teece opened a panel in the side wall, pulling out the resuscitation kit.

Chief Anson pulled a pneumo-ject from the small trauma kit that all Ghatazhak carried in their thigh utility pockets and jabbed it into the side of Cori's neck.

"That's formulated for trauma, not hypothermia," Teece reminded him.

"At this point, we don't know which one caused her to stop breathing," the chief said as he accepted the auto-intubater from the corporal and inserted it into her mouth. Corporal Teece handed him the oxygen tube from the portable oxygenator in the resuscitation kit as the chief activated the auto-intubater, creating a sealed airway through which the resuscitator could breathe for her. Within seconds, the unit began to hiss, and Cori's chest began to rise and fall with each forced inhalation.

As the chief opened the young engineer's jacket and exposed her chest, Corporal Teece pulled out the cardiac pad, removed the backing, and stuck it directly over her heart.

"Nothing," the corporal reported, studying the cardiac display. "I'm setting it to pace," he announced as he made the adjustments. "Sensing...capture... pacing."

Chief Anson felt for a pulse on Cori's neck. "Faint but there," he reported as he tapped his comm-set. "Baris, what's your ETA?"

"Three minutes," Baris answered. *"You get her inside?"*

"Yeah. No pulse, no breathing. Cold as hell. We've got her on the resuscitator and paced, and she's got a load of my trauma nanites in her, just in case."

"*What kind of injuries?*"

"Don't know yet. I don't think we should remove her cold gear until we get her to a warmer part of the ship."

"*Copy that.*"

"Jesus, what the hell was she doing out there?" Corporal Teece wondered. "It should have been one of us."

"From what I hear, she insisted."

* * *

The Tollis spaceport was littered with an odd assortment of private shuttles and small cargo ships. There wasn't enough traffic to warrant a control tower, but just enough that no one paid much attention to ships arriving or departing.

No one had seemed interested in the Seiiki's arrival either, nor at the arrival of a medical shuttle an hour later that had taxied up and parked next to them.

Nathan stood at the bottom of the ramp as the ambulance techs floated the gurney carrying Vlad's medical stasis unit down the ramp and over to their shuttle, with Doctor Chen following closely behind.

"What's the plan?" Jessica asked as she, Chiqua, and Dominic descended.

"Only family can ride in the med-shuttle," Nathan replied. "So, to maintain our cover, that means her," he added, pointing to Chiqua.

"You're fucking kidding."

"You, me, and Kit will meet up with them at the hospital," Nathan added.

"How?" Jessica asked.

Chiqua pointed at two aircars approaching in the distance. "I secured a couple of courtesy cars."

"Dominic and Mori will take one to purchase some fusion reactors, and you and I will take the other to the hospital and meet up with Chiqua and Doctor Chen," Nathan explained.

"How are we paying for these reactors?" Dominic asked, already knowing the answer.

Chiqua pulled out a credit chip and handed it to him. "That should cover the cost of the reactors, including transportation back here."

"How many are we buying?" Dominic asked as he accepted the chip.

"As many as you can get with that," Nathan replied.

"I'll shop around."

"Don't," Nathan objected. "Just go to the best place, and get it done as quickly as possible. I'm not crazy about being this deep into Alliance space, considering all that I've heard so far. The sooner we can get Vlad cured and back to the fringe, the better I'll feel."

"Can I at least haggle a bit?" Dominic asked, half joking.

"A bit."

The two aircars arrived, their gull-wing doors opening to reveal empty vehicles.

"We're ready, ma'am," one of the med-shuttle attendants told Chiqua.

"I'll see you there," Chiqua said as she turned to follow the attendant.

"How much is all of this costing us?" Jessica asked. She wasn't really looking for a number, just reminding Nathan of the risk he was taking.

"What makes you think I plan on repaying her?" Nathan asked.

"Because I know you," Jessica replied, heading for one of the aircars.

* * *

Cameron stood by Cori's bed in the very same trauma bay that Vladimir had occupied a day ago. The young woman's face reminded her so much of herself at that age. Driven and unwilling to accept her own limitations. Cameron had made that mistake many times herself in the past. It had been one of the hardest lessons she had ever needed to learn. But the fact was that everyone had their limitations. The trick was accepting them.

"She's a tough one," Master Sergeant Baris commented as he entered.

"Will she recover?"

"Surprisingly, her injuries aren't that bad. I suspect that her cold-weather gear protected her a bit."

"But she *died*."

"But it was the shock that stopped her heart, not the fall," the master sergeant explained. "Luckily, she was already borderline hypothermic when it happened. Probably bought her a few minutes. If they hadn't gotten her back inside and on the resuscitator so quickly, she would've stayed dead. My only concern at this point is what their nanites will do to her."

"They'll heal her, won't they?"

"Sure, but they weren't formulated for her. The Ghatazhak have developed rather unique metabolisms over time, and their nanites are tweaked for them. I'm not sure what effect they might have on her metabolism. Speed it up, screw with her hormones, I really don't know. I'm just a med-tech, after all. I suspect Doc Chen will have a better idea what to expect."

"Should they not have given them to her?" Cameron wondered.

"She had a tear in her pericardium from a rib fracture. Probably happened when she landed. I'm pretty sure the nanites went straight there. If they hadn't, resuscitation might have failed."

"How the hell do they know where to go?"

"They don't," the master sergeant replied. "But he injected them into her jugular vein, so they reached her heart and lungs pretty quickly. As soon as one of them detected a problem, it communicated to the others, calling for assistance, and as many of those buggers needed to resolve the problem converged on the site and got to work. It's pretty miraculous stuff, really, and the Ghatazhak nanites are *specifically* designed to rapidly deal with trauma."

"You're right, they are miraculous."

"Any idea when the doc will be back?"

"I'm afraid not," Cameron admitted.

"Well, as long as those nanites don't twist her up too much, I should be able to take care of her."

Cameron looked at Cori again. "When will she wake?"

"She's awake now," Master Sergeant Baris assured her. "She's just keeping her eyes closed because she's afraid she's going to get a butt-chewing."

"Not true," Cori said hoarsely, slowly opening her eyes. "I've got a headache, and the light hurts my eyes."

"Probably from the Ghatazhak nanites," the master sergeant commented as he headed out.

"If you weren't injured, you would be getting that butt-chewing," Cameron assured her.

"Sorry, sir."

"You're not on an XK any longer, Chief. You're not supposed to do everything yourself. You're supposed to delegate."

"I'm not a chief, sir," Cori corrected. "I'm only a sergeant."

"You can't run my engineering department as a sergeant," Cameron told her. "So now you're a chief."

"What about Chief Dixon? Surely he knows the Aurora better than I do? He's been on board longer."

"By a few hours," Cameron told her. "Before that, he was working in propulsion assembly. So use him for propulsion issues."

"But..."

"He's never been responsible for an entire ship, either. You have."

"Not one this big."

"Size doesn't matter," Cameron told her. "They all work the same way. You just run it like you did the Lawrence, except let your junior engineers do the dirty work. We can't afford to lose another senior engineer."

"Yes, sir." Cori thought for a moment, letting it sink in. "What about when Commander Kamenetskiy gets well?"

"We'll figure that out when the time comes, Chief. I have a feeling things are going to be pretty fluid around here for the foreseeable future."

"Yes, sir."

"Get some rest, Chief." Cameron patted her on the shoulder then headed for the exit. The young woman didn't have the experience and knowledge that Vladimir had, but she certainly had his passion for engineering, and that was half the battle.

* * *

"This place is huge," Nathan commented to Chiqua as they approached her in the lobby of the critical care department.

"It's the only hospital in the sector," Chiqua explained, "so it has to be."

"Other worlds don't have hospitals?" Jessica wondered in disbelief.

"Most worlds in the outer sectors don't have large enough populations to justify them," Chiqua explained. "So the Alliance builds clinics on them and then builds a hospital large enough to serve all the worlds nearby that are connected by gates."

"What if you get injured on one of those worlds?" Nathan asked.

"The local clinic stabilizes and calls for transport, which usually comes an hour or two later."

"How is it you know so much about how things work in Alliance space?" Jessica asked.

"I didn't always live on Hadria," Chiqua explained.

"How'd you end up there?" Nathan wondered.

"Followed my husband out there. When he died, I took over his business. Simple as that."

"They say anything about him when you checked in?"

"No, but they looked worried as hell," Chiqua admitted.

"Doctor Chen went in with him?"

"Yes, but only because she refused to be kept out. They couldn't find her in the registry. She got angry and rattled off some medical stuff that I think even *they* didn't understand."

Nathan smiled. "Doc's seen a lot, that's for sure."

"So what do we do now?" Jessica wondered.

"You know damn well what we do," Nathan told her. "We sit and wait."

"Not a good idea," Jessica objected. "It's not safe."

"It's a hospital, Jess."

"One that probably has vid-cams and facial recognition."

"You think they keep facial recognition data for people who've been dead for five centuries?" Nathan laughed. "You know how much data that would be?"

"We're five hundred years in the future, Nathan. I'm pretty sure technology has advanced enough to store the identities of a few hundred trillion people."

"She's right about that," Chiqua agreed.

"But *why* do so?" Nathan challenged. "Basic records I could see but facial recognition data?"

"He's right too."

"I still think we should go," Jessica insisted. "We should just pick up some comm-units somewhere and have Chiqua call us when she learns something."

"What if they need to make a medical decision?"

"His *doctor* is with him," Jessica reminded him, "and so is his *wife*. And let's not forget how famous you were five hundred years ago."

"That's two," Chiqua said. "She wins."

* * *

"Are you sure this is the right place?" Mori asked as the aircar touched down. "It looks like a junkyard."

"That's because it is," Dominic replied.

"Okay."

"*Shall I wait?*" the female voice of the aircar's AI pilot inquired.

"Yes please," Dominic instructed.

"*As you wish.*"

The doors opened, and the two men climbed out and headed into what looked like the main building.

"I sure hope you're right about this place," Mori commented as they entered.

"There's an old saying," Dominic said. "The fringe runs on what the Alliance throws away."

"Well, if this place is any indication, then the fringe has an endless supply of crap."

"The trick is in knowing what is crap and what are hidden gems."

"I suppose you're a gem expert?"

"No, but I do know crap when I see it."

"May I help you sir?" a clerk asked.

"Yes, we are looking for fusion reactors, preferably something in the E two hundred series or the Quantor eighteen seventies, and serviceable."

"The Quantors are hard to come by, especially in the eighteen series. They get snapped up as soon as we finish refurbishing them. We've only got a few of the E two hundreds, but they're in rough shape. Probably only good for parts. We do have a few of the three hundred series in good working order, if you don't mind paying a bit more."

"I'm afraid the three hundreds are too large for our ship to haul."

"They're pretty compact. How many do you need?"

"Four," Dominic replied, adding, "without a sales record."

"I assume you will be paying with a credit chip then?"

Dominic placed the credit chip on the counter in

front of the clerk, causing the value indicator to glow just enough for him to read it. "Which three hundred series are we talking about?"

"We have three LX three twenty-fours, and a few of the D three sixties."

"The LX are crap," Dominic stated. "But I think we could make do with three of the three sixties if they're in decent enough shape *and* the price is right."

"They're ten five each," the clerk replied. "Delivered."

"At that price, they'd better be. Eight five, and you've got a deal."

"I can get ten five for them easy."

"Maybe, but not to someone who will be coming back for all sorts of items in the near future."

The clerk studied Dominic and Mori, trying to size them up. "Big project?"

"A crashed Bor two seventy."

"How bad?"

"Bad enough."

The clerk sighed, then said, "Nine even?"

"Eight-five, and we'll keep the balance left over from that chip on your books toward future purchases."

The clerk smiled. "*That* I can do. Right this way, gentlemen."

* * *

As usual, the young population monitoring officer started his shift with a review of what the department referred to as 'ghosts'. Most of these were simply the result of human error. Someone at the local level forgot to check a box that would normally trigger an identity to be stricken from the Alliance's facial recognition database.

The Ghost Resolution Team's sole mission was to reconcile these errors, verify that the identities in question were indeed deceased, and correct them in the database. With a population numbering in the hundreds of trillions, without the GRT, the database would quickly grow unmanageable, rendering their primary method of population monitoring ineffective.

"Good morning, sir," the young officer greeted as he entered his commanding officer's office.

"Good morning, Lieutenant."

"I thought you might want to look at this ghost," the lieutenant said, causing a holographic page to appear in the air between them with a motion of his hand. "Notice the date of death."

The senior officer looked at the record in the air before him, finding the date in question. "That's over five hundred years ago."

"Five hundred and thirty-five, actually. The system was unable to verify this person's death, because there was never any body. He was the chief engineer on a ship that was reported missing and was officially listed as lost."

"What ship?"

"The Aurora, sir."

"The *Aurora*. That ship was destroyed by a singularity. Probably just another doppelganger. Where was this hit located?"

"On Pyru, sir. A patient was brought to the medical center there from the fringe."

"That explains it," the senior officer decided. "The system couldn't find a record for him so it chose the closest match. In this case, a ghost record."

"Shall I return an unidentified to the sender and

strike the ID file from the database?" the lieutenant asked.

"Negative. Procedure for matches to missing Alliance personnel is to kick it upstairs to investigations."

"But surely it's a ghost."

"Of course it is," the senior officer agreed. "But it's not our call to make."

"I'll forward it to investigations immediately," the lieutenant assured his commander before he left.

The senior officer turned to his view screen, calling up the communications screen. After entering a code, he created a secure message, then grabbed the image still hovering in the air before him and moved it into the message itself before sending it.

* * *

"I'm afraid there is not much else they can do," Doctor Chen said over the Seiiki's comms. *"They were able to fully arrest progression and neutralize the remaining venom in his bloodstream, but the damage to the medulla is too severe. At this point, all of his bodily functions are being controlled by automation."*

"What about his mind?" Nathan asked. "His memories, his personality..."

"The damage to those areas of his brain appear minor, but it's difficult to tell how much of his memory and personality are still intact."

"Then we might still be able to clone him," Nathan suggested.

"I inquired about that," Doctor Chen replied. *"I am told that cloning was outlawed throughout the Alliance nearly a century ago. Apparently, the penalties are quite severe."*

"What about *outside* Alliance space?" Nathan wondered.

"*I didn't ask. They seemed quite put off that I even mentioned it.*"

"Damn it," Nathan cursed.

"*What are your orders, sir?*" the doctor asked.

"Stay with him, Doc," Nathan replied. "We'll arrange transport of you and Vlad back to the Seiiki."

"*Not much for me to do really.*"

"We'll get there as quick as we can," Nathan promised.

"*Understood.*"

Nathan closed the comm-channel. "You've been cloned, right?" he asked Dominic.

"Several times," Dominic confirmed. "The last two times by some crazy, old doctor who was forced to leave Alliance space *because* of the anti-cloning referendum."

"Is he still practicing?"

"Considering that he's cloned himself about a dozen times, I expect so."

"Where's he located?"

"I don't know. His practice *used* to be on Pyru, but he moved to the badlands a few years ago, right after my last cloning. Something about trying to get as far from Alliance reach as possible."

"The Alliance reaches into the fringe?" Jessica wondered.

"In cases like his, yes. He performs augments as well, which the Alliance frowns upon even more than just straight-up cloning. They'll go into the fringe to apprehend wanted fugitives, but they rarely venture out into the badlands."

Nathan sighed, feeling as if things were rapidly souring. "Is there anyone else we could use?"

"With the Alliance crackdown on cloning clinics in the fringe, that's going to be difficult. You'd stand a better chance of finding my guy out in the badlands to be honest."

"Do you remember the name of the guy you used?" Jessica asked. "Maybe we can track him down."

"That's easy. Symyri."

Nathan's jaw practically hit the floor. "*Nikolori Symyri?*

"I don't know, maybe. We weren't exactly on a first-name basis," Dominic said.

"No way," Jessica said in disbelief.

"He did say the guy had cloned *himself* a dozen times."

Dominic looked at them both. "You guys *know* Doctor Symyri?"

Nathan looked at Jessica. "We may have just caught a lucky break."

* * *

The elaborate palace gardens had endured for nearly a millennium. Through times of both peace and war, and through multiple rulers, the gardens had survived. Because of this, Jakome felt compelled to appreciate them daily, sometimes taking long walks among the meticulously manicured beds, alone with his thoughts. Without them, he doubted he could handle the pressures of his position as well.

Leadership carried great responsibility. Since birth, he had been groomed for this position, both physically and mentally. Even his genetics had been skewed to make him better able to lead the greatest of all human societies.

As usual, his solitude was interrupted by the duties

of his position. The footfalls of an aide, undoubtedly approaching with news of some pressing matter that only he could deal with.

"Apologizes, my lord," the aid said as he came to a stop a few meters from his leader.

Jakome often found it difficult to handle the level of deference offered him by every person he met. Men such as this aide, a man twice Jakome's age and with decades of experience and service to his people, bowing respectfully to a much younger man with less than a decade in his role. Jakome had to remind himself that, despite his young age, he carried the wisdom and instincts of all those who ruled before him, ever since genetic memory had been integrated into his family's genetic line.

"This message just arrived," the aide continued. "Its content appears to fall under royal edict one four seven."

That caught Jakome's attention. "One four seven. Are you certain?"

"I did not read the message, my lord, I was only told by the senior communications officer to deliver this message to you personally and to convey the urgent nature of its contents."

Very carefully stated, Jakome thought as he activated the message holo handed to him. "Ready my ship and alert my personal guards that I will be traveling."

"Yes, my lord. How soon would you like to depart?"

"Immediately," Jakome replied smartly, heading quickly for the main building.

"Shall I inform your pilot of your destination, my lord?" the aide asked, dutifully following his leader.

"Pyru," Jakome replied. "Tell him we are going to Pyru."

* * *

"We're here to pick up Vladimir Kimbro," Nathan told the receptionist at the critical care desk.

"By yourselves?" the receptionist asked, seeing only the two of them.

"Our medical transport should be arriving shortly," Nathan assured her. "We're just here to get the ball rolling to avoid any delays."

"Of course. I'll check with Mister Kimbro's care coordinator in case there are any instructions."

"Would you let Doctor Chen and Missus Kimbro know that we're here?" Nathan added.

The receptionist looked confused. "Doctor *Chen?*"

"The doctor who was attending Mister Kimbro when we brought him in," Nathan explained.

"I'll check with the care coordinator," the receptionist promised again, rising from her chair and heading to the door at the back of the reception desk area.

Nathan looked at Jessica. "Does she seem a bit off to you?"

"*Nervous* would be the word I'd use."

"Must be because of how tough I look when I don't shave," Nathan joked, stroking the two-day growth on his chin.

"That must be it, baby face." Jessica noticed two hospital security officers taking positions at the exit to the critical care lobby. Both were armed with stunners, which wasn't unusual, but what was odd, at least by Jessica's observations from their previous visit, was to see a pair of guards working together. "Our exit strategy just changed," she commented under her breath.

"What?"

Jessica nodded discretely toward the guards at the exit.

Nathan glanced that way. "That's not good."

The doors from the critical care ward opened, and an unusually fit man in hospital scrubs came out, heading directly toward them. "Captain Tuplo?" the man called.

The use of Nathan's pseudonym was the first thing that Jessica noticed. Neither of them had given their names to anyone at the hospital.

Nathan noticed it as well, but it was too late. He had already turned to look at the man calling him. "Yes?"

"Doctor Chen sent me to escort you back. She is closely monitoring Mister Kimbro and didn't want to risk leaving his side."

"That's okay," Nathan replied. "We don't need to speak with her. If you could just let her know that transportation will be arriving shortly, I'm sure she'll know what to do."

"No reason you can't tell her yourself," the man insisted, gesturing toward the door.

"We really need to get back to our ship and get her ready for departure, but thank you," Nathan said as he turned to leave.

"Please, sir," the man said, grabbing Nathan's forearm and arresting his departure. "Doctor's orders."

At that moment, the two guards at the door took their first steps toward them.

Jessica immediately noticed the movement of the guards and jumped into action. She grabbed the man's arm, breaking his grip on Nathan's forearm and twisting it over and away from the man's body as she struck him in the nose with her fist, then swept one of his feet out from under him, sending him to the floor.

Nathan spun around just as the two guards drew their stunners and took aim. "Stunners!"

Jessica drove her foot into the downed man's face, breaking his nose and sending blood splattering in all directions. She then ran toward the guards as they took aim, stepping up onto one of the lobby chairs and using it as a launching pad. She landed on the shoulders of the guard on the right, using her momentum to twist him around and bring him down.

Nathan tucked and rolled toward the guard on the left as he fired, the stunner's energy passing over him. As Nathan returned to his feet and prepared to attack, there was another stunner blast, and the guard he was about take on dropped to the floor, unmoving. Nathan glanced to his right, in the direction the shot had come from, and saw Jessica pulling the stunner from the man she had just taken down. She jumped to her feet, not waiting for the man to regain his senses, and fired, immobilizing him.

"I have a feeling our faces are still in that database," Nathan said as he picked up the stunner dropped by the first guard.

"Ya think?" Jessica replied, turning and firing at the receptionist who had just pressed the general alarm button.

Nathan glanced in the receptionist's direction as the woman fell to the floor. "Was that really necessary?"

"Yes," Jessica replied, not offering an explanation as she headed for the critical care ward entrance.

"Where are you going?" Nathan asked, falling in step behind her.

"To get Vlad and Doc Chen."

"Jess!"

Jessica kicked the doors open, breaking the meager latch meant to discourage unauthorized entry. Everyone in the room turned, looking at her in shock. To their surprise, Jessica opened fire, stunning everyone in sight.

"Jesus, Jess!" Nathan exclaimed. "These people aren't a threat!"

"This was a fucking setup!" Jessica insisted as she headed for the nearest treatment room.

"We don't even know what room he's in!"

"There's only one way to find out," Jessica insisted as she opened the first door, finding only an unknown patient and someone who was probably the patient's family member, cowering in the corner. Jessica stunned her as well.

"Jess! Stop stunning everyone!" Nathan barked as he pulled out the local comm-unit they had purchased earlier in the day. "Josh! We're going to need some help here!"

"Something's wrong," Kit said as he spotted several black airvans skimming across the tarmac toward them.

"LE?" Mori said.

"Josh, get to the cockpit and spin up for launch."

"I don't have a clearance yet," Josh warned.

"*Josh! We're going to need some help here!*" Nathan called over comms as the sound of stunner fire echoed behind him.

"I have a feeling a clearance is the least of our worries," Kit remarked as he grabbed his weapon. "Ghatazhak! Defensive positions!"

"Uh, we've got a problem here, Cap'n," Josh called over comms as he turned and ran toward the cockpit.

Four armed men spilled out of one of the critical care rooms, but they weren't hospital security. Jessica immediately began firing, but their personal shields protected them.

"Shit," Jessica cursed, diving behind the counter as the men opened fire. The angle of fire changed rapidly, indicating at least two of them were circling to her right. Staying low and using the counter as cover from incoming fire, Jessica grabbed a treatment cart and swung it around the corner, hurtling it toward the two men.

The cart slammed into the two men but only slowed them.

"Side exit!" Jessica yelled to Nathan as she made a dash for the side corridor. Incoming fire splashed against the wall beside her as she shifted from side to side while she ran, in an attempt to make it more difficult to be targeted.

Once she reached the corner, she turned and fired back, dialing her stunner to full power in the hopes that the attackers' personal shields had limited amounts of energy and could not protect against a sustained attack.

Nathan ran for the corridor, slipping past Jessica and heading for the exit. She spun around to follow, firing behind her as they ran down the corridor.

Nathan burst through the door only to find himself face to face with two more armed men. They too were caught by surprise, a fact that Nathan wasted no time taking advantage of. He grabbed an oxygen bottle from an empty gurney, swinging it like a hammer and striking the first man in the side, knocking him into the second. Not waiting for either of them to regain their footing, Nathan jammed the bottle into the gut of the second man, causing him to double over.

Jessica burst through the door and vaulted over Nathan's bent-over body like a gymnast on a pommel horse, jutting her feet forward into the face of the first man, knocking him backward. "Grab their shield generators!" she instructed Nathan as she landed, turned around, and fired back down the corridor which was now full of armed men charging toward them.

Nathan scrambled on his hands and knees, finding the wrist-mounted personal shield generator attached to the first man's wrist. He quickly grabbed it, but the man grabbed Nathan's wrist, trying to stop him. Nathan instinctively twisted the device's face, shutting the shield off, then pointed his own stunner at the man and fired. He reactivated the device, slapping it onto his own wrist just in time to deflect stunner blasts walking across his back in search of a target.

"What the fuck is taking you so long!" Jessica demanded as she fired around the corner at the men slowly advancing with the protection of their shields.

Luckily, the other adversary was unconscious and offered no resistance when Nathan removed the man's wrist-mounted personal shield generator. He then scrambled back to his feet, spun around and opened fire down the corridor, adding his fire to Jessica's. "Here!" he yelled, tossing the device to her.

Jessica caught and activated the shield, stepping out into the open to join Nathan in bombarding the approaching guards. "Pinpoint on the far-right target!" She instructed.

Nathan did as he was told, and they concentrated their fire on the man on the right. In seconds, the man's shield failed and he dropped to the ground, immobilized like the others.

"I fucking knew it!" Jessica exclaimed as four more men suddenly appeared at the far end of the main corridor. "We gotta move!" she said, grabbing Nathan and whipping him around in the direction she wanted him to run.

"Where are we going?" Nathan said, stumbling into a dead run, away from the attackers.

"Our only chance is the roof!" Jessica yelled as she ran after him.

"What's happening?" Dominic wondered as Josh practically exploded up from the ladder well and into the Seiiki's crew cabin.

"Things just went to shit!" Josh replied as he disappeared through the cockpit door.

Josh leapt into the pilot's seat, flipping switches like a madman as he started up the ship.

"We're taking fire back here!" Kit warned. *"Get us in the fucking air!"*

"I'm working on it!" Josh replied.

"Josh! Pick us up on the roof!" Nathan instructed over comms.

"Got it!"

"*How long?*" Nathan asked urgently.

"I'll get there as quick as I can!" Josh replied. "We're under attack here!"

"*What? By who?*"

"Beats the shit outta me!"

"*Get that ship in the air!*" Nathan urged.

"What the hell do you think I'm doing?" Josh snapped back. "Everyone in back there?" he called as he grabbed the flight controls.

"Who's shooting at us?" Dominic asked as he entered the cockpit.

"*We're in!*" Kit replied.

"Hang on!" Josh yanked the grav-lift throttle, jerking it up sharply, causing the ship to moan loudly as it lurched upward.

Dominic stumbled, falling into the side console as the Seiiki veered to the right and spiraled upward.

Josh grabbed the gear lever and pushed it up into the retract position, then reached for the main throttles, jamming them forward. The ship lurched forward, quickly accelerating. That's when Josh noticed the two tiny, black dots on the horizon, both of them with flashing blue and red lights. "Uh-oh."

"*Seiiki, Seiiki, this is Pyru security! Set down immediately, or we will open fire!*"

"Everyone hang on!" Josh warned, yanking the flight control stick hard over and twisting it to the left.

Dominic grabbed the side of the console to keep from falling over as the Seiiki maneuvered wildly. "Jesus, doesn't this thing have inertial dampeners?"

"Reactor's not at full power yet!" Josh replied.

A warning light began flashing, accompanied by an audible alarm.

"What's that?" Dominic asked.

"Threat warning!" Josh replied. "They're locking missiles on us!"

"Those patrol skimmers have smart missiles!" Dominic warned. "They'll..."

The alarm tone changed, becoming more rapid, as did the flashing light.

"Hang on!" Josh warned again, reversing his turn and pitching up.

"Whoa!" Jessica barked, coming to an abrupt stop when she spotted the armed troops on the next landing in the stairwell. She pushed Nathan toward the exit as stunner blasts rained down from above, striking the top of her personal shield. She returned fire, then followed Nathan out the exit.

Nathan burst out of the exit into the corridor just outside of the cafeteria. His sudden arrival, as well as the stunner in his hand and his glowing personal shield, caused an immediate panic, sending cafeteria patrons scattering in all directions. All of them except for one.

Chiqua stood in the corridor in front of Nathan, a drink and a sandwich in her hand, and a surprised look on her face. "What the..."

Jessica burst through the door a split second later, also spotting Chiqua. "Of course," she said, quickly scanning the area. "We're cut off. We're not getting to the roof."

"Josh, you airborne?" Nathan called over his comm-set.

"*Little busy right now, Cap'n!*"

"If we can't use the roof, where are we going to be picked up?" Nathan asked.

"We're not getting out of this building," Jessica said. "They'll have all the exits covered, including the roof."

"What about the dining patio?" Chiqua suggested, pointing back over her shoulder toward the cafeteria.

Kit and the others held on tight to avoid falling out of the open cargo bay door as the Seiiki pitched up hard and went to a full power climb.

"Those are heat-seekers," Dominic warned as he struggled to get into the starboard auxiliary seat and strap himself in.

"Good to know," Josh replied. He glanced at the threat display, noting that the two inbound missiles were closing on them. He reached over and armed the ship's defenses.

"What are you doing?" Dominic asked, his eyes going wide. "You can't fight them!"

"I don't plan to," Josh replied.

"You need to jump!"

"Don't have the power yet." Josh grabbed the throttles and pulled them back to zero.

Dominic's eyes grew even wider. "What are you doing?"

"Watch and be amazed," Josh replied, a wry smile on his face.

As the Seiiki's climb slowed, her defensive turrets deployed. With its mains at idle and her grav-lift systems at minimum, the shuttle quickly stalled, its nose pitching back down toward the planet below.

"Oh shit!" Kit exclaimed as he and the other Ghatazhak became weightless. "Hang on!"

Josh reached up and flipped two switches. The look of shock on Dominic's face changed to a mix of disbelief and horror. "Did you just kill the acceleration chambers? Are you trying to kill us?"

Josh glanced at the threat board again. Now that the Seiiki was in an unpowered dive, the missiles were closing ten times as fast as they had been seconds ago. He jammed the main throttles all the way forward.

Dominic's expression changed to complete confusion. Their pilot was throttling up engines that weren't even lit.

Large amounts of propellant poured out of the main thrust ports on both the port and starboard engines. As their dive had just begun, the propellant gasses seemed to ball up in the freezing temps of Pyru's upper atmosphere, creating a pair of flammable clouds directly behind them.

"You have to shoot them down!" Dominic insisted, realizing that they only had seconds to impact.

The threat warning indicator changed color again,

indicating that the incoming missiles had lost their track on the Seiiki.

Josh smiled, sliding his throttles back to zero as the missiles streaked past his port window only a few meters away.

The port aft topside defense turret fired, but not at the passing missiles. Instead, it ignited the two clouds of propellant now a few hundred meters above. Sensing two heat sources that were spaced the same as the engines they had been tracking, the missiles adjusted their course toward the rapidly burning clouds, detonating within them.

The threat indicator light suddenly went dark, and Josh reached up and relit his main drives, pulling out of the dive and increasing both the mains and their grav-lift systems. "I guess those missiles weren't so smart after all."

Dominic just sat there trying to catch his breath, speechless.

Kit and the others pulled themselves up off the floor, having been put there by the force of the ship's pulling level so sharply. Kit tapped his comm-set. "Any chance you can get the inertial dampeners online, Josh?"

Josh rolled the now-level ship into a left turn, coming to a heading that would take them to the hospital. A quick glance at the reactor display showed him that both reactors were finally at full power. "Inertial dampeners coming up now," he told Kit.

"*Josh! You'll have to pick us up on the dining patio, fourth floor, west side,*" Nathan called over comms. "*You'll have to sweep the roof first, or we'll get slaughtered.*"

"Be there in thirty seconds," Josh replied. "Hot LZ pickup, guys!" he called over his comm-set to the Ghatazhak in the cargo bay.

Nathan and Chiqua burst out onto the dining patio, sending diners running for the exits. "Go! Get out of here!" Nathan barked at them as they passed.

Jessica pushed Chiqua through the fleeing diners out onto the patio. "Where's our fucking ride?"

"Where are you, Josh?" Nathan asked over his comm-unit as heavy stunner fire began to rain down from overhead.

A blue-white flash of light momentarily filled the late afternoon sky, accompanied by a thunderous screech. It was followed seconds later by the sound of energy weapons fire, and not the type that stuns.

Suddenly, the rain of stunner fire ceased, and the Seiiki slid into view overhead, practically falling toward them with her cargo ramp extended.

Dominic had finally begun to pull himself together after their brush with death. He now had his eyes fixed on the external aft camera feed on the center console view screen. His anxiety quickly returned. It looked like their wing tip nacelles might scrape the sides of the buildings on either side. "This is insane."

"Yeah, ain't it great?" Josh giggled.

The Seiiki's grav-lift systems whined loudly as they went to full power momentarily to arrest the shuttle's rapid descent. The ship settled in, coming to a hover with the end of its cargo ramp less than a meter from the edge of the dining patio.

Troops came rushing into the cafeteria, their stunners blazing.

Kit and Mori took up positions on either side of the Seiiki's cargo ramp, pouring energy weapons fire through the windows and into the cafeteria, hoping to deter the advance of the troops with their deadlier weapons.

Nathan and Chiqua ran toward the hovering Seiiki, Jessica hot on their heels, as Ghatazhak energy weapons fire streaked over their heads. Nathan helped Chiqua up onto the railing, and another Ghatazhak reached out and pulled her onto the ramp.

"Move it!" Kit barked.

Nathan was next, climbing up and jumping over to the ramp, followed by Jessica.

Kit tapped his comm-set as he continued pouring red-orange bolts of plasma energy through the cafeteria windows. "We've got them," he told Josh, backing away from the end of the ramp as he fired.

The Seiiki's grav-lift system again raised in pitch and volume, the shuttle rising slowly and drifting away from the dining patio.

Kit and Mori turned and ran back inside, the

ramp already passing a twenty-degree angle as it swung upward to close off the cargo bay.

Jessica came walking across the cargo bay toward Nathan and Chiqua. "You want to tell me how it is that you just happened to be away from the critical care unit the moment we were ambushed?" she asked Chiqua.

"I was hungry," Chiqua defended.

"Uh-huh."

"Enough, Jess," Nathan insisted. He tapped the intercom button on the wall. "Josh, jump us out of this system."

"*Where to?*" Josh asked.

"Anywhere as long as it's not in Alliance space."

"If you use your jump drive, you're marking this ship," Chiqua warned. "You'll never be able to fly it into Alliance space again."

"I'm pretty sure that's already the case," Nathan replied. "We're going home," Nathan told Josh. "Just cover our tracks."

"*Got it.*"

Jessica looked frustrated. "So now what do we do?"

Nathan sighed, the adrenaline already starting to fade. "We figure out how to rescue them."

CHAPTER EIGHT

"Good morning," Erica greeted as she entered the Mirai's cockpit.

"Morning," Aiden replied from the pilot's seat, yawning.

"There's still some hot food back there if you hurry."

"I ate a couple hours ago."

"Anything new?"

"Nope. Reactors are humming along as expected."

"Any word about Cori?"

"Captain Taylor called a few hours ago. Cori should recover."

"That's a relief," Erica said, taking the copilot's seat. "I was starting to wonder if anyone cared."

"What do you mean?" Aiden wondered.

"Well those guys seemed more concerned about the extra work they'd have if they lost another engineer. Not exactly what you'd call a 'close' crew."

"We were all thrown together at the last minute, some of us by circumstance."

"Still, you'd think they'd show a little compassion."

"Trust me, they care. They just joke around. It relieves the stress."

"Yeah, I've never understood that whole 'dark humor' thing."

"Spend enough time under fire together, and you will."

"Let's hope it never comes to that," Erica commented.

"You'd better expect it."

"Why do you say that?"

"Let's just say that Captain Scott and the Aurora have a history of stirring up trouble."

"So I've heard," Erica replied, checking her systems. After a moment of silence, she spoke again. "So, have you thought about what you're going to do?"

"Other than hit the rack for a few hours?"

"You know what I'm talking about. The rumors?"

"All ships have rumors."

"You're telling me you haven't thought about what to do now that you're five hundred years in the future?"

"Of course I have, but the answer is always the same. I follow the orders of my superiors. That's the job. That's the oath I took."

"It might not even be the same organization now. Is your oath still valid?"

"You don't adhere to an oath because it's valid, you adhere to it because it gives you a sense of purpose."

"If you hadn't suddenly been transported five centuries into the future, what would your life be?"

"I'd probably continue serving."

"You never thought about settling down and having a family?"

"Have you?"

"I didn't have any immediate plans, but I figured it would happen eventually."

"Weren't you a cargo ship pilot before all this? Back in the days of long-haul linear FTL? Kind of hard to have a family that way."

"Actually, my plan was to get assigned to an outbound, deep-space colonization mission. Those are one-way trips, so family would've come eventually."

Aiden stared out the window, thinking. "I suppose I thought the same thing. That I'd meet someone… someone worth giving up a life in space. Not sure what I'd do for a living though. This is the only job I've ever really had."

"So you're sticking around then?"

"I don't see any other option at this point," Aiden admitted. "What about you?"

"I'm going to stick around as well if they'll have me. I figure it's the only way I'll get familiar with current systems and such. Maybe after a while, I can find a regular pilot's job somewhere."

"I guess that's as good a plan as any, all things considered," Aiden admitted.

* * *

"I'm telling you, she fucking set us up!" Jessica exclaimed. "We should toss her out the fucking airlock right now!"

"I didn't set you up," Chiqua defended.

"The hell you didn't."

"Jess…" Nathan tried to interrupt.

"Why the hell would I do that?"

"There's probably some kind of reward or something," Jessica opined.

"How could there be a reward, Jess," Nathan argued. "The Alliance doesn't even know we're alive."

"They sure as hell do now, thanks to her."

"Even if there was a reward, I stand to make far more running goods into the badlands," Chiqua insisted.

"Maybe, but a reward is fast and easy, with less risk."

"Not from where I'm sitting," Chiqua replied.

"It's my fault," Dominic said, interrupting them both.

"What?" Jessica said, looking at Dominic. For some reason, she had trusted him, at least until now.

"They probably ID'd one or all of you through facial recognition," Dominic explained.

"I didn't see any cameras," Nathan argued.

"You wouldn't. They're built into the walls and ceilings in all public buildings and spaces throughout the Alliance. Everyone is tracked through the monitoring system, and their movements are recorded and stored."

"Why didn't you tell us this before?" Nathan wondered.

"Honestly, it didn't occur to me. It's ubiquitous in the Alliance. Unless you're in your own home with the shades drawn, you're being watched. I just figured it wouldn't matter, seeing as how you've all been dead for over five hundred years."

"And people just accept this?" Jessica asked.

"It's not really that big a deal to most. Those records can only be accessed by court order, which requires probable cause. Most consider it insurance to guarantee that they won't be falsely incriminated."

"It's also one of the number one reasons people leave the Alliance," Chiqua added.

"So you knew about this as well?" Nathan asked Chiqua.

"Yes, I suppose I did."

"You see," Jessica said. "She knew we'd be ID'd. That's why she was in the cafeteria, away from Vlad and the doc."

"I was only up there for ten minutes."

"I'll bet she went up there the moment we left,"

Jessica said to Nathan, not trying to hide her comment from Chiqua.

"The Alliance doesn't pay rewards," Dominic stated. "In case that helps."

"You see?" Chiqua said. "Wait, they don't?"

"Why would they, with cameras recording everything?"

"That's a good point," Nathan said to Jessica.

"Maybe, but I still don't trust her."

"Why would the Alliance even *want* to arrest you?" Chiqua demanded. "Is there something about your *disappearance* that *you're* not telling *us*?"

Nathan looked at Jessica and sighed, then looked back at Chiqua. "We may have been set up by the Alliance to trigger a war with the Ilyan. If that's true, they wouldn't want us around to tell our side of things."

"Like what?" Dominic wondered.

"Like how the Ilyan ships seemed to be able to track us, despite being cloaked," Nathan explained.

"Or why they sent the two captains they knew wouldn't abandon me," Jessica added.

"If that were the case, wouldn't they have shown up sooner?" Chiqua suggested.

"Not if they truly believed that the Aurora and her crew *were* destroyed five hundred and thirty-five years ago."

"If so, why would they still have our records in the facial recognition database?" Jessica questioned.

"We don't even know which of you was ID'd," Dominic pointed out. "It could've just been a ghost."

"Come again?" Jessica asked.

"A ghost, in this case, is a personal record that never got closed out upon death," Dominic explained. "It happens all the time, but more often with deaths that don't have a body to go with them. The Alliance has an entire department dedicated to sorting out ghost hits. If it were any one of you, then it eventually would trigger a response."

"And armed troops were the response?" Nathan surmised.

"Those were probably local law enforcement. If they were Alliance troops, we'd all be in custody... or dead."

"We've got to get them out of there," Jessica urged Nathan.

"How long would it take the Alliance to respond?" Nathan asked Dominic.

"In most cases, a few days. But in your case, there's no telling. If you *were* set up five hundred years ago, then I expect they'd respond even sooner."

"Maybe there's a chance they've forgotten about us?" Jessica suggested. "It's been five hundred thirty-five years after all."

"That's the trouble with AIs," Dominic warned. "They never forget."

* * *

When Nathan and the others came in from the cold hangar bay, Cameron could tell by their faces that things had not gone well. Once she noticed that Doctor Chen and Vladimir were not with them, she feared the worst.

"What happened?" she asked Nathan. "You were only gone a day."

Nathan didn't answer but turned back to the others as they came through the hatch into the corridor. "Everyone get cleaned up and grab something to eat. We'll meet in the command briefing room in two hours." He looked at Jessica. "Keep everyone together," he told her.

Jessica caught his meaning. "No problem."

Jessica led the rest of the party away, leaving Cameron and Nathan standing alone in the corridor.

"I'm not going to like this, am I?" Cameron said.

"We need to talk."

* * *

The one thing Nathan hated more than anything was to have only bad options. Yet, for the second time in less than a week, bad options were, once again, all he had.

Nathan entered the Aurora's command briefing room, finding everyone already seated at the conference table. "So everyone's here," Nathan commented as he took his seat at the head of the table. "I'd like to start by saying that, for those of us in uniform, this will be an informal meeting completely off the record. I want honest opinions from each of you."

"My honest opinion is that we go in with everything we've got and get Vlad and Doc Chen out of there, and that we do it now," Jessica said without reservation.

"Trust me, that was my first thought as well," Nathan assured her, unsurprised by her statement.

"We have to take into account that less than half of our crew wears a uniform," Cameron reminded them.

"We only need the ones who do," Jessica stated.

"My point is that we have a responsibility to their well-being. We don't have the right to order them to risk their lives. They didn't take an oath like us."

"No one is proposing that we risk the lives of our

civilian techs," Nathan promised. "Nor do I intend to go in full force, guns blazing," he said to Jessica. "If we're going to rescue Vlad and Doc Chen, we'll have to be clever about it." Nathan looked at Kit. "I assume you have a plan?"

"I have a few ideas," Kit replied.

"Let's hear them," Nathan insisted.

"Well, to start, we can't use any of our ships," Kit began. "The Seiiki is marked, and we have to assume that the Mirai will be as well, since both are mint-condition, Navarro-class shuttles, which aren't common in this century."

"What about your shuttle?" Nathan wondered.

"We don't know if the Ghatazhak still exist," Kit pointed out, "let alone what their status is within the Alliance."

"I do," Dominic interrupted.

Everyone turned their attention to Dominic, especially Kit and Jessica.

"A few hundred years ago, the Ghatazhak withdrew their support for the Alliance and simply disappeared. Some say they retired and blended in with Takaran society to live out the remainder of their lives. Others believe they left Alliance space for a world in the fringe or beyond. There's even a theory that they are lying in wait among us, waiting for the right moment to take action and overthrow the Alliance."

"Which story do you believe?" Nathan wondered.

"I've never given it much thought. However, history has not been kind to the legend of the Ghatazhak. Most Alliance citizens consider them traitors for turning their backs on the confederacy that they helped create."

"So we can't use the Ghatazhak shuttle either," Nathan concluded.

"The hospital isn't that well defended, at least not from what we saw," Jessica commented.

"We have to assume that has changed by now," Kit insisted.

"By now, they've already pumped your doctor with forenate, and she's told them everything she knows," Dominic warned. "If the Alliance feels that your existence threatens theirs, they'll come for you, and soon."

"Doctor Chen doesn't know much," Cameron pointed out. "She has been so busy taking care of the wounded and then Vlad, I doubt she even knows what planet we crashed on."

"The fringe is vast," Chiqua reminded them. "Finding you would be difficult."

"They'll trace your route to Pyru and begin their search from there," Dominic said.

"How long do you think we have?" Nathan asked.

"It depends on how badly they want to find you," Dominic replied. "They have thousands of patrol ships they could commit to the search, but that would raise questions. I'd expect they'd prefer to keep your existence a secret, at least for now."

"Then we have time," Nathan concluded.

"A few months I'd guess," Dominic replied. "But that's only a guess."

"If we're going to rescue them, we'll need another ship," Kit told them. "Even if we jumped in right on top of that hospital, if we're in one of our shuttles, it will trigger a massive response."

"And if they're expecting us to rescue them, there would be a massive response waiting for us no matter how we got in," Jessica warned.

"Then we need a way to get into the facility without immediately attracting attention," Nathan decided. "The closer we are to Vlad and Doctor Chen when the alarm is triggered, the better."

"Assume that we *are* able to rescue them," Cameron said. "Then what?"

"We get him to Symyri," Nathan replied.

"We don't even know if it's the same guy," Cameron pointed out.

"It doesn't matter," Nathan replied, "as long as he can clone Vlad."

"I'm sure *my* Doctor Symyri can," Dominic assured them. "The trick will be finding him."

"We'll have to worry about that *after* we rescue Vlad and Doctor Chen," Nathan decided.

"I hate to be the one to bring this up, but we have to consider the risk," Cameron stated. "I know it's Vlad, but do we have the right to risk everything, more importantly every*one*, for two people?"

"You mean two of *us*," Jessica snapped, glaring at her.

"I spent more time serving with Vlad than any of you," Cameron reminded them. "But as XO, I have to think of the well-being of *everyone*, not just my friends."

"She's right," Nathan stated. "As much as I hate to admit it." He paused a moment, thinking. "Call a crew meeting…one hour." Nathan rose from his seat to exit. "They deserve the right to decide their own futures."

* * *

"Got a minute?" Robert asked, standing at the doorway to the captain's ready room.

"Not if it's going to be spent lecturing me," Nathan replied.

"Since when do I lecture you?" Robert asked, moving over to the couch. "I simply offer sage advice."

"There's a difference?"

Robert chuckled. "You're about to make a mistake."

"Your sister said the same thing a few minutes ago."

"I suspect for different reasons," Robert replied. "She undoubtedly declared that you don't give the crew a choice, you just give them commands."

"Something like that."

"She's not much on nuance."

"No she's not," Nathan agreed.

"May I ask what you have planned for this ship? Assuming you get her to fly again."

"I haven't decided yet," Nathan admitted.

"Are you still considering returning her to Alliance control?"

"No I'm not. That much I'm sure of."

"Technically, this ship is Alliance property."

"Technically, this ship is mine to command as long as I do so in a manner true to my oath. And from what I've seen and heard about the Alliance so far, my oath requires that I stand *against* them, not for them."

"You're going to *fight* the Alliance?" Robert asked. "Surely you're not *that* crazy."

"Fortunately, I'm not," Nathan assured him.

"Then you *do* have plans for this ship."

"My only plans are to get her back into space."

"You can't do that without a mission, Nathan."

"A *mission*? And what might that be?"

"Jessica once told me that there was one thing we could always count on you to do."

"And what was that?"

"The right thing."

"I'm pretty sure doing the *wrong* thing is what got us here, Robert."

"Right and wrong depends entirely on one's perspective," Robert told him. "Yes, most would say that we never should have entered the Ilyan, that we should have left Jessica there. But neither of us could have done that. Me, because she's my sister, and you because she rescued you from execution on Nor-Patri. The right thing for you *was* to go in and rescue her."

"Even if it led to the death of trillions?"

"We can't know if that war wouldn't have happened had we *not* gone into the Gamaze. Likely, something else would have sparked that conflict sooner or later. And if the Alliance *did* set us up, then we are victims of that deception, the same as anyone else."

"Then Jessica told you of our suspicions."

"She didn't have to," Robert replied. "Suspicion runs in our family."

Nathan leaned back in his chair, thinking. He'd been running on very little sleep and mere instinct for the past week, and it was beginning to take its toll. "What would you do with this ship if she were yours to command?"

"At my age, sell it and retire," Robert laughed. "But at your age, I'd find wrongs that I could right and right them, one at a time."

"To what end?" Nathan wondered.

"Sometimes, doing good, no matter how small, is end enough."

"For a four-hundred-meter starship?"

"Logistically more difficult, I'll admit, but I may have a solution for that."

"Why am I not surprised?"

"What do you mean?"

"You have a unique way of steering a conversation in the direction you want."

"That obvious?"

"Only to someone who grew up around politicians," Nathan replied. "What's your solution?"

"If you plan to resurrect the Aurora and operate her, you're going to need consumables," Robert explained. "Food, water, propellant, medical supplies, raw materials for the fabricators, and that's just the beginning. All of that has costs, but those costs don't have to be in the form of credits or even trade. What you need is an operational support base. Somewhere safe. Someplace that no one knows about."

"Do you have a place in mind?"

"No, but I haven't even started looking," Robert admitted. "But one thing is certain, it needs to be someplace far away, within easy range of the Aurora, but out of single-jump range of most ships. Especially Alliance ships. And it needs to be hospitable, so that we can grow crops and raise livestock."

"You're talking about establishing a settlement," Nathan realized.

"One that can feed your crew and keep you well supplied."

"That will take years to get up and running you know."

"I know."

"We have no idea where we'll be, or what we'll be doing a year from now."

"No matter what it is, you'll need food and water," Robert pointed out.

"Are you going to lead this settlement?"

"I was thinking about it," Robert replied.

"You're going to give up your life in space?"

"I'm not getting any younger, Nathan. I need to start thinking about retirement. This way, I get that retirement but still have a purpose that I believe in."

"You'll need help," Nathan realized, already seeing where Robert was going.

"Not everyone will choose to follow you. Those in uniform will probably stay, but many of the civilian techs are already wondering why they're here. Perhaps some of them would like to help me create this new settlement."

"How soon were you thinking of leaving?" Nathan wondered.

"It's not like I'm in a hurry. But the sooner we get started, the sooner we can begin seeing results. At the very least, we should start looking for the right world as soon as possible."

"We wouldn't be able to provide much in the way of support, at least not until the ship is flying again."

"I wouldn't expect to start the settlement until then anyway," Robert explained. "You can't spare those techs until she is."

"If they *want* to leave, I don't think I have the right to ask them to stay."

"Well, for now, there isn't really any place for them to go, at least not anyplace where they are guaranteed to have a chance at making a decent life."

Nathan sighed. Again, nothing but bad options.

* * *

Nathan entered the Aurora's mess hall, still uncertain of what he was going to say.

"Captain on deck!" Loki barked from the side of the room, snapping to attention.

Everyone in the room stood, coming to attention as well. Even the civilian technicians stood, although their stance was far less rigid and practiced.

"As you were," Nathan stated, making his way up the middle of the hall. Once he reached the forward doors leading to the patio, he turned around to face his crew. He scanned their faces, each and every one of them. They ranged from the despondent to the hopeful, with those ranges equally divided among military and civilian alike. His people had been through a lot since leaving Earth a week ago, and now they found themselves alone, far from their various home worlds, all ties with family and friends lost, and facing uncertain futures. What could he possibly say to them that would give them hope?

"The Confederated Systems Alliance has fallen," Nathan began, immediately drawing looks of disbelief among his crew. "It was not taken by force, but from within. The greed of the few took advantage of the naivety of the masses, slowly chipping away at its own constitution over the centuries, until its original ideals were no longer recognizable. The Alliance we fought and died to create has become an oligarchy disguised as a democracy. The rights of each member to live and govern as they see fit has been traded in exchange for peace and security. This is not what any of us took an oath to protect."

Nathan paused a moment. He had started down a road too narrow to reverse direction. "Each of you who took that same oath must decide for yourselves whether or not you still feel bound by it. I, for one, do not. At this point, my only oath is to my crew and my ship, and to the *ideals* upon which the Alliance was originally founded. To that end, I intend to get this ship back into space, and to continue providing for and protecting my crew and my ship, while we do whatever we can to uphold the ideals we swore to protect."

Again, Nathan paused. He had stated his intent, but he was only halfway home. "Two of our crew are currently being held within Alliance space. I intend to rescue them. But before I do, I owe each of you the right to choose your own destiny. For we are separated from our worlds and our loved ones, by both time and space, never to return. In the face of such adversity, I have no right to order you to follow me into the unknown. What I can do is offer you three options. Captain Nash will be establishing a new settlement on a yet-to-be-selected world, with the intent of supporting the ongoing operations of this vessel. Those of you wishing to start a new life there will be allowed to leave and will be given as much support as possible. Those of you wishing to leave this ship or her settlement entirely, will be provided transportation to a world of your choice, *outside* of Alliance space. Finally, those of you choosing to remain must understand that our future is uncertain. Pay will be nonexistent for now, and resources will likely be scarce. It will be a difficult life to be certain. But you will be part of a family, one that will always be willing to risk us all for the one. *That* is all I can promise you."

* * *

"Not nearly as cold," Nathan said as he walked across the Aurora's shuttle bay toward Marcus and the Seiiki.

"Dominic got the first of the reactors up and running. Good thing too, cuz there was no way I was getting those bays changed out without power," Marcus explained.

"Then we're good to go?"

"Midship bay has a cargo module in it, and the side bays have weapons modules."

"Great."

"Just so you know, Cap'n, Neli and I ain't goin' nowhere."

"I never had any doubt," Nathan said, patting Marcus on the shoulder as he headed up the boarding ramp.

Jessica came into the cargo bay, meeting Nathan in the middle.

"Everyone aboard?"

"Kit and Mori are in the crew cabin with Hanna and Chiqua, and Josh is in the cockpit, waiting for you. Dominic's not coming with us?"

"He's staying here to hook up the other two fusion reactors," Nathan replied, tapping his comm-set. "Close her up and get us in the air, Josh."

"You got it, Cap'n," Josh replied.

Nathan turned aft as the ramp began to rise, waving to Marcus outside. "Keep the lights on, old man."

* * *

Since Hadria was well within single-jump range from Dencke for the Seiiki, the flight had taken less than an hour, gear up to gear down. Within an hour of touchdown on Hadria, Chiqua had returned as promised, with truckloads of goods to fill their ship.

"There's more here than just medical supplies,"

Jessica commented as she and Nathan examined the cargo being packed carefully into their ship.

"I didn't know you traded in other goods," Nathan said to Chiqua.

"I don't," she replied. "I contacted other traders and sold them space on your ship for the run. We keep fifty percent of their profit."

"Pretty hefty cut," Nathan observed.

"Why would anyone agree to those terms?" Jessica questioned.

"Because it's the only way they'll have access to markets within the badlands."

"What happens if we lose our cargo to pirates?" Jessica wondered.

"Then I have to pay them for their losses," Chiqua replied. "So I'd appreciate it if that did *not* happen."

"We'll do our best," Nathan promised.

Jessica watched Chiqua as she turned and headed back down the cargo ramp. "I still don't trust her."

"Really? I'm shocked."

Jessica sneered at him. "You know, once we go up against these pirates, we'll have both the Alliance *and* the pirates gunning for us."

"Does that worry you?" Nathan wondered.

"Hell no. I like that kind of shit."

"Then what's the problem?"

"I worry about you," Jessica admitted. "You're an idealist. You can't turn your back on injustice."

"Trust me, all I'm interested in at the moment is rescuing Vlad and Doc Chen," Nathan insisted, turning to head forward.

"Uh-huh. Keep telling yourself that."

* * *

"Why can't we just jump straight to...what's the name of this place again?" Josh asked.

"Kataoka," Chiqua repeated.

"What kind of a screwy name is that?" Josh wondered. "Why don't they ever name places something inviting, like Paradise, or Happy-land..."

"Happy-land?" Jessica chuckled. "It's official. Josh never gets to name worlds."

"This part of the badlands is rife with gravity wells," Chiqua explained. "Luckily, most of them are stationary, but there are at least a dozen that shift positions regularly. The further you try to jump through such a region of space, the greater the chance that you will not end up where you intended...and that's if you're lucky."

"And if you're unlucky?" Nathan asked.

"You'll never know."

"I'm starting to understand why they didn't call it Paradise," Josh muttered to himself as he activated the lift-off sequence.

"Is this the only route to Kataoka?" Nathan asked as the Seiiki's grav-lift system began to whine and the buildings outside the cockpit windows began to slowly fall from view.

"From Hadria, there are three other routes, but all of them are twice as long and twice as hazardous. This route hasn't seen a rogue gravity well in years."

"Which means it's also the one pirates are most likely to be monitoring," Jessica concluded.

"Correct," Chiqua confirmed.

"Then why are you recommending it?" Jessica wondered.

"Because she'd rather risk pirates than gravity wells," Nathan stated.

"Me too," Josh agreed as he pushed the main drive

throttles forward, accelerating away from Hadria as they continued to climb.

"An old ship captain I once knew said that the trick to evading pirates was to not linger between jumps. Verify your position, get your jump calculated, and execute. The Vernay passage *is* the best route to Kataoka."

"I guess we'll have to take your word for it," Nathan decided. "Jump us to the rendezvous point as soon as we reach orbit," he instructed Josh.

* * *

Six pairs of people clad in cold-weather gear appeared from the port hatch on the Aurora, quickly moving down the snow-covered ramp, trying their best not to slip on its icy surface. Once they reached the bottom, the pairs moved quickly to the row of six Dragon fighters parked nearby, the sleek ships half buried in snow.

Talisha was the first one to reach her fighter, its canopy sliding back as she climbed up the snowbank to its cockpit. Once there, she stepped inside, standing in the cockpit as she stripped away her cold-weather gear, revealing her flight suit underneath.

"D-d-d-damn," she exclaimed, shivering from the biting cold.

"Gimme that gear and get your canopy closed," Marcus told her. "Before you freeze your ass off!"

Talisha plopped down in her seat, immediately reaching for her canopy control. "Promise me the recovery deck will be working by the time we get back!" she yelled as the canopy began sliding forward over her.

Marcus laughed, giving her a 'thumbs up' as he backed down from the cockpit, turning to head back inside with the other fools who had volunteered to get the Dragon pilots to their ships.

"Crank up the heat, Leta," Talisha instructed her AI.

"*Already done,*" Leta assured her. "*Reactor is at full power. All systems are ready for liftoff.*"

"*Leader to all Dragons,*" Loki called over comms. "*Check in.*"

"*Two,*" Nikolas reported.

"Three," Talisha followed.

"*Four,*" Talisha's wingman, Meika added.

"*Five,*" Kusya chimed in.

After a moment, Loki called, "*Six, check in.*"

"*Six here, sir. Sorry about that. I had a little trouble with my canopy.*"

"*Did you get a good seal?*"

"*Yes, sir. I'm all good now. Just a little cold.*"

"*We'll lift off in five,*" Loki announced. "*That should be time enough for us to get the feeling back in our fingers.*"

"Better make it ten," Talisha joked.

CHAPTER NINE

"The pirates tend to vary their strikes," Chiqua explained. "They almost always ambush inbound flights and take half their cargo as an import fee. If the ship pays, they get a safe passage transponder attached to the ship's hull. However, this only grants them passage to their destination. Anything they attempt to haul out is subject to an export fee. Again, it's usually about half of what they haul."

"How are the ships supposed to make any profit?" Nathan wondered.

"That's the thing," Chiqua continued. "Very few do. Some manage to hide part of their cargo, usually the most valuable part, to ensure their profit. Those who don't, break even at best. That's why people like me don't run cargo into the badlands. Too much risk of loss. That's fine if you're just trying to survive, but it sucks if you're trying to get ahead."

"And no one stands up to these pirates?" Jessica asked.

"A few do, and they end up on a hit list, always looking over their shoulder for assassins. They last a while, but usually not for long. Eventually, they lose their ship, their life, or worse."

"What's worse than losing your ship and your life?" Josh wondered.

"They also kill everyone you loved," Chiqua replied. "Your family, your friends...I heard they once took out an entire settlement that one guy was from, simply because he didn't have any family or friends, so they took the next best thing."

"How do these pirate gangs manage to stay in

business?" Nathan wondered. "It seems like they're ruining their market."

"That's where the Korsan, and others like them, come in," Chiqua told him. "They maintain a balance. They take just enough so that those they rob still manage to make a living. For those who live in the badlands, this is just a part of life. It's the price they pay to live completely free."

"Well not *completely* free," Jessica commented.

"Free in the sense that there are no governments running the worlds on which they live, which is what most of them seek."

"So these worlds have *no* government at all?" Nathan wondered. "No laws, no enforcement?"

"Most adopt similar versions of 'frontier' law."

"What's that?" Jessica asked.

"You know; you wrong me, I kill you."

"Seems a bit extreme," Nathan decided.

"Life in the badlands isn't for everyone," Chiqua agreed. "But I have to admit, it does simplify things."

"So only the strong survive in the badlands," Jessica surmised. "Hardly seems fair."

"If they're not strong, they don't belong in the badlands," Chiqua stated. "No one moves to the badlands thinking things are going to be fair or easy."

"Sounds like a real fun place," Josh decided.

"You'd get killed in a few days," Jessica laughed. "A week at the most."

"I can handle myself," Josh defended.

"You'd hit on someone's wife and get shot," Nathan insisted.

"One fucking time!" Josh objected.

"And people still move to the badlands despite the dangers."

"Like I said, some like it that way, while others move there out of necessity."

"How many settlements are there?" Nathan asked.

"No one really knows for certain," Chiqua admitted. "The frontier is vast, surrounding the fringe and the Alliance within. Where it begins is well understood, but how far it extends varies."

"So hundreds?" Nathan guessed.

"More like thousands," Chiqua corrected, "if not tens of thousands. Originally, the 'frontier' referred to anything beyond the borders of the Alliance. People migrated there in droves during the post-war reformation. That's when the Alliance began exerting more control over member worlds with the promise of peace and prosperity. It was referred to as 'interstellarization'. Those who liked it stayed, those who did not, left. Often with the Alliance's support."

"The Alliance *paid* them to leave?" Nathan wondered.

"More like they *allowed* them to leave. They even sold them discounted settlement packages and provided transportation. It was very profitable for the Alliance, plus, they rid themselves of potential opposition from within."

"What differentiates the fringe from the badlands?" Jessica asked. "Is it just the presence of governments?"

"For the most part, yes, but there are other factors. Population, trade, and civil defense to name a few." Chiqua studied Nathan a moment. "Why so many questions?"

"Just trying to understand what we're getting into," Nathan replied.

The sensor display beeped, and a group of icons appeared on its far left edge.

"They're here," Josh announced.

"*Seiiki, Dragon One,*" Loki called over comms. "*Off your port beam, ready to begin escort.*"

"Good to see you, Lieutenant Commander," Nathan replied. "Divide your flight into three pairs. One pair jumps a minute after us, a few klicks astern, the other two pairs jump in one minute later, to either side. We're sending our route now."

"*Understood,*" Loki confirmed.

"What are you doing?" Chiqua asked, concerned. "You should keep your fighters with you, trust me."

"I have my reasons," Nathan assured her.

"I have to object, Captain. You owe me a tidy sum, one I'm not going to recoup if you get us slaughtered by pirates."

"My ship, my rules," Nathan replied.

Chiqua looked to Jessica. "Does he know what he's doing?"

"Of course not," Jessica chuckled. "He's just winging it like usual."

* * *

"Jump three complete," Josh reported.

Nathan studied the sensor display, still seeing no contacts. "Any idea how far into the passage they usually attack?" he asked Chiqua.

"I really don't know," Chiqua admitted.

"If it were me, I'd attack during the middle third of the passage," Josh commented.

"Since when do you think like a pirate?" Nathan wondered.

"Come on, Cap'n. You know I'd make a great pirate."

"I can see it," Jessica agreed.

"Why the middle third?" Nathan wondered.

"Too far in to turn back, and too far from the end to escape," Josh explained. "Plus, the middle of the passage is the tightest as far as maneuvering goes. Veer too far in any direction and you risk getting pulled into the unstable gravity wells."

"I still don't get where these rogue gravity wells are coming from," Nathan stated. "I always thought it took an incredible amount of dark matter to create a gravity well. And the rogue nature of them doesn't make any sense."

"I wouldn't know either," Chiqua admitted. "It's all way beyond my meager understanding of physics. I'm more of a 'knowledge from life experience' kind of gal."

The sensor screen beeped as two icons appeared directly behind them.

"First two Dragons are with us," Nathan announced. "Doubtful they'll attack us now."

"Don't be too sure," Chiqua warned. "I've heard of escorted ships still being attacked. Granted, they weren't being escorted by *Dragons*, but these pirates might not even recognize your fighters as being a more significant threat than the usual escorts."

"Why don't the ships trying to make these passages just beef up their shields?" Jessica wondered.

"Better shields require more power," Nathan pointed out.

"Most ships running the badlands are old and barely space-worthy," Chiqua added. "Plus, the pirates force them to operate on such thin margins that they can't afford any upgrades. Most of them can't afford escorts either. In fact, some believe that having escorts just makes you a more likely target."

"Second group just jumped in," Nathan announced. "Go ahead and plot our next jump."

"You got it," Josh replied as he began the process.

"This is dumb," Jessica insisted. "We should've just picked the least infected part of space and single-jumped to our destination. They'd *never* expect *that*."

"Because no one is that stupid," Chiqua replied. "Not to mention that most ships don't have much jump range and have to multi-jump between systems. That takes additional time, propellant, and consumables."

"But if they're outside of Alliance space, why don't they use longer-range jump drives?" Jessica asked.

"Long-range drives are rare. With the rise of the jump gate network, manufacturers just stopped making them altogether. Only a few custom makers still produce them. Besides, most operators would rather not risk contributing to the gravity well problem nor backlash from the public. I mean, logically, why would you risk making the problem worse?"

"Then you believe the claims?" Nathan surmised.

"I don't care one way or another," Chiqua admitted. "All that matters is what everyone else believes and how it affects my ability to operate."

"Good point," Nathan admitted.

"Jump four is ready," Josh reported.

"Transmit the jump plot to the Dragons and jump when ready," Nathan instructed.

"Transferring jump plot. Jumping in five."

"I just can't imagine being restricted to short-range multi-jumping," Nathan admitted. "I mean, you're talking days or even weeks of travel time."

"Free-jumping is dangerous," Chiqua said. "You

never know when something too massive to jump *through* is going to be in your jump line, and the further you jump, the greater the risk. Short jumps along known routes are much safer."

The jump flash washed over the Seiiki's cockpit, subdued to manageable levels by the filters built into her windows.

"Jump four complete," Josh reported.

"So when a group of people decides to settle a new world, someplace say, *beyond* the badlands, the ship that takes them there has to use multi-jump systems to make the journey?"

"Usually, yes," Chiqua explained. "They usually have SA pods for the passengers though. There are still a few long-jump transports operating, or so the rumor is. I've never seen one myself. In fact, I haven't even *heard* of one for some time."

The sensor screen beeped and three icons appeared: one directly ahead and one on either side.

"Contacts," Josh reported. "Three of them, and they ain't Dragons."

"*Unidentified ship,*" a gruff voice called over comms. "*State your destination and cargo.*"

Nathan tapped his comm-set, tying it into the ship's external communications array. "Unidentified *caller*, this is the unidentified *ship*, and our destination and cargo are none of your business."

"A bit aggressive don't you think?" Chiqua questioned.

"*State your destination and cargo or be destroyed,*" the voice warned. "*This will be your only warning.*"

"The ones on the sides are turning to intercept," Josh warned.

"Raising shields," Nathan stated as he activated the ship's defenses. "Deploying weapons."

On either side of the Seiiki's main section, long doors split open, sliding to the sides and disappearing into the hull. Once open, a plasma torpedo generator with stubby, multi-segmented, large-bore barrels pointing fore and aft rose up from inside. Once locked into place at hull level, the barrels extended, becoming three times their original length. The generator itself began to glow, its plasma charge building as the weapon prepared for battle.

At the same time, along the underside of the two weapons bays, a single missile launch tube descended and locked into place on either side.

"We have no desire to harm you, but we will defend ourselves," Nathan warned over comms. "And we will do so aggressively. That is *your* final warning."

"Nice trash-talk," Josh complimented. "Torpedo cannons and missile launchers show ready. Shields at full strength. Five seconds until the first two ships reach what I'm guessing is their maximum attack range."

"Shouldn't you be maneuvering, or better yet, jumping?" Chiqua urged, growing concerned.

"He's drawing them in," Jessica explained calmly.

"That doesn't seem like a good idea, if you ask me."

"Nobody asked you," Jessica remarked.

Loki checked his jump sequencer as it counted down the last few seconds to the fourth jump in the passage. "Heads up, Remo," he called to his wingman. "Jumping again in three......two......one......"

The Dragon fighter's jump sequencer activated, and the blue-white jump flash filled the cockpit as the ship jumped ahead to rendezvous with the Seiiki at the next waypoint. Loki's tactical display immediately lit up, the threat warning light flashing wildly. His AI immediately charged the fighter's shields and weapons, locking its defensive turrets onto the nearest targets. A glance out the forward window revealed flashes of red-orange streaking back and forth between the Seiiki and its three attackers less than a kilometer ahead.

"Remo! Three bandits attacking the Seiiki! Put two chasers on target three, I'll put two on target two, then we jump in close to target one and force him off the attack."

"*Copy that,*" Nikolas replied. "*Locking chasers on three.*"

Loki rolled slightly left, turning toward his target, then unleashed a pair of chaser missiles on the unknown attacker. "Two chasers away," he reported as his missiles streaked ahead.

"Two away!" Nikolas announced.

Loki glanced at his tactical display, verifying Nikolas's missile launch against the target attacking the Seiiki's starboard side as instructed, and that he was already turning toward the bandit in front of them.

Loki rolled back to starboard, turning onto an intercept course with the first target. A few taps of virtual keys on his jump nav console, and he had his next jump plotted and ready. "Auto-slave jump to target one in three......two......one......"

Again, the cockpit became momentarily awash

with the flash of the jump. The Seiiki appeared only a hundred meters ahead and slightly below. Although the two bandits attacking from either side of the Seiiki had broken off to evade the chaser missiles that were pursuing them, the lead bandit was still firing with all guns on the Seiiki's forward shields, hoping to pound her into submission, as they had likely done to so many others in the past.

"Starting attack run on target one," Loki announced as he pushed his throttles forward, accelerating and passing over the Seiiki.

"*On your wing,*" Nikolas assured him.

"Seiiki, we'd appreciate a clear attack path if you don't mind," Loki called over comms.

"Surprise, assholes!" Josh chuckled as two Dragon fighters streaked overhead, opening fire on the lead pirate fighter.

"Killing all weapons," Nathan announced. "You're all clear, Loki!"

Nathan and Josh both watched out the forward windows as the lead fighter was forced to dive down under the Seiiki to avoid the Dragon attacks.

"What the fuck was that?" Josh exclaimed. "Did you see that? That thing was uglier than a harvester!"

"It looked like they slapped together sections from different ships and cobbled them together," Nathan commented. "I'm surprised they can even fly, let alone attack someone."

"Well all that weapons fire barely drained our shields at all," Jessica told them, examining the ship's defenses at the starboard auxiliary station.

"What are the other two ships doing?" Chiqua

asked, trying to hide the fact that she had never been in a space battle.

"They jumped out as soon as they had chasers on their tails," Nathan replied. "Which means they weren't stupid."

"Or that they just can't fly worth a shit," Josh commented.

"Will they come back?"

"Without a doubt," Nathan insisted.

"Even with two Dragons backing you up?"

"To them it looks like even odds," Nathan explained. "Which probably means that if they turned tail and ran, whoever they fly for would not be happy."

"One of them just jumped back in astern," Josh reported. "Five klicks and closing fast."

"They must not have missiles, or they'd have launched already," Jessica concluded.

"I'm surprised those jalopies can generate enough power to fire the cannons they *do* have," Josh snickered.

"They may not look like much, but they have done their share of damage to transports in this passage," Chiqua warned.

The contact light illuminated again. Nathan glanced at the tactical display, spotting four new icons directly behind the bandit firing on them from behind. The cavalry had arrived. The four icons immediately split into two pairs, each pair veering toward a different bandit, which once again numbered three. A few seconds later, all three red icons disappeared.

"Fuck yeah!" Josh exclaimed. "Nice kills, guys!"

"*They weren't kills,*" Loki reported. "*They bugged out as soon as the rest of the flight arrived.*"

"I guess they are only tough when the odds are in their favor," Nathan surmised.

"Because they can't fly worth shit," Josh repeated.

"*Orders, Captain?*" Loki inquired over comms.

"They know we have escorts now, so there's not much point in jumping in sequence. We'll jump together and keep our time on waypoints as short as possible," Nathan instructed. "Diamond formation on us. We'll slave jump the group the rest of the way through the passage."

"*Understood,*" Loki acknowledged. "*Leader to all Dragons. Diamond-up on the Seiiki.*"

"I'd be happier if we'd have killed at least one of them," Jessica stated.

"Killing wasn't the point," Nathan explained. "We just wanted them to know we could."

"Well you can bet your ass those bandits went running home to papa and are reporting what happened," Jessica insisted.

"They'll be back," Chiqua warned, "and with more than three raiders."

"They could bring a dozen raiders, and it wouldn't be a problem," Nathan insisted.

"Especially if they all fly that shitty," Josh added, chuckling to himself.

"And what if they bring something bigger?" Jessica asked.

"Do they even *have* bigger ships?" Nathan asked Chiqua.

"I'm not certain. I know they have larger raiders, ones that can carry the cargo they steal, but I've never heard of anything the size of the Aurora."

"Well I'm betting that the small amount of cargo we're moving isn't going to be worth the trouble for them," Nathan said.

"They'll likely try to take it from the worlds we trade with," Chiqua warned.

"I've got an idea on how to prevent *that* as well," Nathan told her.

* * *

The cleared and leveled area at the edge of town had not been occupied for months. Nor had the thunderous crack that announced the arrival of a jump ship been heard in a long time. By the time the Seiiki had made its descent and come in to land, a small crowd had begun to form.

Nathan stood at the cargo door as the ramp lowered to the ground. Beyond were the faces of several dozen Kataokans, a diverse mixture of size, shape, and color. Yet every face had one thing in common. A look of despair. These were not the faces of the brave who had chosen to settle the frontier in the hopes of living in complete freedom. These were the faces of people who had been preyed upon; who had been stripped of the profits of their hard work, left with only the bare minimum needed to survive.

From his position, Nathan could see that the town was not very large. A few hundred people perhaps, most still living in the quick-rise homes they had come with. Others had built whatever shelter they could from rock, fused soil, and local timber. They were all closely arranged, with paths paved with river rock lined with carefully designed trenches to whisk away the rains, which, from the lushness of the greenery, came often.

"Who among you trades on your behalf?" Chiqua called out as she stepped up beside Nathan.

Nathan looked at her, surprised.

"I do," a voice called from the crowd.

Nathan surveyed the crowd as a young man stepped forward, looking younger than Nathan would have expected.

"And you are?" Chiqua asked.

"Darren, son of Rod. My father was our trader. When he fell to a Korsan blade, the responsibility became mine."

Chiqua looked out across the settlement, looking for a larger structure that might be their trading hall. "I see no trading hall."

"We have none," Darren explained. "My father usually conducted business aboard the trader's ship. Shall I come aboard?"

Chiqua looked to Nathan, not wanting to overstep her bounds.

Nathan nodded.

"Please do," Chiqua invited, adding a gesture for the young man to come aboard.

* * *

"As soon as Dominic gets main power back to normal levels, I'd like you to start training the few pilots we have available to fly Dragons," Cameron instructed as she and Robert walked onto the Aurora's battered bridge.

"Of course," Robert replied. "I assume our remaining five Dragons survived the crash intact?"

"They did. The storage tubes run right along the main longitudinal trusses, so they were pretty well protected from the impact."

"How soon will we have access to them?" Robert wondered.

The main lighting began to flicker, coming to full

illumination. Consoles about the bridge came to life as well, most displaying error conditions or flashing nonsensical data.

"Now I guess," Cameron said, pausing a moment to look around the Aurora's bridge. "Damn, we certainly have our work cut out for us," she stated as they headed into the captain's ready room.

"That we do."

The intercom beeped as they entered.

"Go ahead," Cameron answered into the intercom on the desk.

"*Dominic got the last two reactors hooked up and running, sir,*" Melisha reported.

"Then we have normal power available?"

"*Yes, sir, but we're only running the reactors at fifty percent for now. Dominic had to make some modifications to allow them to work with our power distribution system. Something about it being outdated. Different phasing or something. He plans to bring them up to one hundred percent within the hour, at which point we can run full shields or full weapons, but not both.*"

"Very well. Keep me informed," Cameron instructed.

"*Yes, sir.*"

"Get a team together and back-feed the fighters from the storage tunnels and get them into the service bay. Configure them for simulation for now. We'll get them airborne as soon as practical."

"I'd prefer that every new pilot has at least a hundred hours of simulation before they start actual flights," Robert told her.

"So would I, but I suspect that's not going to be possible. If necessary, their AIs will have to back them up."

"It's better not to rely on the AI," Robert reminded her. "If it fails, they'd have to fly without it."

"In a perfect world," Cameron said.

"I'll get started," Robert promised, turning to exit.

Cameron tapped the intercom again. "Mirai, Aurora."

"*Mirai, Bodstein here, ma'am,*" Erica replied.

"Female officers are referred to as 'sir' just like male officers, Miss Bodstein."

"*Sorry, ma…I mean, sir.*"

"Disconnect and return to the shuttle bay," Cameron instructed.

"*Yes, sir,*" Erica replied smartly. "*Right away, sir.*"

Cameron moved to reposition herself directly below the blower vent, relishing the warm air blowing in. Soon, the temperature in all the ship's habitable spaces would be back to comfortable levels, and the rest of Dencke's long night would be more easily survived.

* * *

"You challenged them *in transit*?" Darren exclaimed in dismay. "Do you realize what you've done?"

"I defended myself and my ship, as well as my client's cargo," Nathan replied.

"They would have taken half your cargo and let you pass. Instead, they will come looking to *us* for their cut, and they will punish *us* for your actions. We cannot trade with you!"

"They're going to assume that you did, whether or not you trade with us," Chiqua told him.

Nathan glared at her, realizing she had known

this all along and had said nothing. "We can protect you," he stated.

"We can?" Jessica chimed in, surprised.

"In orbit are the six Dragon fighters that escorted us through the passage," Nathan told Darren. "Even more of them are at our base in the fringe. This ship is also well armed and can handle a few pirate raiders on its own."

"And when they jump past your fighters, landing here, looking for revenge, will you be able to defend us then as well?" Darren challenged.

"To some extent, yes."

"Nathan, may I have a word with you?" Jessica said under her breath.

"No," Nathan replied firmly. "Danger can be mitigated," Nathan told Darren. "We have been hired by Miss Kimbro not only to ensure her cargo, but to protect those who trade with her."

This time, it was Chiqua who was surprised, although she hid it well.

"How many worlds does the passage serve?" Nathan asked.

"Six, including Kataoka," Darren replied. "And ours is the first world the pirates will visit."

"Then we will station our Dragons here for now, keeping two on patrol at all times. We will also keep a small force of highly trained men, with a shuttle of their own, to defend against any surface action."

"You are asking us to take a great risk," Darren objected. "We only number a few hundred. Should they come in force..."

"Have they *ever* come in force?" Nathan asked.

"No, but only because we do not oppose them. But I have heard stories of other settlements they have destroyed."

"Has *anyone* ever fought back against these pirates?"

"Not that I know of," Darren admitted. "But we have witnessed their enforcement *here.* My father fell to such an enforcement, and all he did was hide some goods from them in order to survive the winter."

"How many men were there?" Nathan asked.

"Eight, maybe ten?" Darren replied.

Nathan looked to Kit.

"Two of us could handle that number without breaking a sweat," Kit assured him.

Darren looked at them. "Who *are* you people?"

"*Who* we are is not important. The question is, who are *you?*" Nathan asked. "Or who do you *wish* to be? Do you wish to continue to be victims, barely scratching out an existence, or do you want more? We can help, but you have to *want* our help."

Darren studied Nathan's face a moment. "How do I know you'll keep your word? How do I know you won't just make your trade and then disappear with our payment, never to be seen again?"

Nathan took a breath, first looking at Chiqua, then to Jessica and Kit. Finally, he looked back at Darren. "We'll give you your share of our cargo, free of charge, as a sign of good faith."

"We'll what?" Chiqua objected.

Nathan ignored her.

"Why would you do that?"

"Because we're not here to make a single trade with you and the other worlds at the end of the Vernay passage. We seek to establish a trade *route*, so that all your worlds can flourish, and we can make a regular profit."

"And you believe the Korsan will just allow you to do so?" Darren wondered.

"That's the icing on the cake," Nathan stated. "Not only do we get to make a living, but we get to right a wrong at the same time."

Jessica shook her head. "Yup, still a do-gooder," she muttered so that only Kit could hear her.

* * *

Aiden watched as Erica piloted the Mirai the short distance from where it had been parked on the Aurora's aft hull to the ship's shuttle bay, setting it down precisely and rolling it inside to its usual parking spot. "Not bad."

"Thank you," Erica replied. "I was a bit surprised when you asked me to fly it back manually."

"Sim experience doesn't always translate well into real-world flights," Aiden explained. "I wanted to see what kind of touch you had."

"And what kind *did* I have?"

"Better than I had my first time out."

"Now what?" she asked as she finished shutting down the ship's systems.

"Now you get used to the left seat."

Erica looked confused. "Why?"

"Because I'm being given permanent command of the Mirai, and I'm going to need a pilot if you're interested."

"Hell yes, I'm interested."

"Don't be too hasty," Aiden insisted. "The missions are likely to be somewhat boring in the beginning, and knowing Captain Scott, they will probably become more interesting as time goes on, not to mention more dangerous."

"Can't be much more dangerous than my last job," Erica replied.

"Don't bet on it."

* * *

"What the hell were you thinking?" Chiqua demanded as she followed Nathan through the Seiiki's port corridor. "Do you know how much this stuff is worth?"

"It was the right decision," Nathan defended.

"Yeah, I'm sure little Darren back there agrees with you, but that's *my* cargo back there…"

"*Our* cargo," Nathan corrected. "I gave up my percentage as well, and we need it a lot more than you do."

"I hired you to run cargo, not start a war with the Korsan!"

"It's going to take a lot more than losing control of six insignificant worlds to bring the Korsan down on us," Nathan insisted as they entered the forward boarding compartment.

"How can you possibly know that?"

"You're a businesswoman, I'm surprised you haven't already figured that out."

"What?"

"Ships have operating costs. Crew, consumables, propellant. Pulling them from profitable duties and risking them in battle is a great way to lose a lot of funds and quickly. The Korsan won't take any action as long as the *cost* of doing so is less than what they are losing by ignoring the problem."

"But…"

"Can you make enough profit from these six worlds to satisfy our debt in a reasonable time?" Nathan asked, interrupting her.

"Probably, but I was hoping to service more than just a handful of worlds."

"And we just may do that, but not until *after* the Aurora is fully repaired and back in space," Nathan clarified.

"I've seen the damage to your ship," Chiqua declared as she followed Nathan up the ladder to the crew cabin. "It could take *years* to get her back into space. Especially if we limit this enterprise to *six worlds*. Do you really believe the Korsan will ignore us for that long?"

Nathan reached the crew cabin and stepped to the left, standing just outside the cockpit door. "I'm betting more on this than you are, Chiqua."

"How so?" she asked as she reached the top of the ladder and stepped onto the crew cabin deck.

"You're only risking credits," Nathan told her as he turned to enter the cockpit. "I'm risking everything."

Chiqua stood there, not sure how to respond. Then she started toward the cockpit door herself, determined to push the issue further.

"I'd quit while you're ahead," Jessica commented from behind.

Chiqua turned around, spotting Jessica sitting in the dining booth, picking at a ration pack.

"He's going to get us killed."

"By a bunch of pirates?" Jessica laughed. "Unlikely."

"You don't know the Korsan," Chiqua insisted.

"And you do?"

"By reputation, yes."

"Nathan knows what he's doing," Jessica insisted, finishing up the last of her meal.

"And how do you know that?"

"Because I'm willing to follow him," Jessica replied

as she rose to depart. "And I damn sure know what *I'm* doing."

Again, Chiqua was speechless. She had managed to ally herself with newcomers to this region of space as well as this century. It was the biggest gamble she had ever taken, and at the moment, she had serious doubts about that decision.

* * *

So far, all the settlements at the end of the Vernay passage had been the same. A few hundred people barely surviving, living in ramshackle buildings clustered together for protection. The only real difference had been the environments of each world. While all were habitable, only a few were actually hospitable to human life.

In all his travels, Nathan had never understood why people would bother to live on inhospitable worlds. With all the advances in technology, especially the jump drive, there was just no reason to suffer on such planets. Still, people came to these worlds for a variety of reasons, freedom being only one of them. It seemed a cruel joke that the worlds with the most valuable resources usually had the worst environments for humans.

The other thing he had noticed was the overall lack of labor droids. He had only seen a few on Hadria and Pyru, and none thus far in the badlands.

"This lead had better pan out," Nathan complained as they approached the tavern. "This is the last planet in this area."

"Estabrook is the only port in the area," Chiqua explained. "If we're going to find a ship for hire in the Vernay, it'll be here."

"And you think we'll find their captain here?" Jessica challenged.

"Captains like to drink and boast about their adventures to other captains," Chiqua explained.

"She's right about that," Nathan commented.

"What better place to do both than a tavern?"

They entered the run-down building, pausing just inside the door.

The tavern on Estabrook was dark and dingy. A dimly lit great room with simple wooden benches and tables, and a massive stone fireplace on one wall, in which a fire blazed. People of various ilk drank and ate, swapping stories with full mouths as they lied and laughed their way through the meals and pints. It was like something out of a vid-flick set in medieval times on Earth.

"Have you noticed something odd?" Jessica mentioned to Nathan as they worked their way to one of the few empty tables in the place.

"Take your pick," Nathan replied.

"We're the only ones carrying blasters," Jessica said.

Nathan glanced around, checking waistbands for holsters, but all he found were sheathed knives of various lengths, as well as a few swords. "Well that does seem odd."

"First time on Estabrook?" a gruff voice called from behind.

Nathan turned to see an old man at a nearby table staring at them. "How did you know?"

"The blasters," the old man replied. "No one carries them here."

"Why not?"

"Cuz there's vissian gas leaking out all over this crappy, little world. One blast of that weapon and you're more likely to set yourself on fire than kill your target."

"That explains all the knives," Jessica decided.

"I'd get yourself a few of them if I were you," the old man recommended.

In a quick motion, Jessica drew a combat knife the length of her forearm from the sheath built into the thigh of her pants, twirling it several times before presenting it to the old man. "Like these?"

The old man smiled. "That'll do ya," he said, raising his mug in respect.

"Thanks for the advice," Nathan said, turning to continue on. He paused a moment, then turned back to the old man. "Mind if I ask you for another piece of advice?"

"Depends on what it is."

"We're looking to hire a ship. Nothing big, just something to get us to Pyru and back."

"Why the hell would you want to go to Pyru?"

"Business," Nathan replied.

"What makes you think you can find one here?"

"Someone on Trullen told us we might."

"Well the only ship around here is the Acuna, but I'm not sure she's the kind you're looking for."

"Any idea where we can find her captain?" Chiqua asked.

The old man pointed.

Nathan looked in that direction, spotting two women sitting at a corner table. "Which one?"

"The one on the left. Alex is her name. Be careful, she bites."

Nathan looked back at the old man. "Thanks for the warning."

* * *

The doors to the critical care ward lobby swung open, and a dozen armed men dressed in black uniforms, trimmed in gold, crimson, and blue, poured into the room, followed by Jakome, their leader. They did not stop at the reception desk, nor did the lock on the entrance to the ward itself slow their progress.

"What is the meaning of this?" the charge nurse demanded as the squad of armed men entered the ward.

"You have a patient by the name of Vladimir Kimbro under your care," Jakome stated. "We are here to take him into our care and transport him to Earth."

"Under whose authority?" the charge nurse demanded.

Jakome touched the comm-unit on his left wrist, making a swiping motion as if casting something toward her. "Alliance Medical Command."

The charge nurse examined the holo-document hovering in the air before her. "I cannot release Mister Kimbro without his doctor's approval. I'm not even certain he is stable enough to move."

"Then I suggest you find him and quickly," Jakome warned, a touch of menace in his tone. "I have little time and even less patience."

* * *

Nathan approached the two women at the corner table, with Jessica, Kit, and Chiqua behind him. He paused a moment before speaking, sizing them both up.

"What the hell are you looking at?" the woman on the left snarled at him.

"I'm trying to decide if what that old man over there told me is true," Nathan asked.

"Oh yeah?" the woman said, taking a drink of her ale. "Probably not."

"He said to watch out, that you bite."

"Well, he was right about that," she replied, sharing an amused look with the younger woman next to her.

"He also told me that you have a ship for hire," Nathan continued. "Is that true?"

"Depends."

"On what?"

"On the mission," she replied. "Alex Foruria. This is my engineer, Josi."

"Then you *do* have a ship," Nathan surmised.

"The Acuna."

"Isn't that a kind of fish?" Jessica wondered, drawing a nasty look from Alex.

"Connor Tuplo."

"Where are you looking to go, Connor Tuplo? And what are you hauling?"

"Pyru and just a team of...*specialists*," Nathan replied.

"Pyru's in Alliance space," Alex said.

"Is that a problem?" Nathan asked.

"Not as long as you're willing to pay." Alex downed the last of her ale, then added, "Why are you going to Pyru?"

"Does it matter?" Nathan wondered.

"It might."

"To bring a sick friend back home where he belongs," Nathan explained.

"If he's sick, wouldn't he be better off on Pyru?" Alex questioned. "I hear there's an Alliance hospital there."

"His condition is terminal," Chiqua chimed in. "I just want to bring him home so he can die among family."

"And who are you?" Alex wondered.

"His wife," Chiqua replied, "the one paying for all of this."

Alex didn't look convinced. "How many *specialists* are we talking about?"

"About a dozen, including the four of us," Nathan replied.

Now she knew something wasn't right. "*Eight* specialists?"

"Medical, SA techs, some private security, nothing to worry about," Nathan assured her.

"*Security?* Who is this guy? Is he wanted or something?"

"You don't need to know," Jessica insisted.

"It's *my* ship, lady," Alex objected.

"All you have to do is fly us from Hadria to Pyru and back," Nathan told her. "You choose the route; we choose the spaceport on Pyru. The whole trip will take just over a day, and you can name your price."

"Within reason," Chiqua emphasized.

Alex looked over at her engineer, who shrugged. "We may be interested," she told them.

"We need to see your ship first," Nathan insisted. "Is it nearby?"

"Short walk," Alex replied, standing.

* * *

Nathan and the others followed Alex and Josi through the town, finally following a narrow path between two large buildings that opened out onto a pad of fused dirt hosting what appeared to be a ship.

"What the hell is that?" Jessica asked, almost laughing.

"*That* is the Acuna Dera," Alex stated proudly. "Pretty slick, huh?"

"It's a hunk of junk!" Jessica exclaimed.

"That's the beauty of her," Alex boasted. "From the outside, she looks like she was cobbled together from about half a dozen ships. But on the *inside*, well let's just say she can do whatever you need her to."

Nathan stood a moment, looking the ship over. "How many ships *is* she cobbled together from?"

"To be honest, I lost count," Alex admitted.

"Fourteen, if you include all her internal systems," Josi stated.

"It looks like you built her in a junkyard," Jessica commented.

"That's because we did," Alex admitted, still as proud as before. "Cost us a hell of a lot less that way."

"Yeah, I can tell," Jessica replied. "This is a waste of time," she told Nathan.

"She may not look like much, and her cargo holds may be small, but she's got lots of hidden compartments that are shielded to return whatever readings you want," Alex told them. "Makes it easy to sneak stuff past raiders or even Alliance patrol ships if you get my drift."

"What kind of jump range does she have?" Nathan asked.

"Her multi-jump system can get you anywhere you want as long as you have the time."

"I meant her *single* jump range," Nathan corrected.

Alex looked at them, sizing each of them up again. "You're not Alliance, are you?"

"Not for a very long time," Nathan assured her.

Alex wasn't sure what to make of his response. She looked to Josi, who again shrugged. "One hundred and twenty-three light years."

"Won't the Alliance detect that kind of range?" Chiqua challenged.

"Not the way I built it," Josi assured her.

"She's registered as a low-power, single light year multi-jumper," Alex explained. "And that's what they'll see on their sensor displays when they scan us."

"Then you've done this before?" Chiqua asked.

"A few times."

Nathan looked at Jessica.

"I say we look elsewhere," Jessica advised.

"Got any ideas?" Nathan asked Chiqua.

"Not really."

He looked at Kit next.

"I kind of like it," Kit admitted.

"You just like the girls," Jessica grumbled.

Nathan turned back to Alex and Josi. "How soon can you meet us on Hadria?"

"How soon do you want us?" Alex replied, smiling.

CHAPTER TEN

It was a relief to see the Aurora fully lit once again, and even more so to no longer need to bundle up in cold-weather gear just to move about the shuttle bay.

The Seiiki had only just returned, and already Marcus and the other techs were busily checking her over to ensure she was ready for her next mission.

"What load-out do you want?" Marcus asked Nathan as he and the others descended the ramp.

"Swap the center bay to a med module again but keep the weapons bays and the main cargo bay as they are," Nathan instructed.

"You got it."

"Kit, have the Ghatazhak ready to depart as soon as possible."

"All of us?" Kit wondered.

"All of you."

"What about Kataoka and the other worlds?" Jessica wondered.

"I'm betting they won't see any unwanted pirate visitors for at least a day or two," Nathan replied.

"That's a big gamble," Jessica warned.

"It can't be helped. I can't risk losing Vlad and Melei again."

"You promised them…"

"I know what I promised, Jess, and I meant every word. But we have to do *this* first, and to ensure success, we need *all* of the Ghatazhak." Nathan continued across the bay and through the hatch into the central corridor, running into Cameron exactly as expected.

"I take it things went as planned?" Cameron surmised.

"For the most part, yes. We delivered the goods and secured a ship. We're meeting it on Hadria in an hour."

"Where are the Dragons?" Cameron wondered as she fell into step alongside Nathan as he headed forward down the corridor.

"I had to leave them on Kataoka as protection, in case the pirates we ran into during passage came looking for payment."

"Do they have enough propellant?"

"I left them nearly all of the Seiiki's propellant, so they should be okay until we get back," Nathan promised.

"What about us?" Cameron wondered. "We don't have enough power to run both shields *and* weapons."

"But you got the fabricators running, right?"

"Yes, but it's going to take about a week to get the new containment emitters fabricated. Without the Dragons, we're sitting ducks."

"We've got five more, right?"

"Yes, and I've already got Robert training our other pilots to fly them, but even if they spent every waking minute in the sims, it's going to take weeks to turn them into effective Dragon pilots."

"They'll just have to do for now," Nathan told her. "Besides, we'll be back in just over a day. Then Josh and I can man a couple of the fighters if need be."

"Assuming you *make* it back."

"We'll make it back," Nathan promised. "I'm not going to sacrifice us all for just two people, even if it is Vlad and Melei."

"Good, because we can't afford to lose anyone else."

Nathan stopped in his tracks, realizing her meaning. "How many?"

"Robert says fifteen have notified him that they want to leave," Cameron replied. "All of them are civilian techs. But none of them want to go to an established world. They all want to join Robert to start a new settlement. Even better, they're all willing to stay until we either get the Aurora flying again or determine that she can't be saved."

"Either this ship flies again, or I die trying," Nathan swore.

"Let's hope it doesn't come to *that*," Cameron commented as they continued down the corridor.

* * *

"I don't like it," Shane complained.

"We need the credits," Alex insisted as she calculated the next jump. "We need to replace the starboard heat transfer manifold, or we're not going to have a starboard engine."

"I can patch that thing again if I have to," Josi suggested.

"You've patched it four times already," Alex argued as she executed the next jump. "It ain't gonna hold forever, and you know it."

"I don't trust them," Josi insisted.

"I don't either," Shane agreed.

"You didn't even meet them," Alex scolded.

"I trust Josi."

"And you don't trust me?"

"No," Shane replied. "You take way too many risks."

"You two don't take *enough* risks," Alex retorted.

"We don't need to," Josi stated. "You take enough for all three of us."

"I've got a feeling about this one," Alex insisted as the cockpit of the Acuna filled momentarily with the jump flash. She shook her head, rubbing her eyes. "Maybe we can even make enough to fix the jump flash filters in these damned, cheap-ass windows you put in."

"That's all we could afford, remember?" Josi snapped back.

"Look, it's a cake run for good pay," Alex told them. "It's even *in* Alliance space, so we don't have to worry about pirates."

The sensor screen beeped.

"You mean like them?" Josi said, nodding at the sensor display.

"Crap," Alex cursed. "I was so hoping we wouldn't run into them this time." She turned to look at Josi. "Tell me you got the cargo cloaking fields working."

"I did."

"Why do we need them?" Shane asked. "We're not carrying anything."

"Cuz we don't want them to know about our secret compartments," Alex replied. "How many times do I have to tell you that, Shane?"

"At least a few more I'm sure," Shane replied, turning to head aft.

Alex flipped her thrust reverses on and pushed her throttles forward.

"What are you doing?" Josi asked.

"May as well let them board now while we're empty."

"But we can out-jump them..."

"Yeah, but then they'd be pissed and more likely

to ambush us on the way back, and we don't know if we'll be empty on the way back."

"You planning on bringing cargo in?" Josi questioned.

"I haven't ruled it out," Alex replied. "Besides, it's better to let them keep believing we're cooperative. We don't need a target on our hull."

"Then why the hell did I spend all that time rewriting the jump-calc algorithms to make them faster?" Josi complained.

"Hey, you're the one who's always complaining about me taking too many risks!" Alex exclaimed as she killed the engines and set the autopilot before rising from her seat. "Let's go welcome our guests."

A minute later, Alex and Josi had joined Shane at the Acuna's docking airlock between the forward crew accommodations and the ship's four cargo bays along her midships.

"Weapons stashed?" Alex asked Shane as they entered the compartment.

"As usual. Sabers and stunners in all the right places."

There was a loud thud, and the ship shook momentarily, the decking under their feet shifting slightly.

"You guys know the drill," Alex said, assuming a standard nonthreatening position with both hands in front of her, where they could easily be seen. Josi and Shane also assumed the position as the airlock pressurization cycle began.

A moment later, the hissing of compressed air stopped, and the status light above the airlock door changed from blue to green, indicating that the pressure in the airlock now matched that of the interior of the ship.

Alex reached over and activated the airlock door control, stepping back into position as the inner airlock door unlocked and swung open.

Four men wearing brown long-coats stepped through the hatch. Each of them had sabers and long knives hanging from their belts, easily visible under their coats. None of them had shaved or bathed recently, and each had their own menacing look to them.

"Alexandria Foruria," the lead man greeted, a lecherous smile on his face.

"Vodar."

"Haven't seen you in a while, sweetness."

"Business has been slow," Alex replied.

"Whatcha got for us today?"

"Sorry, we're empty."

"You're making an empty run? That's not like you."

"Some idiot hired us to run them into Alliance space and back."

"Still gotta pay a fee for passage, you know that."

"Ain't got it," Alex insisted. "Like I said, business has been slow. Catch me on the way back. Good chance I'll have a few extra credits then, or maybe even some cargo you can skim."

Vodar stepped closer, looking over Alex and Josi. "I can think of a few other things I'd like to skim a little of," he said, eying them both.

Alex and her crew stood fast, not letting the lecherous, old man get to them. It wasn't the first time Vodar had made such suggestions, and it wouldn't be the last. "Like I said, on the return, and I'll make it worth your while."

Vodar leered at her for a moment. "And when might that be?"

"Couple days, I suspect."

After studying her a bit longer, he nodded. "Uh-huh. Maybe I should search your ship? Make sure you're tellin' me the straight."

"Scanners broke?"

"Nope, they're working fine. I just like it here." The man walked around the bay, looking things over. Your ship's got a lot of character. Ugly as hell, but lots of character."

"Gee thanks," Alex replied.

"Don't suppose you know anything about a shuttle comin' through the passage recently?" Vodar asked, turning back to her.

"How recently?"

"Today as a matter of fact. A Navarro-class shuttle, escorted by six Dragon fighters."

"*Dragon* fighters?" Alex wondered. "I didn't know any of those still existed."

"In good shape, too. I don't suppose that's who hired you?"

"Why would someone with ships like that hire a bucket like this?" Alex said.

"You never know." Vodar turned back to Alex, stepping closer to intimidate her. "You know anything about them?"

"Only what you just told me."

"I suppose you'd tell me if you did."

"Of course," Alex assured him. "You know I don't want any trouble. Just trying to keep flying."

"Family business and all."

"Yup," she agreed.

Vodar smiled. "Say hi to your old man for me."

Alex didn't answer, scowling at the man, since he knew damn well what buttons he was pushing.

Vodar's grin wasn't lascivious like before, but more evil, with a hint of aggression in his eyes. Finally, he turned back toward the airlock. "See you on the return," he announced as he and his men stepped back into the airlock. He turned back and added, "And you'd better have something good to offer me, or you're not gonna like what I *take*."

Alex said nothing as she reached for the hatch controls. Once the door was closed, she spoke again. "I fucking hate that asshole."

"He's the one, isn't he?" Shane realized.

Alex didn't reply. She didn't have to.

* * *

As dusty and raucous as Hadria was, it was a far sight better than anything they had seen at the end of the Vernay passage.

Nathan and his team had found a tavern a short walk from the clearing on the edge of town where they had left the Seiiki. It was about the same distance from the main airfield where the majority of traffic usually set down.

"How are they going to find us?" Josh asked as he wolfed down his stew.

"I've got people watching the main landing fields," Chiqua assured him. "They'll see that they find us here."

"Speak of the devil," Jessica commented, nodding toward the entrance.

Nathan looked over his shoulder, spotting Alex standing just inside, looking around. Her eyes found his, and she started toward them, just as Nathan turned back. Better finish up," he told Josh.

"We just got here."

Alex approached their table and sat down. "Double or I'm gone."

"And eat the cost of getting here?" Chiqua questioned. "I don't think so."

"You should have parked further out," Alex continued. "Which means you're either stupid or overconfident. I'm betting stupid, since you pissed off the Korsan. So double or I walk."

"We're not hiring you to fly through the badlands," Chiqua argued.

"If word gets out that I took a job from the same ass-hats who stood up against the Korsan, I'm dead. My crew is dead. My ship is gone, and my parents lose their entire family *and* their only source of income. So you've got ten seconds to agree, or I'm lifting off and telling the Korsan everything I know about you, such as the fact that you can be found on Hadria."

"To hell with her," Chiqua exclaimed. "We'll find someone else."

"I'm out of here," Alex said, rising from her seat.

"Sit down," Jessica told her.

"Or what?" Alex challenged, standing.

"You don't want to know," Jessica warned.

Alex had been threatened before, but the look in Jessica's eyes was different. It wasn't like Vodar's and others of his ilk. The confidence in pirates was based in their numbers and their reputation. This woman's confidence was in herself, as was that in the man sitting next to her.

"I'd suggest you do as she says," Kit told Alex.

"Everyone relax," Nathan suggested. "Alex, *please* sit down.

Alex looked at Nathan. His look was not the same as the other two. His inspired trust, not fear, so she sat back down.

"We can't pay you double," Nathan began. "But we *can* offer you a lot of future business."

"Business through the Vernay passage, which means dealing with the Korsan," Alex surmised. "No thanks."

"What if I told you that all your runs through the passage would be under fighter escort?" Nathan suggested.

"Fuck, I knew it," Alex said, more to herself than the others.

"You knew what?" Chiqua wondered.

"Dragon fighters?"

"Yup," Nathan replied.

"You do realize what you've done, right?" Alex said.

"Defended ourselves?"

"You put *every ship* that plies the badlands at risk," Alex stated. "What the hell gives you the right to do that?"

"It's complicated," Nathan told her. "But I assure you, that was not my intention."

"It doesn't matter what your fucking intention was."

"What if I told you that the Korsan would never bother you again?"

"I'd tell you you're full of crap."

Nathan leaned back in his chair. "It's my understanding that very few pilots work the badlands *because* of the Korsan."

"No shit."

"I'm going to put them out of business," Nathan stated.

Alex just stared at him. Then she looked over at Jessica, who looked a little surprised herself. Then Alex glanced at Chiqua, who looked completely shocked. "You're serious," she said, looking back at Nathan.

"I am."

"What the hell are you trying to haul out of Pyru?"

"Her husband, just like I said," Nathan assured her. "And his doctor of course."

"You're going to need a lot more than a five-hundred-year-old shuttle and a half dozen fighters to take down the Korsan," Alex warned.

"I'm well aware of that," Nathan stated confidently.

After a moment, Alex said, "Fifty percent more and the *option* for more business, assuming you can do what you *say* you're gonna do."

* * *

Four Dragon fighters sat nestled under the thick green canopies of Kataoka's dense forest just outside of the settlement.

Nikolas sat on the ground, leaning against a tree near the line of fighters. "Why couldn't the Aurora have crashed here?"

"I was thinking the same thing myself," Meika agreed.

"How long do you think we're going to be here?" Nikolas asked Talisha.

"Why, you got someplace else to go?" Talisha wondered.

"Just curious."

"I could stay here for days," Meika insisted.

Talisha spotted Loki sitting alone in the distance,

looking forlorn as usual. She decided to go speak with him.

"How are you doing, Lieutenant Commander?" she asked as she approached.

"You can drop the rank, Sane," Loki replied. "Not much need for it all things considered."

"But we still say 'yes, sir', right?" Talisha questioned. "And we still call the captain 'Captain'..."

"Point taken."

"Thinking about them?" Talisha asked.

Loki smiled. "You always were direct."

"I can't help it," she replied, sitting down next to him. "I think about my family, too."

"I'm sorry, I didn't realize you had any family."

"I haven't seen them in a while," she admitted. "My parents didn't approve of me being a pilot, let alone a fighter pilot."

"I'm sure they were proud of you nonetheless."

"I'd like to think so." After a moment, she added, "I'm sure your family was proud of you as well."

Loki didn't reply, just stared off at the horizon.

"*Leader, Five,*" Allet called over comm-sets.

"Go ahead, Five," Loki replied.

"*We just spotted two of those bandits coming out of the passage. They turned toward Kataoka and then jumped.*"

Loki jumped to his feet. "SCRAMBLE!" he yelled before tapping his comm-set again. "Five, hold position. We're scrambling now."

"*Copy that.*"

Talisha reacted immediately, heading for her own fighter in a dead run. Nikolas and Meika stared in disbelief for a second and then jumped into action themselves.

The first jump clap came as Loki was climbing

into his cockpit, the second clap arriving a few seconds later as Loki was dropping into his seat and hitting the quick-start button. He glanced toward the settlement as his ship's systems began to spin up, spotting two small shuttles similar to the ones that had ambushed the Seiiki hours earlier. He fastened his harness and pulled it tight as his canopy began to slide forward.

"Two bandits setting down in the middle of the settlement," he called over comms as he reached for his helmet.

Talisha was already in her cockpit with her canopy closing when Loki's call came.

"*They jumped in close, so I doubt they've spotted us,*" Loki added.

"They're sure as hell going to detect us now," Talisha warned.

"*Everyone jump in directly over them and take up attack hovers,*" Loki instructed. "*Remo and I will target one, Slider and Dudder on the other. Lock everything you have on them, but don't fire without my order.*"

"You get all that, Meika?" Talisha asked her wingman.

"All I got was don't fire without my order," Meika replied.

"Just stick to my ass and do what I do, Dudder."

Loki's fighter was the first one up, and he wasted no time jumping into attack position. In a flash of blue-white light, he jumped into a hover just above the center of the settlement, a few meters to the side of the two pirate shuttles that had just set down. He yawed slightly to bring his nose toward the shuttles and pitched down, putting his ship into a nose-down hover as his weapons systems automatically locked onto both shuttles.

Nikolas's heart was racing. It was the first time he had ever scrambled from a ground position. It was also the first time he had jumped less than a minute after takeoff. He immediately did as his leader had done and pitched down, putting his nose on the targets as he hovered.

Two more flashes appeared as Talisha and Meika joined the party, taking up nose-down hovers on the opposite side.

"*Lead group, even spacing,*" Loki instructed. "*Leave them nowhere to run.*"

Loki watched out his forward window as three men exited one of the shuttles, taking up firing positions to defend themselves. "You've got to be kidding me." Loki pressed his transmit button. "Pirate shuttles, lay down your arms and lie face down, and you won't be harmed."

The men who had just disembarked raised their rifles and opened fire, sending pinpoint beams of red slamming into Loki's forward shields. Loki focused his eyes on the first man firing, causing his weapons system to take aim on the man. He then squeezed the trigger on his flight control stick, quickly releasing it, sending a single low-power bolt of red-orange plasma streaking toward the man, blowing him into a million pieces and spraying the side of the shuttle behind him with blood and tissue.

The other two men opened fire as the second shuttle began to rise off the ground, hoping to bring one of their side-mounted plasma cannon tubes to bear on Loki's fighter.

Loki sighed. "All Dragons, single missile, fire." Loki pressed the missile launch button, sending one of his own missiles hurtling toward the rising shuttle. The missile slammed into the side of the shuttle, exploding, followed a moment later by one launched from his wingman, also exploding. The shuttle fell back to the ground, rupturing completely upon impact. Meanwhile, missiles from Talisha and Meika found the other shuttle, blowing it apart and killing the last two men standing in the process. "Three and four, fly CAP around the settlement. Remo and I are going high to check for backups."

Loki pulled his nose back level, twisting his flight control stick slightly to swing around before adding both forward power and lift to begin climbing out. He looked out the side of his canopy as he passed over the burning targets, shaking his head. "God that was dumb," he said, as if the dead below might hear him.

* * *

"We'll be making our final jump to Aubrey in a few minutes," Alex told Nathan.

"This ship is a fucking mess," Josh exclaimed as he joined them in the cockpit.

"If you wanna spend the rest of the trip unconscious, go say that to my baby sister," Alex warned.

"No offense," Josh apologized.

"Your engineer is your sister?" Nathan asked.

"And my cargo master is my brother," Alex replied. "Family business."

"How is it you ended up with your own ship?" Nathan wondered.

"It's not mine, it's my father's."

"Where's your father?"

"He took a beating during a boarding a while back. Lost an arm and an eye, and can't get around very well anymore. So we run it for him."

"Impressive," Nathan said. "How'd you learn to operate her?"

"Hell, we all grew up around this ship," Alex told him. "I was flying right seat when I was ten, and Josi was helping Pop keep it running when she was eight."

"What about your brother? What was he doing?"

"Shane's the muscle. He's a good guy, but he doesn't have much going on upstairs if you know what I mean."

"What about your mother?" Nathan asked. "She still around?"

"She takes care of Pop, mostly."

"Where do they live?"

"Estabrook." Alex looked at him. "Why so many questions?"

"Just making conversation," Nathan told her. "What route are you taking to Pyru?"

"We're going to piggyback on a long-hauler direct to Pyru. Cheaper and a tenth the travel time."

"What's a long-hauler?" Nathan wondered.

"Big-ass cargo ship. Their captains will let little guys like us land on their hull and carry us through the gates...for a fee of course."

"How much of a fee?" Nathan asked.

"Usually about ten percent of what we'd pay on the up. That's how they retire in style. *And* it has the additional benefit of getting us through the gate network without being tracked by the Alliance."

"Don't they detect you?" Nathan wondered. "They must have sensors."

"The ship captains running piggyback ops are paying off the sensor officers on the gates as well. The smart ones have cloaks like ours that make us look like part of their ship. As long as you're using an uncontrolled port on the surface, the Alliance won't even know you're there."

"And I suppose you pass the savings on to your clients?"

"Hell no," Alex laughed.

"Don't Alliance worlds have sensors and air traffic control?" Nathan wondered.

"Some do, some don't. Most of the outer worlds aren't that heavily populated, so they don't have ATC, except maybe around their main spaceports. For the most part, no one really cares about who's flying in and out of the outer worlds. The *majors*, however, are a different story. You do *not* want to try sneaking onto one of *those* worlds."

"How do you know if a world is a *major* world?" Nathan asked.

Alex cast a quizzical look Nathan's way. "You just do." After a moment, she added, "You haven't been privateering long, have you?"

"Yes *and* no."

That caused another curious look.

"It's all in the charts," Josh told Nathan.

"I take it *he's* your pilot," Alex concluded.

"Best there is," Nathan replied.

"Aw, I don't know about *best*," Josh chuckled. "*Greatest* might be more accurate…or *greatest ever*… or maybe…"

"Time to jump," Alex announced.

The jump flash washed over their cockpit. Alex closed her eyes ahead of time, but the brightness of the flash caught Nathan and Josh by surprise.

"Crap," Josh exclaimed, rubbing his eyes. "You ever heard of flash filters?"

"Sorry, I should have warned you. They're on the list."

"The list?" Nathan wondered, opening and closing his eyes in an attempt to get them to function properly again.

"Of things that need fixing," Alex explained. "It's a pretty long list, and filtered windows is pretty far down it."

"I take it that's Aubrey," Nathan said, pointing out the window at the nearby planet now that he could see clearly again.

"Yup." Alex pointed left of dead ahead. "And *that's* a long-hauler."

Both Nathan and Josh squinted to focus in the direction Alex had pointed. At first, neither of them saw it, but then they noticed tiny flashes of red and green light. At first, the flashes were so close together that they appeared to be from a single light source. After a few seconds, the flashing lights became further apart, growing further still with each passing second.

The two lights became four, then eight, as the ship grew closer and its relative attitude angle became obvious.

Alex pulled down her comm-mic from the overhead

panel. "Jorla-Den, this is the Acuna Dera. We're approaching from your upper, forward port quarter."

"Acuna, Jorla-Den. How can we help you?"

"Just lookin' for a place to set down for an hour so we can make repairs to one of our heat transfer arrays."

"I believe we can accommodate," the man replied.

"Any place in particular?"

"Pick a spot that suits you. Should be plenty of room aft. Ventral side is probably your best bet."

"Copy that, thanks." Alex placed her mic back in its cradle overhead, then pressed a couple of buttons before hitting the 'transmit data' button.

"What was that all about?" Josh wondered.

"Code?" Nathan surmised.

"Yup."

"How did you even know their name?" Josh wondered.

"The Jorla-Den is the only long-hauler that runs the Aubrey-Pyru-Trullan loop," Alex explained. "She comes around Aubrey once every four hours, give or take. You ask to set down to make repairs. You ask for an hour, it means you're getting off at the next stop. Two hours means two stops and so on."

"How do you pay them?" Nathan asked.

"I just did," Alex replied, pointing up at the button she had just pushed on the overhead comm-panel.

"It's that simple?"

"Pretty much."

"And the Alliance doesn't know about this practice?"

"I doubt they really care. There are ferry boats that do the same thing but all legal-like, but they only operate on the dedicated, single-stop routes between majors. I always figured the Alliance allowed the piggybacking because it permits more goods to flow between their outer worlds and the fringe."

"Why would they care about that?" Josh wondered.

"I'm a privateer, not an economist."

By now, the details of the long-hauler were becoming more apparent, as was its size. "That thing is *enormous*," Nathan exclaimed.

"It kinda looks like the Glendanon," Josh commented.

"But bigger," Nathan agreed. "*Much* bigger."

"If you think *that's* big, you should see the ferry ships," Alex commented.

* * *

Loki walked up to the site of the two destroyed pirate shuttles, where more than a dozen locals were working to remove the debris and clean up the mess. He glanced around, noticing a few broken windows and some scorch marks where burning debris must have struck the surrounding buildings.

"Sorry about the mess, Loki said to Darren as the young man approached. "Maybe you should wait until everything has cooled down before you try to remove the debris."

"No time," Darren replied.

"Are you expecting retaliation?"

"I don't really know," Darren admitted. "If that was just a regular visit, then we're likely the first of their six stops, so they won't be expected back for a while. But if they came here looking for you, then we have far less time. And if they see this, they won't even bother landing. They'll just bombard us from the air."

"How are you going to hide all this?" Loki wondered.

"Haul it off and dump it in the lake. Fix the broken windows and paint over the scorch marks. Could be worse I suppose."

"You'd better remove and replace the first few inches of soil as well," Loki suggested. "It'll be full of plasma residue from our weapons that their sensors can probably detect."

"We'll do that, thanks."

"I'd volunteer my pilots to help, but it would probably be best if we stayed close to our fighters just in case."

"Probably best," Darren agreed.

Loki looked around again, sighing. "Again, I'm sorry about all of this."

"Don't be," Darren told him. "Most people think this is long overdue."

"What about you?" Loki wondered.

"I'm not sure," Darren admitted. "To be honest, I'm afraid they'll come back with a lot more firepower. More than you can handle with six fighters."

"Not to brag, but you'd be surprised how many targets one of those fighters can handle."

"I hope you're right," Darren replied. "For all our sakes."

* * *

Jakome entered Vladimir's room for the eighth time in just as many hours. "I assume your presence means that Mister Kimbro is ready to transport?" he questioned the attending physician.

The physician was not intimidated by Jakome's

tone. "This man is critically ill, and I find your cavalier attitude toward his well-being abhorrent."

"Under *your* care, this man is *terminal*, not *critically ill*," Jakome corrected. "His *only* chance is with us."

"There is still a chance the serum may turn him around."

"I applaud your optimism, Doctor, however misplaced." Jakome locked eyes with the doctor. "May I move him now?"

"I will be filing a formal complaint with the medical review board."

"If that will ease your conscience, then by all means do so. Now will you have your people load him into our medical SA unit, or do we have to do it ourselves?"

The doctor handed Jakome his data pad. "Sign this, and the responsibility for this man is no longer mine."

Jakome signed the data pad, then handed it back to the doctor, who promptly left the room in a huff. Jakome walked over to Vladimir, staring down at his face. "This will all be over soon enough, Mister Kimbro," he said as his men rolled their SA unit into the room.

* * *

In the emerging light of dawn, six men in civilian attire stepped out of the Acuna onto the Tollis tarmac and loaded their gear bags into the waiting aircars.

"What's in the bags?" Alex asked Nathan as the four of them stood beside the ship, watching.

"Nothing you need to worry about," Jessica answered for him.

"Everything you people say and do worries me."

"Just be ready for a quick departure," Nathan told her.

"And that worries me even more," Alex complained. "What's to stop me from taking off now and leaving all of you on Pyru to find your own way home?"

"Because you need us as much as we need you," Nathan stated plainly.

"The hell I do."

Nathan looked at her. "Look, I've been where you are. Barely keeping my ship flying. Barely keeping my crew fed. Worrying about clients ripping me off or worse. We're offering you regular work. Work that will get you ahead, maybe even shorten that list of yours. All we're asking you to do is trust us."

"You're asking a lot," Alex grumbled as she headed back inside.

"She's going to be a problem," Chiqua muttered under her breath.

"What makes you say that?" Nathan wondered.

"She wants to know more than she needs to."

"I'd be asking the same questions if I were in her shoes."

"In my experience, the best privateers are the ones who *don't* ask too many questions."

"Those are also the ones who don't last long," Nathan replied. "Trust me, she'll be fine."

"And how do you know that?"

"Because I'm a good judge of character."

"You can't be that good," Chiqua stated. "You trusted me."

Nathan glanced at her. "I didn't have much choice."

The med-shuttle pulled through the gates,

heading across the tarmac as the Ghatazhak climbed into their aircars and headed out.

Nathan turned his head back toward the open cargo door on the Acuna. "Med-shuttle is here."

"*We're ready,*" Kit's voice replied from inside.

"You're about to commit a federal crime, you know," Chiqua warned. "The Alliance has some pretty severe penalties for those kinds of things."

"I'm sending armed men into a hospital to forcibly steal a five-hundred-year-old engineer who's dying so that we can illegally clone him. Abducting some med-techs and hijacking their shuttle for an hour is the least of my worries," Nathan replied.

The med-shuttle came to a stop a few meters from the Acuna's loading ramp. The back door opened, and two med-techs stepped out, pulling their anti-grav gurney behind them.

"Good morning, gentlemen," Nathan greeted. "The patient's inside."

The med-techs headed inside with their gurney as Josh came down the ramp, his hands in his pockets. He exchanged a glance with Nathan as he passed, heading for the med-shuttle's cockpit.

"Your pilot's up for this?" Chiqua wondered.

"My pilot's up for anything," Nathan chuckled.

Josh stepped up to the cockpit, tapping on the window.

The pilot opened the cockpit door. "How can I help you?"

"Change of plans," Josh told him. "Can you step out?"

"Why?" the pilot wondered.

Josh pulled his right hand out of his pocket, revealing a small stunner. "So I don't have to *drag* your unconscious ass out."

The pilot looked confused at first, then started to reach for something inside, but froze when he heard Josh's stunner charging up to fire. "What do you want from me?"

"Your uniform, to start," Josh replied.

The man stepped out, his hands still up.

Josh looked the man over, stepping back to keep a safe distance from him. The man was considerably taller, and probably twice Josh's weight. "Of course," Josh muttered, gesturing for the man to head inside.

Jakome stood in the corner of the room, his head and face shrouded by his cloaking hood, watching his med-techs prepare Vladimir to be moved to the special transfer pod they had brought with them. Now that the shunts had been installed, and Vladimir's blood was being oxygenated and cleaned by the pod, his tube and ventilator had been removed, giving Jakome his first real look at the man's face.

Jakome found that he couldn't stop staring at the man. He had the oddest feeling about him, as if he had seen him before or had even known him. He had seen many pictures of the famous engineer and had even watched vids of his various meetings and presentations during the design phase of the Alliance's original Expedition-class vessels. Dozens of those ships had been built, and they had been responsible for the Alliance's defeat of both the Ilyan Gamaze and the Jung Empire. The success of the class had been largely due to the genius of the man lying on the bed before him.

A man from five hundred and thirty-five years ago. The reality still haunted him, which was surprising since so many people these days lived incredibly long lives. Yet here Jakome was, a clone of his former self, and an illegal one at that.

Two identical aircars, each bearing the same logo of the Tollis spaceport, came in to low hovers over the hospital parking lot. As they descended, they turned in different directions, heading to opposite ends of the lot before landing and rolling into their parking spots.

Once down, their doors opened and three men, each carrying small bags from their shoulders, climbed out and headed toward the hospital.

The door opened, and Doctor Chen was brought in by two of Jakome's men.

Doctor Chen looked around, noticing what they were doing to Vladimir. "What's going on here? What are you doing to him?" she demanded.

"We are preparing him for transport," Jakome replied.

Doctor Chen stared at Jakome, trying to see his face, but the scattering field of the cloaking hood made its wearer's face appear out of focus and without detail. "Transport to where?"

"To someplace where he can be saved, I assure you."

Doctor Chen studied the man's distorted features, finding a need to see who he was. "Who *are* you?" she asked. "Are you Alliance?"

"Not exactly," Jakome replied. He removed his

hood, causing the cloaking field around its rim to dissipate, revealing his face in complete clarity.

Doctor Chen's eyes widened, her jaw dropping open. "This...this isn't possible..."

"I will explain everything," Jakome promised, "in good time. For now, you need to believe me when I tell you that we *are* Commander Kamenetskiy's only hope."

Josh glanced out the side cockpit window as he guided the med-shuttle toward the hospital's rooftop flight deck. There were already three shuttles down there, one of which was large and black. "Not much room down there," he warned Kit and Mori in the back.

Kit peered out the side window of the patient compartment, taking in the view below as their shuttle circled around to land. "That is *not* a medical shuttle," Kit realized.

"What was your first clue?" Josh said.

"Can you squeeze us down in there?"

"No problem," Josh assured him.

"What do you think it is?" Mori asked Kit.

"Probably some VIP shuttle," Kit replied, still staring out the window. "It's got guards."

"Alliance maybe?"

"No markings that I can see."

"Problem?"

"I don't think so," Kit replied.

Jakome watched as Doctor Chen carefully monitored the med-displays on the transfer pod.

"This thing can display data down to the *cellular* level. I've never seen anything like it."

"Actually, it can see down to the genetic level," Jakome corrected.

A med-tech pulled out some sort of skullcap that had a bundle of carefully dressed wires connected to it and began placing it on Vladimir's head.

"What is that?" Doctor Chen asked.

"It's just a precaution," Jakome assured her.

"You're going to monitor his brain activity?"

"Something like that," Jakome replied, nodding at the med-tech to continue.

Doctor Chen realized what was going on. "You're going to scan his memories, aren't you? You can't do that. We don't know how that might inhibit his recovery."

"Assuming he recovers," Jakome pointed out.

"Why are you doing this?"

"The commander has valuable information in his head," Jakome told her. "Information that we *cannot* risk losing."

"Even if it costs him his life?" Doctor Chen asked. "Who are you really?"

Jakome sighed. "I am who I appear to be, Doctor."

"I'm not sure you are," Doctor Chen insisted.

"He's ready to move, my lord," one of the med-techs announced.

"He's not even in SA," Doctor Chen objected.

"We're not putting him into SA, Doctor," Jakome replied, nodding to the med-tech.

The med-tech closed the lid of the transfer pod.

Doctor Chen stared at Vladimir's face through the lid's large window, feeling that she had failed him. "So help me, if you hurt him…"

Jakome pulled his hood back over his head,

activating the cloaking field once again. "For the well-being of your patient, I recommend that you cooperate. I have no wish to carry you out, but I will if I must."

Jokay, Abdur, and Jephen entered, walking through the weapons detectors at the hospital's east entrance, each of them spaced out in the line by a few locals seeking entrance as well.

Jokay was the first up, remaining calm as he stepped up to the scanner, hoping the special equipment that had been developed over five centuries ago was still undetectable by modern-day devices.

Jokay and the other Ghatazhak had already sized up the guards, the weapons they carried, and the doors, instinctually preparing alternate plans in case things went wrong.

Fortunately, they did not. Jokay stepped through without alarm, ushered along by complacent guards. He moved directly toward the elevator area, waiting for his two cohorts to pass through the scanners before boarding.

Kit and Mori, dressed in med-tech uniforms, unloaded their gurney from the med-shuttle and moved quickly toward the elevator lobby on the far side of the rooftop shuttle deck.

Kit nodded at the two guards standing outside the hatch of the jet-black shuttle, noting the emblem on the side of the ship.

Once across the deck and through the lobby, they

entered the medical elevator with their gurney, the doors closing behind them.

"Odd choice of colors," Mori commented. "Black, with gold, red, and blue trim."

"Did you notice the emblem on the side?" Kit asked.

"Yeah. Any idea what it meant?"

"None," Kit replied. "But I think we should try to find out once this is over."

Derel, Uray, and Cas got into the elevator, having just entered the hospital through the west entrance. They waited for the three medical personnel who had boarded with them to get off on another floor before pulling their stunners out of their bags and attaching them to each wrist.

"Remember," Derel cautioned the other Ghatazhak as he pulled his sleeves down to hide the stunners, "this has to be as covert as possible, so don't stun anyone you don't have to."

Josh was not good at sitting still, and that big, black shuttle outside had him curious as hell. It took very little time for his curiosity to get the better of him, forcing him to open his cockpit door and climb down.

He pretended to stretch his body, as if he'd been sitting in that shuttle all day, before sauntering over to the black shuttle.

"Damn," Josh exclaimed, looking the shuttle over as he walked alongside her. "That is one sharp-lookin' ship," he exclaimed as he neared the guards standing by her boarding hatch. "Is it a Toridor?"

The guards just looked at him.

"Is your pilot on board?" Josh asked. "I'd love to pick his brain a bit. I'm hoping to get a *real* gig someday instead of flying that piece of shit around."

"Move along," one of the guards told him.

"I promise I won't bother him too much," Josh promised as he headed toward the ramp.

The near guard put his hand out. "No one boards, orders of our lord."

"Your *lord?*" Josh wondered. "I'm hoping you mean your *employer,* and not, you know...*God*?"

The guard's expression suddenly changed, becoming more threatening.

"Sorry," Josh apologized, "no offense intended." Josh looked at the emblem on the side of the shuttle, next to the hatch. "Is that a Lion?" he asked. "Where have I seen that before?"

The first guard looked sternly at Josh. "Go away."

"I'll just go over there," Josh said, pointing to the other side of his little med-shuttle. "Nice talkin' with ya though."

Jakome's team floated the transfer pod out of the critical care ward and across the lobby, followed by Doctor Chen and Jakome, his face once again obscured.

The receptionist watched them cross the lobby and enter one of the east elevators, saying nothing. She and the rest of the medical staff had spent most of their shift being intimidated by the menacing hooded man and his team, and they were just happy to see them leave.

"You know this is going to go to shit really fast, right?" Abdur commented as the elevator came to a stop and the doors opened.

"I know," Jokay replied as they exited.

Jokay stepped out, surveying the critical care lobby as the doors to the next elevator to his left closed. A glance across the massive lobby showed that they were the first ones to arrive, but a moment later, the second group of three Ghatazhak stepped out of one of the elevators on the opposite side.

Jokay and his men fanned out, taking seated positions at predetermined locations on their side of the lobby, doing their best to appear to be family members waiting for word on their loved ones.

Josh stood at the corner of the med-shuttle as the doors from the elevator lobby opened and a group of men in black uniforms emerged, two of them maneuvering an anti-grav gurney. The group was followed by a man in a black cloak, and...

That's Doc Chen, Josh realized. He tried not to stare as the group neared, only glancing at the window on the transfer pod as they passed. But that glance was enough. He locked eyes with Doctor Chen for a brief moment, but it was enough for him to get the message. She was not happy.

Once they passed, Josh turned and headed forward as he tapped his comm-set. "Uh, guys?" he called as he climbed into the med-shuttle's cockpit.

"*They're here! They're on the roof!*" Josh called over comm-sets.

"What?" Kit replied in disbelief. "Are you sure?"

"*Of course I'm fucking sure! They went right past me! I even locked eyes with the doc, and she looked scared as hell! They're loading them onto the black shuttle!*"

The doors to the elevator opened, and Kit immediately pushed 'close', then selected the rooftop. "Everyone scrub and get back to the roof ASAP!"

"*What do I do?*" Josh wondered.

"You stop them, that's what you do!" Kit replied.

"How the fuck do I do that?" Josh replied as he started powering up the med-shuttle's systems, figuring that one way or another, they were going to be lifting off soon.

"*Whatever it takes!*" Kit ordered. "*Just don't let them take off!*"

"Shit," Josh cursed to himself. "What the hell do they expect me to do in a tiny little piece of crap like this?" He glanced out the right window. The black shuttle was already spinning up its grav-lift.

Josh took his controls and advanced his lift throttle, causing the med-shuttle to rise up into the air. At the same time, he twisted his flight control stick, swinging his tail around and sliding his shuttle over in front of the much larger shuttle, blocking it from lifting off.

On the top of the black shuttle's hull, a door

opened and a small defensive turret popped up, quickly swinging its double barrels upward to take aim on the medical shuttle. A second later, it adjusted its aim slightly, then fired a single burst of energy from both barrels.

The bolts slammed into the med-shuttle's aft end, causing one of its grav-lift emitters to explode. The shuttle rolled sharply over, sliding sideways as it rapidly lost altitude.

"Oh shit!" Josh exclaimed as he struggled unsuccessfully to regain control of his falling shuttle. "I'm going down!" he called over comm-sets. "I'm going down hard!"

Josh glanced out the forward window as the parking lot full of aircars below rushed toward him. "Fuck!" he cursed, bracing himself for impact.

Kit and Mori were the first ones to reach the roof, leaving their gurney in the elevator lobby and bursting through the doors on the shuttle deck.

The black shuttle was already in the air, rising and turning away as they opened fire with their stunners, knowing that it would do nothing.

As they reached the edge of the rooftop deck, the black shuttle began to accelerate away. Kit could hear people yelling down below, and he looked downward, spotting the crashed med-shuttle below. "Team One, get to the med-shuttle crash site on the west side," Kit instructed over his comm-set. "Team Two, provide cover for Team One. Mori and I will get the vehicles."

"One copy."

"Two copy."

The black shuttle disappeared in a blue-white flash, and Kit felt his heart sink. "Damn," he cursed. "If we'd gone in fully armed, that shuttle would be on the ground instead of Josh."

"And Vlad and the doc would both be dead," Mori pointed out. "Let's go. We're not home yet."

* * *

The two aircars came in quickly, skipping the gate and flying over the fence so that they could reach the Acuna faster.

"Nathan!" Jessica called back toward the ship.

Nathan came down the ramp, seeing the approaching aircars but no medical shuttle. "This isn't good."

"What's going on?" Chiqua wondered, coming out behind him.

"Go tell Alex to get ready to lift off," Nathan told her.

The aircars came to a hover a few meters aft of the Acuna, setting down rather abruptly, their doors opening before their grav-lift systems had even begun to spin down.

"What happened?" Jessica asked, approaching the aircars.

"Where's the med-shuttle?" Nathan asked.

Kit didn't answer, instead turning to help Josh out of the vehicle as the Acuna's grav-lift systems began to hum.

Nathan's eyes widened when he saw Josh. His head and face were bloody, and his uniform was singed.

"Shit," Jessica exclaimed.

"Jess, get the med-shuttle team out of the ship. We're leaving," Nathan instructed.

"What the fuck happened?" Jess demanded.

"Now, Jess!" Nathan snapped, before running over to help them with Josh.

Two flashing red and blue lights appeared on the horizon, barely visible in the dawn light.

"Are you okay, Josh?" Nathan asked.

"I'm sorry, Cap'n, I tried to stop them," Josh sputtered.

"What happened?" Nathan asked Kit as they all headed back to the Acuna.

"Someone got to them before us," Kit told him. "If we had gotten there just a few minutes earlier..."

"Incoming!" Jessica barked from the ramp as she escorted the med-shuttle crew down onto the tarmac in their underwear. "You should all start running," she told the med-shuttle crew.

Nathan didn't reply to Kit, turning to look at the incoming security shuttles closing on the spaceport. "Jess, get everyone inside and buttoned up fast!"

"I told you these people were trouble," Josi insisted.

"Not now, Jo," Alex snapped as she prepared the ship to lift off.

"Out of the way," Nathan barked as he entered the Acuna's cockpit. He forced his way past Josi and climbed into the copilot's seat.

"What do you think you're doing?" Alex demanded.

"I'm helping you get us out of here," Nathan explained. "You need to jump us...NOW!"

"What?" Josi asked, shocked by Nathan's orders.

"We don't even have a clearance," Alex added, equally as shocked.

"We don't have time," Nathan insisted.

"I'm not jumping from the fucking tarmac," Alex objected.

"Then get us the fuck in the air!" Nathan barked.

"You don't get to tell me how to fly my own ship!" Alex exclaimed.

"I'm taking control," Nathan told her.

"The hell you are!" Alex objected, reaching for the weapon she kept tucked next to her seat.

"Don't even think about it," Jessica warned from the hatch, her blaster whining as its plasma cell came to full charge.

Alex looked back at Jessica. "You miss and you'll blow a hole in the hull. Then we won't be jumping anywhere."

"I don't miss," Jessica replied.

Alex stared back at her a moment, then put her hands up to indicate her submission.

"*We're buttoned up!*" Kit called over the intercom.

Nathan eased the grav-lift throttles forward, causing the ship to rise slowly from the tarmac. At the same time, he pressed the jump button, filling the cockpit with blue-white light.

───────

The med-shuttle crew stumbled and fell to the ground as the Acuna jumped away behind them. When they got back up and turned around, there was a gaping hole in the tarmac where the ship had been a moment ago.

───────

A blue-white flash appeared far out in the Pyru system, revealing the Acuna and a chunk of tarmac floating below them.

"Jesus!" Alex exclaimed. "You just blind-jumped us!"

"Better than getting a missile up our ass," Jessica told her.

"You people are fucking insane!"

Nathan rose from his seat. "Max-range jump us back to Hadria," he instructed as he headed aft.

"Max range? Are you nuts?"

Nathan turned back. "Don't make me repeat myself," he said, pointing a figure at her.

Alex began calculating the jump. "Your captain doesn't give a shit about anyone but himself."

"My captain just lost his best friend and our only doctor," Jessica told her. "He cares more than you know." After a moment, she added. "Now jump us the hell out of here."

CHAPTER ELEVEN

Nathan stared out the windows of his ready room aboard the Aurora. The jagged, near vertical rock face that formed the end of this valley was so close, he felt as if he could reach out and touch it. The thought that the only thing that had saved them from certain death had been the bog at the end of the valley seemed almost comical. One never knew what unexpected elements might change one's destiny, for better or worse.

Yet none of those unexpected elements had played out in his favor when it had come to Vladimir and Doctor Chen. Nathan had done everything possible; had gone out on a limb and risked not only himself, but his entire ship and crew. He had even jeopardized the lives of people he had just met, sucking them into his dangerous endeavors. All to no avail.

"It's not your fault," Cameron commented from the doorway.

"It's entirely my fault," Nathan insisted. "All of it. Vlad, Doc Chen, being stuck here, five hundred years in the future…even the war and the current state of the Alliance is my fault."

"If you're going to become that self-loathing wuss you were the first time you were in command, we're all going to mutiny."

Nathan turned to look at her. "Self-loathing wuss?"

"Jessica's description."

Nathan turned back to the windows. "You want to hear something ironic?"

"Why not?" Cameron said, entering the ready room and taking a seat.

"Laza says that ninety percent of the raw materials we need to repair the ship are in that rock face out there. It almost killed us, and now it could end up being our salvation."

"They're still alive, Nathan," Cameron reminded him.

"You can't know that."

"Whoever took them did so for a reason. I doubt killing them was part of their plan. If it had been, they wouldn't have taken them both out of there *alive*."

Nathan turned back around. "They could be anywhere, Cam. How are we supposed to find them?"

"I don't know," Cameron admitted. "But I *do* know that it all starts with getting this ship back into space."

"That will take months, perhaps years."

"Maybe. But all we can do is try."

"He was my *best friend*."

"I understand, Nathan. Truly I do. This is how we all felt when *you* died. *Especially* Vlad. But we carried on. Not because it was what *you* would have wanted us to do, but because there was nothing else we *could* do."

"Everything in me is telling me to do the same as Jessica did for me," Nathan admitted. "To forget about the risks and just do whatever has to be done to get them back."

"And if someday we see an opportunity to do the same for Vlad and Melei, we'll do that as well," Cameron assured him. "But the closer we get to being fully operational, the more options we have toward that end. So it's time to get back to work. Two days of brooding is enough." Cameron rose from her seat.

"Now are you going to conduct the morning briefing, or do I have to make excuses for you again?"

* * *

Everyone seated around the conference table in the command briefing room watched as Cameron entered, expecting her to take the seat at the head of the table nearest the exit, as she had for the last two days. But this time, she walked past it and headed for the seat at the opposite end.

Their heads turned back toward the entrance, and when Nathan entered, they immediately moved to stand.

"Don't even think about it," Nathan warned before they could rise. He headed straight for his seat. "First, I'd like to thank Dominic for all his hard work. With Commander Kamenetskiy and Doctor Chen still missing, his assistance has proven invaluable."

"Thank you, Captain," Dominic replied with a nod. "It's been a real pleasure working on such a classic ship."

"Well I apologize for our outdated systems," Nathan remarked. "How are things going with main power?"

"We finished fabricating enough emitters for one reactor. I took the liberty of incorporating some of the improvements made to the original design. It wasn't much, but it will make them less prone to failure in the future."

"How long until the first reactor is back to full power?"

"Tomorrow morning at the latest. The second reactor should be back online a few days later."

"Excellent."

"We currently have enough power to run all environmental systems normally," Cameron reported. "We can also run either shields or weapons at full power, but not both."

"How are we doing on consumables?" Nathan asked Neli.

"We're good for a few months, more if we ration," Neli replied. "But I wouldn't recommend rationing though. Our people are working awfully hard, and they *need* to eat."

"Make up a list of what you think we need to acquire in the near future, and I'll see that Chiqua gets it," Nathan instructed. "Marcus, how are our ships?"

"Seiiki and Mirai are fully operational. I'm keeping them both fitted with med and weapons bays, along with the usual cargo bay for now. Seems to be the best configuration for the time being."

"And the Dragons?"

"All eleven are fully functional, and we've got plenty of ordnance for them, assuming we don't get into a prolonged conflict."

"Let's hope we don't," Nathan agreed. "How are our trainees doing?" he asked Robert.

"Tika and Mick are taking to Dragons pretty easily, which was expected, since they were my Lightning pilots on the Lawrence. Evan and Lannie will need a bit more work before I'm confident in their abilities to handle combat."

"How are we looking on the Vernay worlds?"

"There have been no other contacts since the first one two days ago," Robert reported. "We're keeping four Dragons there and four here for now. Two Dragons on the ground and two on patrol, swapping every eight hours."

"Hard duty," Nathan commented.

"The Kataokans are taking pretty good care of them, keeping them fed and rested as well as they can. We also dispersed comm-drones to each Vernay world, so they can quickly notify our people on Kataoka if pirates show up in their system."

"We're doing the same with the Ghatazhak," Jessica added. "Four there, four here. The alert team on Kataoka can be anywhere in the Vernay within a minute of activation."

"Are four enough?" Nathan wondered.

"For now, yes."

"I've calculated a single-jump path directly between Dencke and Kataoka for our comm-drones," Laza chimed in.

"What about the gravity wells?" Nathan wondered.

"I found a path with only a twenty-three percent chance of a rogue gravity well popping up. I wouldn't use it as a regular route, but it could serve as an option when a timely response is critical."

"Good thinking," Nathan agreed. "Have you established a regular communication schedule with our people on Kataoka?" Nathan asked Ensign Dass.

"The Ghatazhak are currently following a four-hour contact schedule," Sima replied.

"Have we heard from Chiqua?"

"She contacted us this morning, using the comm-drone we gave her. She should be ready for her next run into the Vernay by tomorrow."

"Will we be using the Acuna?" Cameron asked.

"Not until we catch up on our own debt," Nathan replied. "How's your new pilot doing?" he asked Aiden.

"She's ready," Aiden assured him.

"We should rotate our fighters at the same time

as the cargo runs," Cameron recommended. "Two Dragons should be enough if the Mirai is carrying weapons pods."

"Agreed," Nathan said.

"You want me to change the Mirai's med bay for another cargo pod?" Marcus wondered.

"Probably a good idea," Nathan agreed. "But keep a med bay in the Seiiki in case she needs to respond to a surface attack."

"*Captain!*" Loki called from outside the command briefing room. "*We have a contact!*"

Nathan eschewed the customary dismissal of the briefing, jumping to his feet and heading out of the room to the bridge just outside.

"It's a big one," Loki reported from the tactical console. "At least as big as us."

"Is she armed?" Nathan asked as he moved quickly to Loki's side, the others pouring out of the room behind him.

"Not that I can tell," Loki replied.

"Doesn't mean she isn't," Jessica commented, taking Loki's place at the tactical station.

"She's got weapons," Laza reported from the sensor station, having gone directly to her post like everyone else.

"Sound general quarters," Nathan instructed.

"General quarters, aye," Ensign Dass reported as she took her seat at the comm-station.

"Who's on deck?" Nathan asked Loki.

"Nikolas is my wing, but other than that, just our trainees."

"Grab Josh and one of your trainees, and get four birds in the air just in case," Nathan instructed.

"I'm on it," Loki replied, tapping his comm-set to call the others as he headed for the exit.

"What are we looking at?" Nathan asked Jessica as the updated sensor feeds appeared on her console.

"She's not a warship, but in our current state, she's got enough firepower to squash us like a bug."

"Marcus, swap out the shuttle cargo bays with anti-ship missile systems, starting with the Mirai."

"You got it," Marcus replied, heading for the exit.

"Aiden, as soon as he swaps your bay, get up there. If you can put a few missiles into them, they might not press an attack."

"Have they even targeted us yet?" Cameron asked.

"Negative," Jessica replied, "but they're moving into a synchronous orbit overhead. If that's not positioning for an orbital assault, I don't know what is."

"Incoming call," Ensign Dass announced. "They're hailing us."

Nathan shared looks with Cameron and Jessica. "On screen," he instructed, stepping over to the command chair.

The view screen snapped to life, and the image of a very proper-looking man in his late fifties appeared. He was wearing a crisp, black uniform sporting red, black, and blue piping, and appeared to be standing on his bridge. "*Greetings, Captain Scott,*" the man began.

Nathan glanced at Jessica and Cameron again, concerned that the man knew his name. "I don't believe I've had the pleasure," Nathan replied, turning back to face the view screen.

"*I am Captain Elias of the Bonaventura. You can stand down from general quarters. We mean you no harm.*"

"That's good to hear, but I'm going to stay at general quarters for the moment if you don't mind."

"*Of course.*"

"I am curious as to *how* you know my name?"

"*Our lord knows much about you,*" Captain Elias replied.

"Your *lord?*"

"*He wishes to meet with you and present you with a... a gift of sorts. May he come down to speak with you?*"

"If he comes alone," Nathan replied.

"*I'm afraid that won't be possible,*" Captain Elias objected. "*However, I can promise you that no one in his party will be armed.*"

"Very well," Nathan replied. "You may land on our dorsal flight deck, in between the fighters parked there."

"Would it not be better to meet inside your shuttle bay?" the captain suggested. "The conditions are far more favorable."

"No offense to you and your *lord*, but I'd prefer the meeting to take place *outside* of my ship," Nathan stated.

"A wise precaution," Captain Elias agreed. "My lord shall depart immediately." The captain nodded respectfully. "Good day, Captain."

The view screen shut off. Nathan turned to Cameron and Jessica, as well as the others who were about to depart.

"Gotta be Alliance," Jessica said.

"Agreed."

"At least this means they may *not* want us dead," Cameron concluded.

"Continue readying our Dragons and shuttles for combat just in case," Nathan instructed. "And have the Ghatazhak meet us in the shuttle bay."

"I'm coming with you," Jessica insisted.

"I can handle things here," Cameron assured him.

"You might want to keep our dorsal weapons and a few jump missiles locked on that ship," Nathan suggested.

"Just in case," Cameron finished for him. "Good luck."

* * *

The Aurora's shuttle flight deck was nestled between her port and starboard drive nacelles, extending from the shuttle bay entrance along the backside of the forward sections to the cargo door on the upward slope of the aft section. With the pressure shield activated, the entire deck was enclosed in a pale blue, nearly transparent dome. The arrangement was another one of Vladimir's ingenious ideas, meant to provide a pressurized, environmentally controlled space that could serve as a temporary bay to service ships too large to fit in the Aurora's hangar bay.

With their three fusion reactors generating more than enough power to run the pressure shield and the flight deck environmental systems, and four days still remaining in Dencke's long night, the space had served as the staging area for their Dragon fighters; a fact that their pilots had greatly appreciated due to the sub-zero temperatures beyond the shield.

Even with the flight deck heaters running at maximum, the deck still felt like the inside of an ice rink.

Josh, Tika, Loki, and Nikolas were waiting just inside the hangar bay doors, dressed in Dragon flight suits.

"Shouldn't you be in your Dragons?" Nathan asked

as he, Jessica, and four heavily armed Ghatazhak walked toward them.

"This is as far as we got when you canceled our launch," Josh explained.

"Their reactors are hot and ready for immediate launch," Loki assured him.

"If they had intended to destroy us, they'd have already done so," Jessica insisted.

"Why the big guns?" Josh wondered, pointing at Kit and the other three Ghatazhak.

"In case their intention is to *capture* us," Kit replied.

"*Nathan,*" Cameron called over comm-sets. "*They're on approach now. About a minute out.*"

"How many life signs are you picking up?" Nathan wondered.

"*Only four, and no weapons that we can detect,*" Cameron replied.

"*Captain, Ensign Soray here. Since we were unable to detect their weapons until they were activated, they may have the capability to cloak them, perhaps even their portable ones.*"

"Understood," Nathan replied.

"It might be a good idea to activate the ventral defense turrets on our ships," Loki suggested. "They could easily spray the deck *if* Lieutenant Vasya's suspicions turn out to be correct."

"I like that idea," Jessica agreed.

"Why do you think I suggested they land between the Dragons?" Nathan stated.

"Finally you're starting to think like me," Jessica teased.

"I prefer to think that I'm starting to think like them," Nathan said, pointing at Kit and his men.

"I'll set my Dragon's AI to control all four ships'

weapons systems," Loki said. "That way, we'll have two guns on each person."

"Nice little crossfire," Kit said with a smile. "No way they're defending against that." He looked at Nathan. "We may just make a Ghatazhak out of you someday."

Josh was looking up, barely able to make out the approaching shuttle through the translucent pressure shield. "Uh, is it my imagination, or does that shuttle look familiar?"

Everyone looked up.

"It's not your imagination," Kit confirmed. "That's the same type of shuttle that took Vlad and Doc Chen."

"I'm getting a bad feeling about this," Jessica told them.

"Me too," Kit agreed, charging his rifle.

Nathan was beginning to feel the same way. But he couldn't think of a better way to control whatever was about to happen. And with his ship grounded, with insufficient power for both shields *and* weapons, refusal to meet might make matters worse.

The large, black shuttle came to a hover directly over their landing spot, then descended through the pressure shield as its landing gear deployed. Its grav-lift systems were surprisingly quiet, especially for a shuttle larger than their own.

The shuttle's gear touched the deck gently, all four wheels kissing the deck simultaneously. The discrete hum of its grav-lift dropped sharply, and the shuttle settled, its gear compressing slightly as it took on the weight of the shuttle.

"Same red, gold, and blue trim," Josh commented.

Kit made a gesture, and the Ghatazhak fanned

out, taking up positions abreast, just outside of the hangar doors.

Exterior lights on the shuttle lit up, flooding the poorly illuminated flight deck and making it difficult to see the shuttle's side boarding hatch.

"That's not good," Jessica muttered.

Nathan said nothing, just stood confidently, squinting to see the hatch despite the glare of the shuttle's floodlights. The hatch cracked open, splitting vertically, each side sliding into the hull and disappearing as the boarding ramp deployed and extended down to the deck.

A figure appeared in the shuttle's hatch, stepping out onto the boarding ramp and stopping. The person was wearing a hooded cape, with the hood covering the wearer's head. By the size and build, Nathan assumed it was a man.

The hooded man came down the ramp, his hands held out from his sides, palms facing forward to show that he was not holding any weapons. He moved slowly, taking each step down the ramp in an almost rhythmic fashion. Once at the bottom, he stopped, slowly taking hold of the front seams of his cape and opening it to show that there were no weapons underneath.

Nathan studied the man, still unable to see his face under the hood.

"I am unarmed," the man announced.

Nathan felt a chill go up his spine. *That voice*, he thought. There was nothing sinister about it. It was just familiar, yet unfamiliar at the same time.

"Advance...slowly," Kit commanded from the side, his rifle aimed at the hooded man.

"Perhaps I should present to you the gifts that were promised," the hooded man suggested.

Again the voice bothered Nathan. He had heard it before, he was now certain of it. Yet he still couldn't place it. "As you wish," Nathan told him.

The hooded man turned slowly back toward his shuttle. "Doctor, if you please?"

A woman appeared at the hatch, immediately descending the ramp, her hands held out with palms forward in the same fashion. She was of average height and shapely, with shoulder-length blonde hair, but Nathan could not make out her face because of the floodlights behind her.

Nikolas, however, could. "Mom?" Nikolas suddenly ran toward her.

"Remo, wait!" Loki warned, reaching for him. But it was too late.

"Abby?" Nathan realized. He still couldn't make out her face, but her silhouette was suddenly unmistakable.

Nikolas reached his mother, throwing his arms around her, just as she did with her son, both of them sobbing with tears of joy.

"This can't be," Jessica muttered in disbelief.

Two more people appeared at the shuttle's hatch: a tall, broad-shouldered man and a petite woman.

Even with the lights, Nathan recognized their shapes and began walking forward to greet them, pushing past the hooded man. He put his arms around them both, relief overcoming the shock of seeing them.

"How did you manage to get the power back on without me?" Vladimir asked as he hugged his friend.

"I thought I'd lost you," Nathan said, overwhelmed with joy. "Both of you."

"You'd never survive without me," Vladimir insisted. "Not the way you keep breaking ships."

Nathan turned around, looking at the hooded man, expecting to see his face now that the shuttle's floodlights were no longer back-lighting him. But something was obscuring his face, making it seem out of focus. "Who are you?" he asked.

"You're not going to believe this," Vladimir warned, a broad smile on his face as he waited for his friend's reaction.

"I am Jakome Ta'Akar," the man replied as he removed his hood. "Clone of the late Casimir Ta'Akar."

Nathan's jaw dropped as he saw what appeared to be a younger version of the man he once knew as Tug.

CHAPTER TWELVE

Crowden was one of the most dangerous settlements in which to live. It was rocky and barren, with very little vegetation. Only its equatorial regions were habitable, and even then just barely. The rest of the planet was frozen over most of the year, with the permafrost only receding ten degrees in latitude annually.

To make matters worse, it was located in the middle of a dense asteroid belt, which meant that it was struck every few years by some sort of rocky debris from space. All of that, combined with a gravity of twenty percent over normal, was more than enough to keep most people from living there.

The one thing Crowden had going for it was that it served as the base of operations for the Brodek clan, one of the more notorious members of the Korsan syndicate. Because of this, the people of Crowden had access to just about everything that was traded between the fringe worlds and the settlements of the badlands. They also had regular visits by all manner of cargo ships, which allowed them many options and provided a constant influx of new dreamers for Crowden to chew up and spit out.

But for those who could handle themselves and could tolerate the Brodeks, Crowden was a good place to live. With all the traffic, there were plenty of businesses where one could find work. Bars, brothels, restaurants, banks, shops, schools, medical clinics, everything one could think of. About the only types of employment not available on Crowden were agriculture and manufacturing. Everything that the people of Crowden needed was imported, and thanks to the Brodeks, goods were relatively inexpensive compared to other settlements in the badlands.

At the center of Crowden stood the Brodek headquarters. At four stories, it was the tallest building on Crowden, as well as the most solid structure to be found. It was also the preferred entertainment venue on the planet. With the entire first floor as a tavern and gambling establishment, and the second floor acting as a brothel, it was a popular place among pirates, ship crews, and even the locals.

Ottar DePaz had lived on Crowden for thirty years and had seen it grow from a dusty cluster of temporary buildings into a thriving settlement. His own penchant for violence had served him well, getting him into the upper echelon of the Brodek clan. When he spoke, Halvor Brodek listened. Few men on Crowden could claim that, and it meant a lot to Ottar.

Ottar entered the den of Halvor, knowing that he had to give his leader news that he would not like. It did not happen often, but when it did, Halvor often reacted harshly.

Halvor sat in the middle of his den, being fed by women his men referred to as 'Halvor's Harem'. The man was a master of excess and took great pleasure in reveling in his own abundance.

"Ottar!" Halvor greeted. He was happiest when he was dining, which was a lucky break for any bearer of bad news.

"Come, dine with me!" Halvor insisted.

"I'm afraid I bring bad news, Hal."

"Lucky for you, I have the cream of the crop feeding me today," Halvor chuckled. He studied his lieutenant's face a moment. "That bad?"

"The men I sent searching for those ships that challenged us did not return."

"Any chance they deserted?" Halvor suggested.

"Doubtful," Ottar replied. "They were some of my most trusted."

"How many men?"

"Six, three in each ship."

Ottar could see the blood beginning to boil in his leader's eyes.

"Go!" he yelled at his feeders. "Leave us!" Halvor rose from his seat and began pacing the den. "I want this ship found. I want their escorts found. I want them all dead. The pilots, the crew, the owners... everyone they know! Dead! Do you understand?"

"I will see to it personally, Hal," Ottar promised.

Halvor turned to glare at his lieutenant, fire in his eyes. "You are not immune from the consequences of failure, DePaz."

"I will bring their leader back alive so that you can have the pleasure of beheading him yourself."

That was exactly what his leader wanted to hear. "If you do, you will become my second," Halvor promised. He raised his arms up, gesturing around. "And all this will be yours upon my passing."

"Brodek!" Ottar barked, striking his fist off his chest in salute. He turned and headed for the exit, an evil smile on his face. Finally, here was the task that would secure his future.

Thank you for reading this story.
(*A review would be greatly appreciated!*)
Visit us online at
frontierssaga.com
or on Facebook
Want to be notified when
new episodes are published?
Join our mailing list!
frontierssaga.com/mailinglist/

Manufactured by Amazon.ca
Bolton, ON

26175801R00189